FORBIDDEN EMPIRE

INCLUDES SERIES PREQUAL GAMES OF DECEPTION

SINFUL GODS

BOOK ONE

SIENNA SNOW

Cover Design: Artscandare Book Cover Design

Editor: Silla Webb

www.siennasnow.com

ISBN - eBook - 979-8-88535-033-4

ISBN - Print - 979-8-88535-034-1

ISBN – Hardback - 979-8-88535-035-8

AI Disclosure

No generative artificial intelligence (AI) was used in the writing of this work. The author expressly prohibits any entity from using this publication for purposes of training AI technologies to generate text, including, without limitation, technologies that are capable of generating works in the same style or genre as this publication.

Content Disclosure

This book is a dark romance with subject matter
that may trigger some readers.

- Graphic Violence
- Explicit Sexual Content
- Torture / Interrogation
- Dominance themes
- Kidnapping
- Psychological Manipulation / Gaslighting
- Morally Gray Characters
- Weapons & Violence
- Trauma & PTSD
- Revenge Killing
- Dubious Consent (Dub-con)
- Captivity
- Rough Sex / Degradation Kink
- Power Imbalance

- Family Betrayal
- Threat of Sexual Violence (Implied)
- Toxic Relationship Dynamics
- Drug / Substance References
- Psychological Manipulation / Gaslighting
- Blood / Gore Detail
- Degradation

Tropes List

- Dark Mafia
- Cat-and-Mouse Obsession
- Antihero
- Morally Gray
- Villain romance
- Forbidden love
- Obsession / Possessive Alpha Hero
- Touch her and die
- Age Gap
- Obsessive love
- Enemies to Lovers
- Second Chance / Past Lovers
- Forced Proximity / Captivity
- Hate Sex / Enemies in Bed
- "You're Mine" / Ownership Declarations
- Love-Hate Dynamic
- Crime Lord Hero

- Mafia Princess Heroine
- Rival Crime Families
- Dark Obsession
- Twisted Redemption
- Rough Sex / Degradation Kink
- Revenge
- Violent Showdowns
- Dominant Hero/Submissive Heroine dynamic
- Fueding families
- Power couple dynamic
- Claiming and ownership

Before You Dive In!

Welcome to The Underground, where Sinful Gods battle their enemies to maintain power, notoriety, and influence in their criminal world. (Or Las Vegas) To begin the series, I've included the Games of Deception prequel. It's a juicy, fast hit that sets the vibe, stakes, and tangled loyalties of this sinful world. You can absolutely dive straight into Forbidden Empire—no map required—but if you enjoy a decadent warm-up before the plunge, start here...then meet me in Chapter One for the fire. 💋

Games of Deception

Forbidden Empire Prequel

ONE

Aidon

As a predator caught the scent of something dangerous...

I felt the shift in my private booth, a fortress of shadows looming above Vegas' most dangerous and elite haven, the Underworld. Here, the pulse of bass music reverberated through the club, matching the primal rhythm of the crowd below.

From my elevated perch, I sipped on my whiskey and watched everything unfold like a king surveying his kingdom. Shadows danced on the walls, embracing the dark and seductive atmosphere of the club. Underneath the flickering lights, another world hummed with secrets traded, deals sealed, and alliances broken.

Just another night.

I leaned back in my chair, relishing the cool leather against my tailored suit. The view from up here was perfect—no one moved without my notice.

My bouncers, dressed in sleek black suits and wearing earpieces, patrolled the edges of the crowd. This was my dominion, my sanctuary, and I ruled it with absolute control.

Suddenly, the air crackled and charged with electricity—something unrelated to the club's sound system.

Heads turned, conversations faltered, and a collective pause swept through the room.

My sharp eyes scanned the crowd before landing on her.

Esme Theodorus.

She moved through the throng like a queen reclaiming her throne, clad in a form-fitting black gown that shimmered under the lights and revealed every curve. Her raven hair cascaded over one shoulder in loose waves while her crimson lips curled into a smirk that dared anyone to challenge her presence.

Esme was chaos wrapped in beauty, a storm in human form. And someone who should be far, far away from me.

My jaw tightened as I clutched my glass tighter than necessary and rose to my feet.

This was the last place I expected to see her. Not in my city. Not in my club. And for certain, not strolling in with such confidence, as if she owned the place.

Yet here she was, commanding the room without saying a word.

Her emerald eyes met mine, and a mischievous glint lit up her face. She knew I'd be here tonight. Of course, she did. Esme never did anything without purpose.

I set down my tumbler, my fingers itching to crush it. But I held back, reining in my impulses and maintaining an impassive expression as I waited for Esme to come to me.

And she did. Slowly.

She walked past my security team, expecting them not to stop her. As expected, they didn't resist. She climbed the staircase to my lair, her heels echoing on the metal steps like a ticking clock.

She moved with the confidence of someone with nothing to lose and everything to gain. When she reached the top, Ares, my enforcer stationed at the door, looked to me for guidance.

At least he understood how to handle things.

I gave him a subtle nod.

Esme stepped into the booth, and her perfume wafted toward me—a mix of spiced vanilla and something darker. She closed the door behind her, leaning against it with casual defiance.

"Aidon," she greeted, her voice smooth as silk. "It's been a while."

"Not long enough," I replied, leaning forward with my forearms resting on my knees. My dark eyes locked onto hers without wavering. "What are you doing here, Esme?"

She let out a soft, teasing chuckle.

"Straight to business? No, 'how have you been?' No, 'you

look stunning tonight'?" She sauntered closer with a sway in her hips until she stood just out of arm's reach. "I'm hurt."

"You'll survive," I said with a clipped tone. "Now answer the question."

Her smirk faltered for a fraction of a moment. "I'm here to talk."

"Talk fast." I leaned my shoulder against a wall, my gaze narrowing as I studied her from head to toe with wary eyes.

The air between us crackled, tense and dangerous.

Esme raised a brow, her lips curving again in an alluring yet deceptive smile. "You've changed, Aidon."

She stepped closer, her voice dipping lower as she continued to play her games. Her words were laced with a teasing lilt, tempting me to let down my guard.

"The old you would have at least offered me a seat. Perhaps, poured me a drink. Or should I get you one? But you won't take it from my fingers. You're too scared I'd poison it."

I snorted, passing a cursory glance at the club behind her. "And risk wasting good whiskey? That's not your style, Esme."

"Oh, so you do remember my style." She leaned in just enough to tease but kept her distance, trying to manipulate me with her proximity. "Careful, Aidon. You're starting to sound like you missed me."

"Don't flatter yourself," I said through gritted teeth, unable to hide the bitterness in my tone. "Whatever game you're playing, get to the point."

She'd destroyed me once. It wouldn't happen again.

"I thought I was getting to the point." Her voice was soft now, almost pleading. But I knew better than to trust anything that came out of her mouth.

"Not fast enough." My tone was sharp as a blade. "Let me guess. Is this about big brother Zeno?"

Her half-brother, Zenobius "Zeno" Theodorus, believed he controlled the Vegas syndicate world and used his influence to wreck everything in his way. Once, I considered him an ally, even a friend. Still, his underhanded dealings turned us into bitter rivals.

However, we couldn't outright eliminate each other. We were part of a sub-economy linked to every aspect of Las Vegas's legitimate economy. If one of us falls, all of us fall.

"Zeno is planning something big," she said, her emerald gaze meeting mine. "And he's coming for you."

"He's always coming for me," I replied, my voice dry and devoid of any emotion. "That's not news."

Her hand brushed the edge of my tie, straightening it in a gesture that felt too personal, something I would have accepted long ago. But now, it reminded me of how effortless it was for her to manipulate me.

The faintest pressure of her fingers sent a ripple through me, and my body betrayed the discipline I had fought so hard to maintain. Anger flared hot like lightning, but just as fast, something darker and more consuming smothered it, the need to make her feel the same way.

I hated her ability to slip past my defenses with a simple touch.

I remained still, allowing her to linger. My pulse

drummed in my ears as I tried to regain control over my physical reaction to her presence.

"This time, he'll win unless we work together. I have a lot of information you need, Aidon," she said, her tone soft yet cutting like a blade wrapped in silk.

I caught her wrist, feeling her pulse beat faster than the calm facade she presented. "And what's in it for you?"

"Survival. Isn't that what we're all after?" Her words were laced with dark humor and held a hint of something sinister hiding beneath the surface.

"And how do I know you're not just setting me up?" My grip on her tightened just enough to remind her who held the upper hand.

Esme tilted her head, her lips a hairsbreadth from my cheek. "If I wanted to betray you, Aidon, you'd already be dead."

Why was she here? Was this another of her endless games, testing how far she could push me before I snapped?

I studied her face, looking for cracks in her confidence or signs of deception. But Esme was an enigma, wearing a perfect mask of defiance and allure. The faint scent of her perfume, that maddening blend, clouded my mind and made it hard to think clear.

My warning came out as a low growl, my voice filled with frustration and concern. "You're too damn confident for your own good," I stated. "One day, it'll get you killed."

But she smirked, a glint of amusement dancing in her emerald eyes. The way the light hit them made them seem almost ethereal, like pools of shimmering jewels.

"Then I guess it's a good thing you're here to protect me, Aidon," she replied, her voice dripping with mischief.

The challenge in her tone sparked something in me, igniting a fire I couldn't ignore. Logic told me to focus on the danger Zeno posed, but all I could think about was her. The way she cocked her head just right, daring me to act and react. The way she moaned in my arms. The way it felt to fuck her unconscious.

But I couldn't fall into her web and give her the satisfaction.

"You have one chance," I warned, my voice low and lethal. "But if you cross me, Esme, you won't walk away this time."

I meant for my words to chill her, but instead, they seemed to fuel the tension between us. Her green eyes locked onto mine, daring me to push back.

We stood there staring, neither willing to back down.

In the end, I released her and took a step back, needing some space between us.

Her smirk returned victorious and infuriating. "Fair enough," she conceded.

"Meet me in my penthouse. You know the way."

She turned to leave, the fabric of her gown swaying with each step. But before she disappeared, she threw one last glance over her shoulder at me. "You'll thank me later," she called out.

I exhaled, my fingers curling into tight fists at my sides.

Circling Esme's orbit was always a risky move.

It was similar to playing with fire.

You were always close to getting burned, yet the temptation kept drawing you back.

One thing was certain: Esme Theodorus was going to make things very interesting.

Two

E^{sme}

The moment I stepped into Aidoneus Erebus's penthouse, I sensed the energy of wealth and power. The floor-to-ceiling windows offered a breathtaking view of the dazzling Vegas skyline, which shimmered more like false promises than real opportunities. Every piece of furniture in the apartment was sleek and dark, matching its owner's persona but with a hint of danger woven into its design. It was as if he wanted to remind anyone who entered that they were on his turf.

My heels clicking against the polished marble floors echoed through the large rooms. Art and sculptures decorated the space, making it welcoming yet intimidating, curated to evoke that feel. A whiskey decanter sat on a low table near a plush leather sofa, accompanied by two crystal glasses.

Was this his way of showing me that he would always be watching, always in control? This polished luxury felt more like a gilded cage.

I wandered through the living room, again drawn toward the floor-to-ceiling windows. As I looked out at the city lights below, I couldn't help but wonder how many people down there understood the amount of power Aidon held from this very building. The thought sent shivers down my spine, both exciting and sobering at the same time. My fingers traced along the edge of the glass coffee table, considering what it would take to shatter its pristine surface. For a moment, I even entertained thoughts of doing something similar to Aidon himself.

But before I could dwell on those dangerous ideas any longer, a soft chime broke through the silence.

Following the signal, I headed to the bedroom that the butler indicated was mine. Inside, I found a folded set of clothes on the bed, my suitcases already unpacked, and my belongings organized in the drawers.

Aidon's efficiency was almost invasive, but I couldn't help but smirk. He thought he could control me by keeping me here, but little did he know I had learned to navigate his games long ago. The key was never letting him see me sweat.

I poured myself a glass of whiskey and headed to Aidon's office. If he wanted me under his roof, I might as well get comfortable. What better way to stake a claim on his territory than by making myself at home there?

As I walked down the hallway and entered his office, the warm, amber glow of the desk lamp cast long shadows across the room, enhancing its commanding presence. The massive black oak desk shone in the light, and I couldn't resist running my fingers along its edge, imagining all the deals and power plays that had taken place there.

A smile appeared on my lips as I relaxed into Aidon's chair, kicking up my feet on the desk. Its comfort was undeniable, and I could see why he favored it. From here, he had a clear view of his empire, monitoring everything.

I couldn't help but imagine Aidon's voice warning me to stay out of his space. He would hate to find me sitting in his chair, which made it more tempting to claim a bit of it myself. As I swirled the whiskey in my hand, soaking in the warmth of his office, I knew this was just another game between us, one that I intended to win.

The sound of the door opening behind me sent a jolt of adrenaline through my veins, but I didn't flinch. His dark eyes locked onto mine, unflinching and filled with that signature mix of irritation and intrigue.

The door swung shut with a decisive click, the sound sharp in the tense room. Aidon entered, his dark suit sharp and precise, every step deliberate and predatory. I watched him, noticing the tight lines of his posture and the narrowing of his eyes as they settled on me lounging in his chair.

"I see you've made yourself comfortable," he said, his voice quiet and tinged with annoyance.

I raised my glass in a teasing toast. "Nice chair. I can see why you like it."

His jaw tightened, but he didn't take the bait. Instead, he walked toward me with purpose, stopping just short of the desk and leaning forward until his hands rested on its edge. His presence filled the room, making it feel smaller and more suffocating.

"Get out of it," he commanded, his gaze piercing.

I arched a brow, enjoying the flicker of frustration crossing his features. "And here I thought we were supposed to be partners. Or is this how you treat all your allies?"

Aidon's eyes flashed with anger as he moved closer. His hand came to rest on the armrest of the chair, caging me in.

"Partners require trust," he growled. "Something you haven't earned."

"Trust is overrated," I replied, though my heart was pounding under his intense gaze. "Besides, I wouldn't be here if you didn't trust me even a little."

He didn't deny it, instead moving around the desk to grab the back of the chair, spinning it so I was facing him.

He leaned against the edge of the desk, his hand still on the armrest as if to block my escape.

"Are you trying to provoke me, Esme?" he asked, his voice dangerously soft.

I tilted my head, meeting his glare without flinching. "Maybe. Is it working?"

A smirk tugged at the corner of his lips, but the tension in his jaw betrayed him. "You've always had a talent for pushing limits. But this?" His eyes flicked toward my legs, now sitting tucked on the seat of the chair. "This might be your boldest move yet."

I leaned forward and closed the gap between us. "You know I've never been one to play it safe, Aidon. That's why you like me."

"Like you?" He leaned in closer, his breath brushing against my cheek. "You're a liability I tolerate."

I laughed, the sound echoing through the charged air between us. It was my one defense against this man who smelled so good and prickled every one of my senses.

"Keep telling yourself that." I reached out to run my fingers along the edge of his tie. "If I'm just a liability, why haven't you thrown me out?"

His hand shot out, grabbing my neck and holding it in a firm grip. The sudden contact sparked a buzz over my skin, and neither of us moved for a moment. It was as if years of memories flashed before us.

His eyes darkened, and my pulse hammered.

"Don't mistake my patience for weakness, Esme," he warned, his voice a low growl. "You're here because I need you. Nothing more."

I tilted my head, letting my lips form a slow, teasing smile. "And yet, here we are. You could have left me to fend for myself, but instead, you brought me here. Into your domain. Your sanctuary. Why is that, Aidon?"

His grip on my hand tightened for a fraction of a second before he released it and stepped back. The absence of his touch made me feel colder than I expected. This reaction to him wasn't fair. He tormented me, and he knew it.

"Don't overthink it," he said with composure once more. "Stay out of my office and don't get in my way."

No, I wasn't going to let this be the end.

"Are you afraid of what might happen if I don't?"

He paused at the doorway, his back turned. "Afraid? No. Curious? Always."

With that, he disappeared, leaving me alone in his office, with the lingering heat of his presence and the ache deep inside me.

I leaned back in his chair and shot back the last of my whiskey, savoring the burn as it made its way down to my belly.

I took a deep breath. Aidon thought he could control me, but I was always at my strongest when operating on the edges of control. And I had no intention of playing by his rules.

Later that evening, as I sat in my armchair, I watched the distant city lights flicker against the window, casting a soft glow in the darkened room. I couldn't shake the heavy weight of Aidon's words. They pressed down on me, suffocating and stifling.

His warning echoed in my mind in a non-stop look, cutting deeper than a knife.

After years of mastering indifference, pushing people away, and keeping them at arm's length, why was it Aidon Erebus who affected me this way? Why couldn't I shake off what he made me feel or think? It was so easy with everyone else.

Why not him?

I stood up from the chair, walked to the bar cart, and poured a glass of whiskey. Lifting the glass to catch the last rays of sunset, I watched the amber swirl inside.

I stared into the spirit, hoping to find some answer or clarity. Perhaps it was the challenge he presented, the way he refused to let anyone outplay him, or was it something else, a lure toward him that I couldn't explain or control?

With a heavy sigh, I placed the glass on a nearby table and pressed my palms against its smooth surface. That was when a realization hit me.

At some point in this dangerous game we began playing long ago, I stopped caring about the rules.

I was fucked.

THREE

E^{sme}

Aidon's gaze burned into me as I paced back and forth in his dimly lit penthouse office. The air was thick with unspoken tension, contrasting with the positive energy of the bright sunlight shining down on Las Vegas this morning.

Aidon leaned against the desk, his arms crossed in front of him, demanding answers without speaking a word.

"You're wasting time," he said after he was tired of the wait. "If you have a plan, lay it out."

I stopped mid-step and turned to face him, giving him a mocking laugh. "A plan? Do you think we can take down Zeno's empire with just one plan? This isn't a game of chess, Aidon. It's war."

"Then tell me where to aim," he retorted. "Because all you've been doing is talking in circles."

I moved across the room and stood just inches from him. "You think it's that simple? Taking down Zeno doesn't happen by barging through his front door. He's not stupid."

Aidon straightened, his tall frame casting a shadow over me. His body warmth pressed against me without ever touching, and for a moment, I wondered if he might close the distance.

But he didn't. He never showed me more than a glimpse of his intensity, just enough to unsettle me. Just enough to keep me hanging on the edge. Just enough to remind me of everything I lost when I walked away.

"Then enlighten me," he challenged with dangerous softness. "What do you need from me, Esme?"

I hesitated, feeling my confidence waver under his piercing gaze.

For a few moments, memories surfaced, from Zeno's smug grin as he warned me what would happen if I ever stepped out of line to the lies I told for him to survive.

I pushed the past away and focused on Aidon, uncertainty rising up.

Was Aidon the answer, or was I making another mistake? But I pushed those thoughts aside and steeled myself.

"I need your access," I said, my voice steady. "Your resources. Zeno has a vault that very few know about. And those who know, only a trusted one or two can access. I know the location and how to get in."

Aidon raised an eyebrow. "A vault? What's inside?"

"Leverage," I replied. "Enough to bring Zeno down from the inside out. But it isn't in a typical location and protected by a system that perhaps your connections can bypass."

There was a tense pause as we both let the weight of my words sink in.

A heavy silence lingered between us, filled with unspoken questions and doubts. I saw Aidon's mind working, taking in my words, dissecting them, and looking for any cracks in my story.

Finally, he spoke up again. "If I agree to this, there's no turning back. You betray me again, Esme..."

You'll kill me, I said with a roll of my eyes. "Yes, Aidon, I've heard the threat before. But if I betray you, I'll face much bigger problems than just you. Zeno doesn't forgive traitors."

Family or not, I was a tool to Zeno, a pawn to use as he pleased—no more. I couldn't do it anymore.

"We'll plan this together," he declared with finality. "But understand this, Esme, the moment I sense you're playing me, our partnership ends."

I couldn't help but smirk at his warning as I leaned against the desk he had just vacated. "Then you better hope I don't play you."

The tension lingered long after our exchange had concluded. It was like a thick fog hanging around us, suffocating and filling every part of the office with its heaviness. The walls felt too close, the room too small, and every look from Aidon was like a spark just waiting to ignite.

Needing some fresh air to clear my head, I approached the window. But his voice stopped me in my tracks.

"You're holding back."

I turned to face him, my heart pounding in my chest. "I have told you what you need to know."

"No," Aidon countered, moving closer until we were a breath apart. "You have told me what you want me to hear. There is a difference."

The room seemed to shrink as he closed the distance between us until I felt his warmth radiating off him, hot and suffocating.

My back pressed against the cool glass, a stark contrast to the fiery intensity of his presence. He didn't touch me yet, but his nearness alone overwhelmed me.

"What are you so afraid of, Esme?" His voice was low and dangerous, like a growl. "That I'll see the truth? That I'll see you?"

"You don't know anything about me," I shot back, my voice wavering as his eyes locked onto mine, unyielding.

His question tore into my resolve, revealing the cracks I work so hard to hide. It felt like a sharp knife, cutting through my defenses and leaving me exposed. His hand brushed my cheek as he pushed a strand of hair behind my ear, leaving an electric charge that sent shivers down my spine.

Don't I?" His voice was soft but laced with frustration and hurt. "You want me to trust you, but you won't give me a reason to. Why is that, Esme? What are you hiding?

My heart felt heavy with guilt and longing as his words hit me harder than I wanted to admit. I considered telling him everything for a moment, letting him in just enough to quiet the growing storm between us. But the weight of all the unsaid words between us charged the air further, threatening to snap at any second. My breath caught in my throat as his fingers lingered near my jaw. His intense gaze searched mine for answers I couldn't give.

"Aidon," I began, but before I could finish, he closed the gap between us and kissed me.

I responded without thinking, my hands clutching his shirt as I pulled him closer. It was as if a raging storm exploded within me, a mix of anger and desire that stole my breath away.

His grip on my waist tightened, our bodies pressed close as our lips moved in an urgent dance driven by passion and frustration.

"You're impossible," he muttered against my mouth, his voice rough with emotion.

"And you're predictable," I shot back in defiance.

His low laughter vibrated over my skin as he retorted, "You drive me insane, Esme."

"Good," I hummed, feeling alive in this chaotic moment as I held onto him. "Then we're even."

The kiss deepened, our tongues battling for control as they slid, rolled, and dueled against each other.

My pulse pounded in my ears, and goosebumps prickled down my spine. Aidon's overwhelming presence, oppressive and electric, filled the room, making it clear that something dangerous simmered beneath the surface.

"I should walk away from you right now," he growled in a

low and rough voice. "You're chaos, Esme. You unravel everything you touch."

"Then let me go," I replied, my body betraying me as I leaned into him despite knowing nothing could come of this. "You hate me, remember? I'm just a liability."

His grip tightened, not meant to harm but to remind me that he held the reins, even as the fire in his eyes may make me believe otherwise.

"Hating you would be easy," he murmured, his lips so close they almost brushed against mine. "But I don't. And that's the problem."

The weight of his words hung between us, undeniable and heavy. My heart raced in my chest, and my breath caught as the air grew thick with an unspoken tension. He was so close now, his woodsy scent enveloping me like a vice.

"Aidon," I whispered, but he cut me off.

"No more talking," he commanded, as his free hand slid up to cup the back of my neck and his fingers tangled in my hair, tilting my head back.

His lips crashed down with a primal force, igniting a fire that burned through me hotter than any wildfire.

This wasn't a gentle, sweet seduction but a battle of wills and a surrender all at once. The intensity building was years in the making, raw, untamed, and desperate.

Logic said to push him away and end this before it went any further. Except I found myself pulling him closer and fisting the fabric of his shirt.

He groaned against my lips, a sound filled with pent-up

desire and longing. His arm wrapped around my waist, pulling me flush against him, and I gasped at the feeling of his hard, thick cock locked between us as if it were a brand marking me.

"Is this what you wanted?" he rasped, his lips trailing from my jaw to my throat. His teeth grazed the sensitive skin there, sending shivers down my spine.

"You tell me," I managed to say, my voice trembling with need as I tangled my fingers in his hair. "You're the one in control."

He chuckled against my skin, the vibration of his voice sending tingles through me. "Control? With you, that's a luxury I don't have."

The tension between us kept growing, driven by a fiery passion that blurred the borders between anger and desire. Every touch, every kiss, deepened the ache inside me.

"You drive me insane," he muttered against my neck, his breath hot and ragged.

"Good," I whispered back, tugging on his hair just enough to make him groan.

He pressed himself against me with determination, teasing and tormenting me until I couldn't handle it anymore. At that moment, nothing else mattered except us being locked in this fierce dance of lust and desire. But then he pulled back, meeting my gaze with dark, burning intensity.

"You don't play fair, Esme," he growled, his tone laced with desire and frustration.

I smirked at him, my desire fueling my confidence. "And you love it."

A flicker of dangerous intent flashed in his eyes, hinting he saw right through my bravado. He kissed me again, all traces of gentleness replaced by dominance and need.

The sound of our ragged breaths filled the room, adding to the palpable lust consuming us. He pulled back, resting his forehead against mine as he cupped my face. It was a small gesture that cut straight to my core, making me want something I couldn't have.

"You're exhausting," he murmured, a smirk tugging at the corners of his lips right before he brushed his mouth over mine.

This time, the kiss was slower but no less intense. It was a lingering exploration.

Aidon's hand followed the same directive, gliding over every curve and dip of my body, igniting sparks wherever he touched. With deliberate movements, he cupped my breast through my shirt and pinched the hardened tip, eliciting a moan from between my lips.

I clutched at him as my core spasmed and arousal pooled between my legs.

His other hand slipped beneath the hem of my shirt, brushing against the bare skin of my inner thigh.

I moaned and whimpered, dropping my head to Aidon's shoulder. His scent surrounded me, a heady mix of spice and danger that made every nerve in my body come alive. He tilted my neck, his breath coasting over my skin, sending shivers down my spine.

With skilled fingers, he grazed over my throbbing clit.

"Aidon," his name escaped my lips like a desperate plea.

Each touch sent electric shocks through me, igniting the fire inside until it turned into an inferno begging for more.

"You're so fucking wet."

"It's only like this with you."

My confession seemed to unlock something primal in him as he shifted and lifted me into his arms. I wrapped my legs around his waist, needing to hold him close. The room blurred as he carried me to the primary suite, his weight pressing me into the soft mattress beneath us.

He captured my lips again, then moved lower, scoring his teeth and tongue down my neck. His mouth left a fiery trail in its wake, igniting every nerve in my body.

"Say it again," he murmured, his voice rough and commanding. "Tell me you want this."

"I want this," I whispered, arching my back as he buried his face against my pelvis.

He reached up and tugged the straps of my dress down my shoulders, exposing my body to his gaze.

"You're fucking beautiful." His eyes seemed to glitter with hunger as if he were a man possessed.

No one had ever looked at me with such intensity before. Aidon's palms settled on my hips, his touch electric and setting fire to every inch of my skin.

"I have to taste you. It's haunted me for too fucking long."

In an instant, he removed my underwear and delved between my legs without hesitation.

"Oh, God," I cried out, my back arching off the bed as I fisted his hair in my hands.

He devoured me, driving my need higher and higher. Everything inside me tightened, reaching that point I craved so desperately. Then he thrust two fingers into my pussy, curving them to hit the right spot inside me, and I shattered.

It was exhilarating and what I needed.

But it also made me realize that Aidon was the one man who could do this for me, and I hated how much control he had over me.

He pulled away from my body and stepped off the bed to shrug off his clothes. He was a Greek god with a body designed for both fighting and fucking a woman senseless.

He climbed over me and caged me with his large body. His touch was electric, setting fire to every nerve I possessed. His lips found mine again, deeper and hungrier, a battle and surrender all at once.

The room seemed to pulse with the intensity between us, every sense heightened. His taste was an intoxicating blend of whiskey and something darker, something uniquely Aidon.

"Please," I whimpered, lifting my hips in desperation to feel him inside me.

His response was a low growl that vibrated against my lips. "What do you want, Esme?"

"You already know," I breathed out.

"Make it crystal clear," he demanded against the shell of my ear.

His voice was rough and commanding, impossible to ignore, igniting a deeper desire within me.

I held his gaze, unflinching. "I want you to fuck me."

"Are you saying that's all we do?" He fisted my hair, a

crease forming between his brows as he positioned himself at my sopping entrance.

I responded without thinking, "It's all I can say it is."

"I see." He slammed into me with a ferocity that took my breath away.

The heat between us surged, wild and unrelenting. There was no more talking, just the primal sounds of carnal lust filling the room. Aidon pounded into me with a brutal and unrelenting rhythm.

I raked my nails down his skin, desperate to leave my mark on him. Our actions were raw and emotional, and neither of us would acknowledge them once it was over. But for now, we kissed, touched, and consumed each other.

My orgasm rushed over me like a volcanic explosion, my pussy clamping down on his pistoning cock, flooding him with my arousal.

This man could play my body like no one else.

It wasn't fair.

"One more time," he growled, and before I could even process what he had planned, his palm slid between us to circle my sensitive clit.

I lost myself in the sensations, knowing deep down that there was no future for us, no matter how much we both wanted it. But in this moment, as we came together again, calling out each other's names, nothing else mattered.

FOUR

E^{sme}

On the day of the heist, the trip to Zeno's guarded vault was just as dangerous as the mission itself. We sneaked through the back alleys of Vegas, dodging patrols and bypassing security systems with ease. Using our forged credentials, we entered the building, our heartbeats pounding with every step.

We planned every move and action with meticulous care, right down to clearing the armed final checkpoint. Now was when we faced the real challenge of our quest.

My body trembled with nerves and adrenaline as Aidon and I waited, hidden in the shadows near the building housing Zeno's vault.

I'd waited for this moment for so long. My plan was coming to fruition right before my eyes. The air around us seemed to pulse with this electrifying energy, adding to my anticipation.

Except I couldn't allow myself the freedom of too much excitement. We were about to invade the monster's lair. That knowledge alone should frighten me.

Then, there was the low hum of the building's intricate security system, which constantly reminded us of the danger that lurked around us. The moon's faint glow illuminated our surroundings, casting long and ominous shadows that seemed to writhe and move on their own accord. Every second felt crucial despite our planned timeline. Even the most foolproof plans were not immune to disaster.

"Are you sure about this?" Aidon whispered beside me, his warm breath tickling my ear as his deep voice reverberated through my body and sent shivers down my spine.

I turned to him, a small smile playing on my lips. "Would you believe me if I said yes?"

He released a resigned sigh, amusement and annoyance flickering across his features. "Not for a second."

I pressed my body against the cold stone wall as I neared the security panel, the sharp chill piercing through my clothing. My fingers moved over the controls, each code coming to me as if it were a second language I had mastered through years of precise manipulation. Zeno built his vault to be an unbreakable fortress of secrets, but he never expected someone like me.

Aidon stood beside me, his presence both reassuring and

unsettling. His dark eyes kept sweeping the corridor for any sign of movement. "You've done this before," he muttered.

I shot him a smirk, my lips twitching with amusement. "What gave it away?"

"The confidence," he said, suspicion lacing his tone. "And the recklessness."

"We have three minutes before the secondary alarm goes off," I informed him in hushed tones, ignoring his commentary. "Are you ready?"

He didn't answer. Instead, his sharp gaze lingered on me, assessing and calculating.

"Always," he finally growled, his words carrying more weight than they should have.

The lock disengaged with a soft click, and I pushed open the door. A sleek and high-tech chamber greeted us, shimmering with faint blue light. The stark brightness was jarring compared to the darkness we had just left behind. Steel cabinets lined the walls, their surfaces gleaming like secrets locked away.

"Impressive," Aidon murmured, his tone neutral, but his narrowed eyes betrayed his thoughts. "Zeno doesn't do subtle."

"No," I agreed in a softer voice. "He doesn't."

We moved in perfect synchronization, silent and efficient, as if we had been partners for years instead of just tolerating each other out of necessity. I fixed my gaze on the far end of the room where a small, ornate case sat on a pedestal. The surface was etched with intricate patterns, and the gold caught the faint glow of the security lights like a beacon.

"There," I whispered, pointing toward it. "That's what we need."

Aidon wasted no time, moving toward the pedestal with a predator's grace. He reached for the box, his broad frame casting shadows that danced across the walls. His jaw tightened as he studied it, his fingers brushing over the ornate surface as if testing its reality.

"Do you know what's inside?" he asked, his voice cutting through the quiet.

I hesitated, the truth threatening to escape from my lips like an unspoken confession I wasn't ready to share. The weight of what was inside that box felt heavier than all the secrets I kept.

"It's leverage," I said, my voice calm but subdued now. "That's all you need to know."

His gaze flicked to mine, suspicion darkening his expression. His intense stare made me want to look away, but I held his gaze, refusing to back down. Whatever doubts or questions he had at that moment, he let them go, at least for now.

Without saying another word, he lifted the box from its pedestal, holding it as if it were delicate and risky. The tension in his jaw eased just a little as he nodded toward the door.

"Let's go," he said.

The sound of approaching footsteps echoed down the hall, shattering our fragile quiet. My pulse quickened with adrenaline, sharpening my focus.

"Too late," I muttered, drawing a slim dagger from my belt. "We have company."

Aidon's expression darkened, his free hand moving toward the concealed weapon at his hip. "How many?"

I listened for a moment, counting the steps. "Three. Maybe four."

His lips twisted into a grim smile. "Easy."

The door burst open, and chaos erupted. The guards encircled us, but they did not expect Aidon's ruthlessness or my unpredictable nature.

Ducking low, my heart pounded as adrenaline raced through me. My blade flickered in the dim light as I struck the nearest guard with a quick blow to the leg. He collapsed to the ground with a grunt, and I spun around to face another opponent. Aidon moved like a flash, his attacks precise and deadly. In moments, the guards lay groaning on the ground.

Wiping a streak of blood from my cheek, I couldn't help but remark, "Remind me never to piss you off."

Aidon shot me a look that almost seemed amused, his lips curling into a faint smirk. "Too late for that."

Together, we moved into the shadows, with our target tucked away in Aidon's hold. Tension simmered between us, driven by the adrenaline of battle and something even more perilous. Every accidental touch of our hands felt electrifying, and each stolen look sparked a blazing fire inside us.

Stepping into the cool night air, with the shimmering lights of Vegas in the distance, my breathing slowed. But relief didn't flood my senses, and an electric charge refused to dissipate.

"We're clear," I said, my voice betraying a hint of unsteadiness.

Aidon turned to face me, his dark gaze lingering on my face. "What's next?" he asked, his tone softer now with an edge of something undefinable.

Stepping closer, I could feel my pulse quicken at his proximity. "We use what we took to destroy Zeno," I said.

"Is that all?" he asked, his eyes dropping to my lips.

"Not even close," I admitted, feeling a hitch in my breath as his fingers brushed against my cheek.

His lips captured mine in a fierce kiss, unapologetic and driven by need. It was a clash of fury and desire that consumed us both. There was no hesitation, no pretense, just the raw intensity building between us since we met. My hands gripped his jacket, pulling him closer until there was no space left between us. His hands, strong and commanding, wrapped around my waist as if he couldn't bear to let me go.

The kiss grew more intense, his tongue exploring every part of my mouth, claiming me in a way that made my knees weak. A low growl rumbled from his chest as my fingers tangled in his hair, tugging just enough to make him take a sharp breath.

"Esme," he murmured against my lips, his voice thick with desire. "You make everything so complicated."

"Good," I whispered back, my voice trembling as his hands roamed lower, igniting a fire within me. "Complicated is more fun."

He chuckled at my reply, causing a chill to run down my

spine. His lips parted from mine, leaving a trail of hot kisses along my jaw and down to my neck. The scrape of his teeth against my sensitive skin made me gasp, and I arched toward him.

"You're going to be the death of me," he growled, his voice dripping with need and danger, each word like a promise.

"If you're lucky," I replied, unable to control the rush of heat pulsing through my body as his hands traced the curve of my hips.

In that cold, dark alleyway, our fire burned brighter than anything else. Each touch and kiss was a battle, a surrender, a constant reminder of everything we couldn't say. And as we pulled apart, our breaths mingling in the cool night air, the world seemed quieter and the stakes higher for what was yet to come.

The sound of distant sirens reached our ears, and reality crashed in.

"We need to move," I said, stepping away.

"Let's go," he agreed, though his hand lingered on mine for longer than necessary.

As we disappeared into the shadows, the tension between us remained unspoken but potent, a volatile current charged with the weight of what had happened and the undeniable pull of what was still to come.

FIVE

A idon

The ornate box sat untouched on the polished coffee table, its intricate designs catching the light and reflecting it in myriad colors. It was a mesmerizing display that seemed to promise secrets and danger. My eyes couldn't help but be drawn to it, my mind racing with thoughts of what could be inside. I leaned against the edge of the desk, arms crossed tight over my chest as I watched Esme pace back and forth across the room. Every step she took seemed purposeful yet hesitant, a contradiction in her usual confident demeanor that left me feeling on edge.

"You still haven't told me what's inside," I said, my voice low and even but laced with an underlying sharpness. The question felt like a blade aimed right at her, a challenge to reveal the truth.

She stopped mid-stride, her back still, her shoulders rising and falling with each controlled breath.

She turned and spoke, her words clipped and measured. "I told you, it's leverage."

I repeated, 'Leverage,' then stepped away from the desk and moved behind her.

My voice was sharp, and I was losing patience. "That's not an answer, Esme. What is it inside that Zeno would risk everything to keep safe?"

She turned to face me then, emerald eyes flashing with defiance as she met my gaze head-on. But beneath that familiar steel was something else, a flicker of uncertainty, a hint of vulnerability she was trying to conceal.

"It doesn't matter," she said. "You wanted a way to destroy Zeno. This is it."

"It matters if it's going to backfire on me," I growled, closing the remaining distance until we almost pressed against each other. The tension between us was palpable, crackling like electricity in the air. "Tell me what's inside, Esme. Now."

Her lips pressed into a thin line, her shoulders squaring as if bracing for a fight. Her fingers twitched, a nervous energy coursing through her body.

"You'll find out soon enough," she finally replied, her voice hollow but still tinged with defiance.

I closed the space further, backing her up against the wall until we were almost nose-to-nose. The live-wire tension pulsing around us grew stronger, sparking every nerve in my body and rendering me unable to think straight.

"Do you think you can manipulate me, Esme?" I growled, my hands braced on either side of her head as I trapped her against the wall. My voice lowered to a dangerous whisper. "After everything we've been through, you still don't trust me?"

Her chin lifted, an unspoken challenge in her gaze that dared me to call her bluff. "Trust is a luxury neither of us can afford in this game, Aidon," she shot back.

The tension between us was thick and charged, like a spring coiled tight and waiting to snap at any moment. As I leaned in closer, our bodies almost touching now, I couldn't ignore the heat radiating off her or the intoxicating scent of her perfume that seemed to lure me in further. Every second felt like a high-stakes game, one I couldn't afford to lose, yet couldn't seem to stop playing.

"This isn't just a game to me," I said, as I closed the final inch between us. "And if you're lying to me..."

"You'll what?" she interrupted, her voice sharp but breathless. She tilted her head, the moonlight glinting off her emerald eyes as she stared at me with an unreadable expression. Her lips curved into a daring smirk that didn't quite reach her eyes, giving her an air of confidence and defiance. "Kill me? Turn me over to Zeno? We both know you won't."

Her words were a taunt, her tone a challenge to push me closer to the edge. I could feel my control slipping, my emotions and desires warring inside me.

I remained quiet.

Instead, I let the silence stretch between us, heavy and charged. I watched the way her chest rose and fell with shallow breaths, her pulse visible in the hollow of her throat. Her defiance was a shield, but cracks were starting to show, and I couldn't help but wonder what lay behind it. Was it fear? Or something darker, something even she couldn't control?

For a moment, I thought she might crack, that she'd let the truth slip from behind her mask. Her lips parted, revealing a hint of vulnerability in the hesitation flickering in her eyes. It was a fleeting moment where she seemed unsure whether to push or pull away.

But then she did the one thing I wasn't expecting.

She kissed me.

It wasn't gentle. It wasn't sweet. It was fierce, desperate, and unapologetic, a clash of anger and need that left no room for doubt. Esme's hands fisted the front of my shirt, pulling me closer as though she could silence every question I would dare ask her. Her nails dug into the fabric, and I could feel her strength and frustration in every movement.

I should have pushed her away and demanded answers. But instead, I surrendered to the chaos; my hands slid to her waist and pulled her against me. The taste of her was intoxicating, a mix of defiance and fire that left me craving more, each second more consuming than the last. My grip tightened, my fingers tracing the curves of her body as her breath hitched against my lips, a sound that sent a jolt through me like a live current.

"Esme," I groaned against her lips, my voice thick with desire and frustration. "You're impossible."

She pulled back just enough to meet my gaze, the moonlight casting shadows on her face and giving her a hint of mystery. Her emerald eyes blazed with a mix of triumph and something softer, something unspoken.

"You're just figuring that out?" she whispered, her lips curling into a wicked smile.

I didn't give her time to say anything else. I captured her mouth again, deepening the kiss and consuming her. My resolve unraveled with every touch and every sigh. The world outside ceased to exist, reduced to nothing more than the feel of her in my arms and the heat of her skin beneath my hands. There was no room for doubt, no space for questions, just the raw, unrelenting need that consumed us both in that moment.

Then, just as fast as it started, she pulled away, leaving me breathless and off balance.

Her gaze was unreadable. It was a mix of determination and something darker, something I couldn't place but knew would haunt me.

Her jaw tightened as though she were holding back words she wanted to say or truths she feared to reveal.

"You'll thank me for this," she said, stepping around me with a fluidity that made her feel untouchable, untethered. She moved toward the box with purpose, her shoulders set with the resolve that came before something final.

"Esme," I warned, my voice sharp, a thread of desperation bleeding through.

But she ignored me and opened the case, the lid creaking in a way that made my chest tighten with a sense of foreboding and dread.

Inside the ornate wooden box lay a collection of documents, photographs, and a small flash drive. Despite their unassuming appearance, I felt the weight and power emanating from these objects.

She turned to me, her once gentle expression hardening into something resolute and unreadable. "This is everything. Zeno's empire, his secrets, his vulnerabilities. It's all here."

I stepped closer, my eyes examining the evidence with a narrowed focus. The air grew heavier with each step, like the secrets within the box pressed against me.

"And you're just handing it over?"

Her smile lacked any real joy as she replied, "Do you think this is easy for me? That I haven't considered every possible outcome?" She snapped the box shut with trembling hands, betraying her calm facade. "You want to destroy Zeno? Here's your chance. But don't expect me to stand by and watch."

Her words hit me like a physical blow, and I stood frozen, trying to make sense of her meaning. "What are you talking about?"

She avoided my gaze and clenched her fists at her sides. For the first time, I saw cracks in her armor, the vulnerability she was so desperate to hide.

"I can't stay here, Aidon. Not after this. If Zeno finds out I'm involved, he'll..." Her voice broke, and she shook her head, unable to finish her sentence. "He'll kill me before you can stop him."

The thought of losing her sent panic surging through me, an unfamiliar feeling that I struggled to push down beneath a mask of control. "Then stay. We'll deal with Zeno together."

But her bitter laughter, filled with disbelief and regret, cut through the tension like a knife. "You still don't understand, do you? This isn't just about Zeno. It's about survival. And the way I survive is if I disappear."

Her words felt like a gut punch, and I needed something to ground me—anger, frustration, anything but the hollow ache of watching her slip away. But before I could argue, footsteps outside the door froze us both in place. Her eyes darted toward the noise, her expression shifting from defiance to dread in an instant.

In a swift motion, she snatched up the box and spun toward me. "Trust me, Aidon," she pleaded. "This is how it has to be."

"Like hell," I growled, reaching out to grab her wrist, but she slipped through my grasp like smoke.

The door burst open as Zeno's guards flooded the room, their weapons drawn. But my focus was on her as the betrayal gutted me like a knife twisting in my chest.

A call from one of my men snapped my focus away from Esme and to the chaos ensuing around me. I shifted, ducking a blow from one of Zeno's soldiers, and retaliated with all the fury churning up from Esme's treachery.

With my team at my back, the fight was short-lived but

brutal and merciless. My fury and determination for retribution grew for every bruise I received or drop of blood I spilled.

Esme would pay for this. It was obvious she planned this double cross from the very beginning.

It wasn't until hours later, right as I believed Esme disappeared without a trace, that Ares arrived at my club office.

"I found something, Sir." Ares handed me an envelope.

I tore open the seal and pulled out the contents. Inside the container was a confirmation for admission to a high-stakes poker tournament in Monte Carlo.

"Have you followed up?" I asked.

"A woman with Ms. Theodorus's description arrived in Paris this evening. It is safe to say the information we have is accurate."

I nodded. "Arrange to have our prey captured."

Ares inclined his head.

I turned and stared out of the window, gazing at the city's glittering lights. I clenched my fists and made a silent vow: "No one betrays me and gets away with it, Esme. Not even you. Get ready to pay your penance."

Time to turn the page and watch Aidon and Esme's cat-and-mouse game begin.

FORBIDDEN EMPIRE

One

A IDON

My heart pounded a wild beat as I stared at the monitor, transfixed by the flickering image of the woman on the surveillance footage. Esme Theodorus's presence on the screen was like a live wire, sending jolts of electricity racing through my veins, setting every nerve ablaze.

It was maddening how just the sight of her could unravel me so completely. Since the last encounter we had in person, I'd been locked in a futile battle to extinguish the fiery reaction she ignited within me. Esme had an uncanny knack for drawing out the most primal urges from the depths of my being.

I found myself caught in a tempest of conflicting desires: the longing to lose myself in her until she was insensible and the urge to squeeze the life from her until she hovered at the brink of consciousness.

No one else in the world evoked such intense emotions in

me. And no remedy seemed able to quench this unrelenting obsession.

I tried everything. Other women were mere shadows, leaving a hollow ache in their wake. Alcohol, like gasoline, fueled the blaze of my desire for her.

Even the thrill of a high-stakes brawl couldn't match the way my heart raced for her, though it beat with a darkness as black as night.

It was absurd to be so consumed by one woman, to feel as if I were a marionette dangling on the strings of my infatuation for Esme. The realization that she could make me feel like a lovesick fool infuriated me to my very core. After all, I was a kingpin in the glittering city of Las Vegas, a man whose mere name could cause both allies and adversaries to pale in fear or reverence. My enemies feared me as much as they aspired to emulate me.

As I strode through the vibrant, pulsating streets bathed in the glow of neon lights, I was a figure of awe, respected not only for my immense influence and wealth but for the empire I had constructed with my own two hands.

I demanded respect in every area of my life, and as a result, it was given to me by everyone I met. Everyone except Esme, that is. Damn, I couldn't shake the feeling that Esme had never truly respected me. If she did, she had a strange way of showing it.

Sitting in the quiet of my personal office in The Underworld, my mind spun as I fixated on the image of my nemesis and obsession on the screen.

"Fuck," I muttered under my breath, watching as she

slipped into a private elevator at one of the most opulent resorts in the world.

I tapped the button on my laptop to replay the footage, my eyes narrowing in concentration as I scrutinized every frame. The video was grainy, and the angle was distant, obscuring her face more than I'd like.

However, I was sure it was her. There was no doubt in my mind, not even a little. Esme had a unique walk, one that no one else in the world could imitate.

She carried herself with the regal grace of a queen, her long raven hair flowing down her back, catching the light as she moved. Her emerald eyes, bright and sharp, scanned her surroundings with an alertness that suggested nothing escaped her notice.

But it was the confident sway of her curvy hips that was unmistakably Esme.

As I watched her stride purposefully toward the elevator in the grainy security footage, my cock twitched, a familiar jolt.

This was the last image of her we had recorded, a haunting video loop I examined for any missed clues about her current location. Each replay was pointless, but I still hoped to find something new.

I tried to tell myself I was analyzing the footage for details I might have missed, but deep down, I knew I was fooling myself more than ever. I pretended I didn't ache for her presence. I convinced myself that the endless, restless nights filled with tossing and turning were unrelated to her absence.

And most of all, I tried to believe I could move on, that

life would continue seamlessly even if I never laid eyes on her again.

But the truth was as persistent as the image of her in that video—inescapable and undeniable.

I was obsessed with finding her.

She'd fucking used me, betrayed me, and then disappeared.

Now, here I was, pressing the rewind button once again, at least the hundredth time, as my eyes traced every detail of her image on the screen.

My thoughts drifted back to the last time I saw her, her laughter echoing in my ears, the warmth of her skin beneath my fingertips, the lingering taste of her lips.

Damn it all.

I shook my head, trying to snap out of this trance that deceptive woman had me trapped in. Forcing my gaze away from the screen, I let my eyes drift over the dance floor below, where colorful lights flickered and bodies moved to the rhythm. It was a reminder that I was more than just a man consumed by an impossible woman.

I'd constructed this place from the ground up, every beam and brick set according to my design.

The Underworld Club was a dimly lit sanctuary adorned with plush velvet drapes and crystal chandeliers, where the city's elite gathered in secret.

This was where the titans of industry and shadowy figures met to network, negotiate, and seal the deals that would alter the city's power dynamics.

Were most of those deals bordering on illegality? Maybe.

But that was standard in Vegas, after all, a city built on risks and whispers. I had created a refuge where the wealthy could indulge in their high-stakes games, free from prying eyes and the relentless noise of the Strip.

From my shadowy perch on the balcony above the club, I could see everything unfold below me. The dim lighting cast an intriguing glow over the scene, where the most fascinating displays of human behavior took center stage.

In the dark red plush leather booths, men in tailored suits whispered into the ears of women in slinky dresses, their conversations masked by the ambient noise.

Deals were made with a nod or a subtle hand gesture, the currency being lives and fortunes rather than cards or chips.

This was where the real gambling occurred in this town, with not a slot machine in sight.

Beautiful women dressed in shimmering, barely-there outfits weaved through the crowd with trays of champagne flutes, their laughter blending with the clinking of glasses.

This was Vegas, after all, a place where dreams were made and destroyed in the blink of an eye.

Watching over it all, I felt a thrill surge through me, knowing my business was thriving.

The Underworld, as I called it, offered a front-row seat to the secrets that kept my power in this city unbreakable.

I dealt in information, gathering whispered confessions and hidden truths, turning them into leverage and influence. My skill in manipulating this knowledge was unmatched, which earned me respect and sometimes fear. Did I have to seize it through darker means at times? Certainly, but in this world, that was the norm. The empire I had built was vast, a testament to the power I wielded from the shadows.

It should have been enough for me. It might have been enough, too, in some alternate universe where I'd never even heard the name Esme Theodorus, but I would never truly know. Esme had snatched my focus like a hawk plucking a rodent from a field, and I could think of hardly anything else but her.

I was grateful when I saw Ares ascending the curved stairs that led up to my suite. I needed the distraction, but as soon as he saw that I was watching the footage again, he shook his head with disappointment.

"Boss, you're just playing right into her hands. You know that, right?" he asked.

His eyes, as sharp as steel, fixed on mine with an understanding gaze. Ares was not only my most loyal enforcer, but also one of the few I regarded as a friend. His loyalty was unwavering, and I trusted him with my life. That was why he was the only one permitted to speak so frankly about personal matters like this.

And, unfortunately, he was right about Esme.

That knowledge twisted in my gut like a knife. Her ability to manipulate my emotions was infuriating, and the realization that I was falling right into her trap was maddening.

Rather than responding, I clenched my teeth and reached for the double rye whiskey bottle on my mahogany desk.

The amber liquid sloshed against the glass as I poured another shot, the third in just a couple of hours. Yet, despite the burn of alcohol sliding down my throat, the frustration inside me churned relentlessly, a violent river refusing to be tamed.

I hated the fact that Esme consumed my thoughts, an obsession I despised yet couldn't shake.

Ares understood this unspoken torment. He refrained from uttering the obvious, but the concern etched across his face was as clear as a silent accusation.

"Where the hell could she have gone?" I muttered.

I poured him a whiskey, the amber liquid swirling in the glass in hopes of wiping that judgmental look from his face. His eyes were sharp like daggers, assessing every movement.

"You checked Reno?" I asked, watching him lift the glass to his lips.

"Yep." He nodded, taking a sip with a twisted smile that didn't quite reach his eyes. "She's a fucking ghost in the wind."

"What about Los Angeles?" I pressed, leaning back against the worn leather couch.

"She's too smart to go there." He shrugged, setting the glass down with a soft clink. "But I checked, just in case. No sign of her anywhere."

"What about Tahoe?" I suggested, picturing the dense woods and secluded cabins. "Maybe she's hiding in a cabin or something."

"If she is, she's hiding very well," he replied, running a hand through his hair.

"She will slip up." I gritted my teeth. "Then she won't have a chance."

"In the meantime, Aidon, we have other priorities." He leaned forward, eyes narrowing. "We need to evaluate the threat from Rhea and the Shadow Syndicate. Whatever Zeno had in that box contained a lot of intel on them. We're not the only ones after Esme now. Maybe we should handle Rhea and Zeno first?"

His words hung heavy in the air, the gravity of the situation settling in.

Zenobius "Zeno" Theodorus, a former friend turned rival, was yet another thorn in my side. I'd handle him after I took care of my business with his baby sister.

"Fuck that," I growled, with a dismissive wave. "I'm much more focused on finding Esme."

"That's obvious. Look, I know she betrayed you, I know you want revenge, but—"

We turned at the sharp click of approaching footsteps echoing down the hallway, and I couldn't suppress a groan as Helena Karras appeared at my door. Her silhouette was unmistakable, with her sharp suit and piercing gaze.

Helena Karras, my operations manager, burst in like a thunderstorm. The only person besides Ares who wasn't afraid of me and who told me what I needed to hear, especially to clear my mind. She handled logistics, felt the pressure, and heard the voice that reminded me that "protection isn't absolution," even when I was reluctant to listen.

Helena was straightforward, sharp-witted, and her honesty was often brutal. She maneuvered through the world of casino bosses and syndicate leaders with a skill that was almost like art.

Her ability to earn their trust, while uncovering their deepest secrets was nothing short of impressive. She moved through their ranks like a shadow, with every interaction carefully planned, her presence a mix of charm and intimidation.

"Fuck," Ares muttered under his breath, his eyes narrowing as he spotted Helena striding toward us with an all-too-familiar air of superiority.

We both understood that Helena's visits were infrequent, like a solar eclipse, and usually signaled trouble.

"Helena, hello," I greeted her.

Her presence was like a storm cloud rolling in, and I braced myself for whatever news she carried.

"Aidon, how's your day?" she inquired, her heels clicking against the marble floor.

Her overwhelming confidence radiated off her like a noxious perfume, and the smug grin stretched across her lips was enough to churn anyone's stomach. No one held Helena in higher regard than Helena herself.

"It was great, until now," I replied, attempting to mask my irritation.

"Cute." She chuckled, her laughter echoing like a taunt. "Great to see you, too, my friend."

"What are you doing here?" Ares demanded, stepping beside me with his shoulders squared, his disdain for her as plain as the scowl etched on his face.

The air between them crackled with tension as they locked eyes, a silent duel of wills unfolding in the charged atmosphere.

"Ares, are you still here?" she said with a mocking tilt of her head. "I was sure you'd have been knocked off long ago, considering what a terrible shot you are."

I stifled a groan, sensing the coil of anger winding tighter in Ares. He stood rigid beside me, every muscle taut like a cobra poised to strike.

"You want to volunteer for target practice?" Ares suggested, with a low, menacing growl that carried a clear warning. "I'll show you what a good shot I am."

Helena's laughter cut through the tension, her manicured fingers splayed in mock surrender.

"Down, boys!" The gold bracelets on her wrist jangled as she tossed her hair back. "Don't shoot the messenger!"

I leaned forward, knuckles white against the edge of my desk. "Messenger?"

Her red lips curled into a smile that didn't reach her eyes. She glanced at her watch, a Cartier that cost more than most people made in a year.

"I would've gotten to that if your attack dog hadn't bared his teeth the moment I walked in."

Ares stepped closer, the floorboards creaking under his weight. "Spill it."

Helena's shoulders stiffened. She crossed her arms, the fabric of her designer blazer pulling tight across her chest. "Rhea sends her regards."

"Playing errand girl for the Shadow Syndicate now?" My eyebrow arched. "Does big brother approve?"

"Please." She gave a one-shoulder shrug, her perfume, something expensive and floral, wafting through the air between us. "Zeno's chess pieces are right where he wants them."

"And?" I asked.

Helena's manicured fingers extracted a cream-colored note from her blazer pocket. She flicked it across my desk like a playing card. The paper skidded to a stop against my whiskey glass.

I unfolded it with one hand, the expensive stationery crisp between my fingers. Rhea's handwriting, elegant cursive in blood-red ink:

Aidon,

Still searching for your runaway queen? Be careful what you wish for.

Best,

Rhea

My jaw clenched so tight I tasted metal. "This is your urgent message?"

"My job was delivery, not content." Helena's lips curved into that practiced smile.

Ares moved between us, shoulders blocking my view. "Door's that way."

"Always a pleasure, gentlemen." Her heels click-clacked a staccato rhythm down the marble stairs.

The note crackled as my fist closed around it. I hurled it toward the bin, missing. The paper bounced off the rim and settled on the floor like snow.

Ares's eyes tracked the movement. "She's trying to rattle you."

"Let her try." I slammed my palm against the desk. The

whiskey bottle jumped. "Rhea thinks she's untouchable in her little shadow kingdom."

"So, what's our play?"

The image of Esme's face floated before me—her knowing smile, those eyes that saw right through me.

"Find. Her." Each word punctuated the air between us. "I want every camera in this city watching for her. Every informant on alert. Every hotel room searched, if necessary."

"Aidon, Rhea's people are—"

"Did I fucking stutter?" The vein in my temple throbbed. "Esme first. Everything else burns until I have her back."

Two

Esme

The black sequins on my dress shimmered like tiny stars under the strobe lights on the dance floor as I strolled past them.

The club pulsed with life, a sea of young, stunning faces moving to the beat. Laughter and conversation blended with the music as people sipped on cocktails garnished with exotic fruits and mint leaves, their glasses clinking.

The rooftop of the Ida Hotel and Casino offered a panoramic view, but above us, the glow from the relentless neon signs of the Strip swallowed the night sky, concealing any real stars.

I made my way to the balcony's edge, my fingers curling around the cool metal railing.

Below, the sidewalk teemed with tourists, a constant flow of bodies moving from one spectacle to another. The horizon was a dazzling display of flashing casino signs and towering hotel façades, each vying for attention with its kaleidoscope of colors.

Cars crawled along Las Vegas Boulevard, headlights creating a slow-moving river of light.

The sky above was a swirling masterpiece of orange and pink hues, remnants of the setting sun casting its final glow over the towering hotels and endless casinos of this manufactured paradise.

Palm trees swayed in the warm evening breeze, their elongated shadows stretching across the bustling concrete sidewalks, grasping at the vibrant chaos of street performers and hawkers below.

I allowed myself a small, satisfied smirk, savoring the thought that I'd survived another day in the heart of the beast. I was hiding in plain sight, a shadow among the multitude of sunburnt tourists clutching cameras and ice cream cones.

It was a risky move, but I had kept ahead of the men chasing me. I considered escaping the city, yet I knew Aidon and Zeno's relentless followers wouldn't give up, no matter where I fled. Rhea's keen senses and fierce determination probably had her closing in too.

The information I'd spirited away was a ticking time bomb, capable of dismantling their entire operation, and they were aware of the threat I posed.

At least in this city, I navigated its labyrinthine streets with the ease of a seasoned local. I knew how to walk with purpose, to draw attention, when necessary, but more important was how to blend into the crowd, becoming invisible amidst the endless waves of people who never seemed to tire of the neon-lit allure of this place.

But I wasn't naive. I knew the cloak of anonymity wouldn't shield me forever. I would have to confront Aidon and Zeno, face the repercussions of my daring theft, and pay for the chaos I'd unleashed. Sooner or later, my streak of luck would come crashing to a halt.

This was Vegas, after all. In this town, the constants seemed to be the ache of longing, the shadow of despair, and the insatiable hunger for more. Luck was just a mirage in the desert heat. But true to the spirit of a seasoned Las Vegan, I was savoring the streak of good fortune while it lasted, relishing my freedom like a rare delicacy.

The neon signs of Vegas flickered their empty promises across the Strip.

Here today, dark tomorrow.

I tossed back my drink, savoring the burn. Seven days in that Green Valley rental had left me twitching behind identical beige curtains, counting stucco ceilings that mirrored the ones next door, and the next, and the next.

Tonight, sequins bit into my skin as I adjusted the straps of a dress that did the bare minimum to cover what it needed to. My calves ached from six-inch stilettos, and sweat gathered beneath the blonde wig tickling my shoulders. I'd chosen the Ida Hotel's rooftop for this.

Bodies pressed against bodies, music drowning thought. I caught my reflection in a stranger's sunglasses. I was just another party girl, black frames obscuring half my face, invisible in plain sight.

I savored the sweetness of my third Bellini, bubbles tickling my nose. My thoughts drifted to Aidon, who was probably seething now, frustration boiling over in waves of anger. I pictured him storming around his sleek Underworld office, face flushed, fists clenched. A sly smile crept onto my lips, feeling a wicked delight. Aidon's magnetic intensity made him a force to be reckoned with. It drove me mad.

My fingers touched the tiny sequined purse slung across my body, brushing against the cool, metallic surface of the USB drive inside. It was my constant companion, and I kept checking it throughout the day. Each time I felt its reassuring weight, a wave of relief and anxiety swept over me.

A sharp, remorseful pang struck my heart as I snapped the purse shut. I had orchestrated an elaborate heist to snatch that box from Zeno, betraying Aidon, my lover, in the process. I vanished with it, spiriting away its hidden treasures. Yet, the power it granted me was irresistible, a temptation I couldn't ignore.

But I wasn't the only one who valued its contents. I knew they wouldn't hesitate to do anything to get it back. Staying in Vegas was a risk I couldn't take much longer. I needed to come up with a plan, a way out, even though I didn't know where I was heading. Every second here brought me closer to danger.

My phone buzzed insistently against my hip, a reminder of the world outside my thoughts. I opened my purse again, fishing out the device to answer the call.

"Hey."

"Esme, it's me."

"I know, Selene. You called me from an encrypted phone number."

Selene was my secret weapon, a digital phantom who could slip through firewalls, a ghost through walls. Her fingers danced over keyboards like a musician's, composing symphonies of code.

She had been my eyes and ears on Aidon and Zeno, tracking their every digital move, sending me a steady stream of intel about their whereabouts and schemes.

"Right. Listen, we have a problem. I don't know how, but Aidon's getting close to finding you. You need to get out of that city as soon as possible, Esme."

"Oh, yeah?" I replied, letting her words swirl around my mind like smoke. I closed my eyes, feeling the pulse of my instincts.

Today, the city felt like a fortress of anonymity. The risk was palpable, a tingling in my veins, yet Selene's warning barely registered as more than a whisper in the wind. Instead of fear, a rebellious thrill surged through me.

There was something intoxicating about living in Aidon's shadow, slipping past his notice for so long.

As for Zeno, he was a different story.

My half-brother's rage was a storm that might have swept others away, but I had weathered it before. He wanted the information I held like a gambler clutching a winning hand, but I doubted he'd resort to violence.

I wanted to savor this daring game, stretch the tension like a rubber band, knowing the longer I stayed hidden, the sweeter Aidon's defeat would taste when he realized how close I'd been all along.

"I'm not worried," I said with a smirk, feeling the corners of my lips curl upward. "Let him try."

"You're playing with fire, Esme."

She was right, of course. Aidon was a dangerous man, with a temper that simmered like a volcano about to erupt. I'd seen the fury in his eyes up close, felt the tension in the air crackle when he was displeased. He was not just intelligent, but possessed a sharp, calculating mind that made him both cunning and ruthless. It was as if he had a sixth sense, able to see through every façade I put up, predicting my moves before I even knew what they would be.

This time, I felt the thrill of being ahead, at least for the moment. A tiny spark ignited in my chest, a flicker of fear, though I questioned whether it was fear at all.

What would happen if Aidon caught up with me?

I pondered this question once more, replaying every scenario in my head like a broken record.

Would he kill me in a fit of rage?

Harm me, leave me bruised and broken?

Keep me locked away, a prisoner in his twisted game?

Or would he fuck me with an intensity that bordered on madness, pushing me to beg for mercy?

For some reason, none of these possibilities stirred genuine fear within me.

"I'm fine, Selene. Don't worry. I know what I'm doing," I reassured her, trying to sound more confident than I felt.

"So do I, remember? I'm good at my job, Esme. So,

believe me when I tell you that your time is running out." Selene's warning crackled through the phone, urgent and insistent.

"I hear you, my friend," I replied, forcing a casual tone. "Thanks for the information. I'll be in touch soon."

I ended the call, cutting off her protests. She worried too much.

I brushed off any lingering doubts, squared my shoulders, and stepped away from the balcony, leaving the cool night air behind.

With a cool glass in hand, I navigated through the pulsating sea of people, my mind set on enjoying the night.

The thumping bass reverberated through the air, and I scanned the scene, a hobby I indulged in often. A shadowy corner caught my eye near the club's casino, where an unclaimed chair beckoned.

I settled into it, the dim light casting long shadows.

My gaze roamed the crowd, soaking in the kaleidoscope of couples swaying to the music and groups chatting, their laughter bubbling up like champagne.

I inhaled deep, the scent of perfume and cologne mingling with the faint odor of smoke, trying to dismiss the echo of Selene's warning that still lingered like a distant thunder.

Sure, coming here was a gamble, a reckless decision given the circumstances, but hell, I'd already rolled the dice on the biggest gamble of them all by choosing to run.

This wasn't the time to worry. Not tonight. I took another sip of my drink, savoring the sweet, juicy burst of peach that danced across my taste buds. The alcohol hummed through my veins, leaving a warm, fuzzy sensation that started at my toes and spread through my entire body.

It was just what I needed. My shoulders began to sway to the rhythm of the music playing softly in the background, and I let all the worries melt away like sugar in hot tea.

Tomorrow, I promised myself, I would take the time to analyze everything in detail. If I concluded it was time to leave, then I would make my move.

But for now, I needed another drink. I stood up, my empty glass in hand, and weaved my way through the room toward the bar. As I passed a poker game in full swing, I couldn't help but smile at the palpable tension hovering over the table. A group of men sat hunched over their cards, jaws clenched, and brows furrowed, with a single woman among them.

My eyes caught her face as I was passing by, and I paused, intrigued. Her features were taut with concentration, yet inscrutable, embodying the essence of a perfect poker face.

The men around her, however, were far less composed. Sweat beaded on their foreheads, and their hands trembled as they clutched their cards. When I noticed the massive stack of chips in the center of the table, I understood the stakes.

A growing crowd gathered around them, and I joined in, our collective breath held in anticipation of the woman's next move. She exuded sophistication and beauty, her raven hair elegantly coiled into a French twist.

Her appearance was immaculate, from her impeccably

tailored dress to her long, black, sharply manicured fingernails, which tapped rhythmically on the table's edge.

My eyes were locked onto her, a sense of familiarity tugging at my memory like a persistent itch.

Who was she?

The question echoed in my mind, just out of reach. She splayed her cards on the green felt table, and the crowd around them collectively inhaled, a sharp gasp slicing through the tension-filled air.

The men facing her turned ashen, their bravado crumbling as they slumped back in their chairs, the weight of defeat heavy on their shoulders. With a confident sweep of her arms, she pulled the pile of chips toward her, a wide grin lighting up her face.

Her expression of triumph was intoxicating. She met the searing stares of the defeated men with a smile that was as victorious as it was serene, before sweeping the chips into her luxurious Birkin bag. With a graceful ease, she stood, her presence commanding the room, and walked away, leaving a trail of astonishment in her wake.

I couldn't help but be impressed. She had outplayed them with elegance, catching each one off guard with her undeniable skill. They had clearly underestimated her, and I found myself resonating with her audacity. It mirrored my own experience, living in the shadows day by day.

Aidon and Zeno were undoubtedly hunting for me relentlessly, yet I remained hidden, right under their very noses. The thrill of evading them sent a rush of adrenaline through my veins, making me feel alive. Each day, however, it became more evident that I needed to leave. If I didn't, I'd be forced into a confrontation that I wasn't interested in participating in.

Staying in Vegas was too risky, as Selena reminded me with her worried eyes and stern lectures. But leaving meant abandoning unfinished business, which went against every fiber of my being. I hated the thought of walking away from a game before it reached its conclusion.

As the crowd began to disperse, I scanned the faces surrounding me. The pulsing lights of the club cast colorful shadows on the dancers, who moved to the throbbing beat of the music. Most people were returning to the dance floor, their bodies swaying, or heading to the bar for another drink, just like me. I wove through them, my gaze darting from face to face.

I froze in place when my eyes landed on a man near the front door. He stood out, not because of his appearance, but because of his demeanor. He was rigid, his posture unnaturally stiff, as if poised for action. His eyes swept over the crowd with a calculating intensity, just like mine.

And then, as if in slow motion, his eyes locked onto mine. They widened in recognition, and my heart skipped a beat as I realized I recognized him, too.

He was clearly one of Aidon's men, his dark coat and steely demeanor making him stand out in the dimly lit club. His eyes locked onto my face with a laser-like focus as he lunged forward, determination etched into his features.

Panic surged through me.

Damn it. I was too late.

They had tracked me down.

Still, I hadn't been captured just yet.

In a split second, I spun around, blending into the thrumming crowd. My small frame was an advantage as I slipped between the towering figures, their laughter and movement providing the perfect cover. With nimble steps, I edged along the perimeter of the crowd, sidestepping dancers until I reached the club's front door.

I risked a glance back and saw him on the balcony, his head swiveling like a hawk searching for prey. He hadn't spotted me again, not yet. A triumphant grin tugged at my lips as I made my way to the elevator, leaving behind the pulsating lights, the intense music, and Aidon's enforcer lost among them.

Leaning against the cold metal wall of the elevator, I watched as the doors slid shut. My heart thundered in my chest, adrenaline coursing through me.

That had been too close. The closest encounter yet. Selene's words echoed in my mind. Maybe she was right. Perhaps it was time to disappear. For good. Now.

THREE

AIDON

My persistence had paid off, and the sweet taste of victory finally settled in my mouth.

I stepped out of the blistering Las Vegas sun, squinting against the harsh light, and pushed through the revolving glass doors of the Olympus Casino. Instantly, the cacophony of the casino floor engulfed me.

The clatter of slot machines mingled with the rhythmic clinking of poker chips, while dealers called out bets in voices that rose above the din.

Each casino in this city was a fingerprint of its own, unlike any I'd encountered in places like Monte Carlo, Venice, or even Salzburg, where elegance mingled with a more subdued atmosphere.

Here, the flashing lights dazzled with relentless rhythm, casting a kaleidoscope of colors over the sea of eager faces. The air was thick with a heady mix of cigarette smoke and spilled cocktails. That unmistakable scent of money mingling with the bitter undertones of disappointment lingered like a heavy perfume. The desperation etched into the gamblers' eyes was palpable as they clung to their chips, their hopes pinned on the next roll of the dice or flip of a card.

It was a heady cocktail of pain and pleasure, a concoction I found intoxicating, and I was addicted to its allure.

That addiction had driven me to open my own exclusive club, a sanctuary designed to cater to the city's elite. I tailored my establishment to indulge in the unique desires away from the prying eyes of the bustling casino floor.

I walked through the corridors, tourists shuffled like zombies, their eyes darting from one glittering attraction to another. The fleeting dream of sudden wealth lured them forward, a siren's song promising riches.

They all believed it could be their moment, a single card game, one lucky pull of the slot machine.

But those of us working behind the curtains of this neon-lit paradise knew the truth. The occasional lightning strike of fortune was a spectacle, a rare occurrence meant to fuel the myths. Real wealth in this town wasn't found on the casino floor.

It was amassed far from the glittering chaos I had just stepped into, in the shadows where deals were made and fates were sealed.

Today was different. I was a man on a mission, focused, and nothing was going to distract me. The bustling scene around me was a blur.

I ignored the elderly women bustling in and out of overpriced boutiques, their shopping bags rustling with every step. The children, with sticky fingers and chocolate-smeared faces, dripped melting ice cream onto the vibrant carpets, oblivious to the world. I maneuvered through clusters of young women, their sequined dresses catching the dim casino lights as they sipped colorful cocktails, not even glancing their way.

A thrill coursed through me, a tingling sensation that danced along my skin.

Esme was close.

I could feel it deep within, an unshakable certainty that only grew stronger. Just yesterday, one of my men had caught a glimpse of her at the Ida, but she had slipped away, leaving him empty-handed and me seething with frustration.

Right now, fortune smiled upon me.

Ares had rung me up not thirty minutes ago. He'd seen her at the Olympus Casino, of all places, calmly seated at a poker table as if she were just any other tourist passing through.

Her audacity staggered me. It was almost admirable.

Esme, who had deceived me and stolen from her own brother Zeno, was now brazenly sitting in the very casino he owned. It was as if she dared him and every syndicate family from here to Los Angeles to come and find her.

In a twisted way, I couldn't help but respect her boldness. She had vanished with invaluable information, having duped me into aiding her, and took with her the power to topple many influential figures.

The whispers had been relentless, though only Zeno

knew what the contents of that box and USB drive held. Judging by Zeno's frantic search for her, whatever was on there was undoubtedly explosive.

I halted at the perimeter of the bustling crowd, my eyes sweeping the room with hawk-like precision.

Across the sea of people, I locked eyes with one of our men.

My gaze followed his direction, and there she was, Esme, her presence as electrifying as ever. I gasped, the thrill of the chase surging through me once more.

She sat with her chin tilted at that precise angle I remembered—the one that made her look both regal and dangerous. Her fingers tapped the edge of her cards in a rhythm I'd watched a hundred times across my sheets.

Ten feet away, a man with shoulders like a linebacker pretended to watch the roulette wheel, his gaze returning to her every seven seconds, but she didn't spare him a glance.

I moved closer, each step heavier than the last. My collar tightened against my throat.

The air between us vibrated with the same electricity that had once left claw marks down my back.

Fuck.

My mouth went dry. The memory of her taste flooded back, salt and honey and that goddamn expensive whiskey she always stole from my cabinet.

My pants grew uncomfortably tight, the fabric straining as blood rushed south to my cock, betraying me like it had every night for weeks as I'd lain awake staring at the ceiling, sheets twisted around my legs.

As I navigated the perimeter of the bustling crowd, my eyes drank in every detail of her presence. Her long black hair was concealed beneath a short wig of auburn hue, revealing the graceful curve of her neck, pale and delicate. I swallowed hard, the memory of the soft skin at the nape of her neck beneath my lips sending a shiver down my spine.

Her tight cocktail dress clung to her body, its neckline plunging daringly to expose the swell of her creamy cleavage. The vivid image of her bare breasts seared into my mind, leaving me breathless and propelling my feet to move faster.

Within moments, I was standing behind her, my mind racing as I considered my next move. Ares's urgent phone call had propelled me here in such a rush that I hadn't paused to formulate a plan. All I could focus on was her face, her presence consuming my thoughts. Now that she was within reach, I wrestled with what to do next.

Conflicting urges surged within me, the desire to both harm and possess her battling for dominance.

Here, amidst the eyes of the public, I knew I could do neither. But once we were alone? In that private moment, all constraints would vanish, and anything could happen.

The possibilities were limitless.

I took a deep breath, the cool air rushing into my lungs. I caught the faint, floral scent of her perfume, jasmine and amber. It was a familiar fragrance that tickled my memory and set my nerves on edge.

This woman was going to be the death of me if I wasn't careful. Just the sight of her, with her elegant posture and confident smile, left my heart pounding and my hands trembling. I prayed that nobody else noticed the turmoil within me.

Ares's man sidled up beside me, his presence a steadying force. His neatly pressed suit and sharp gaze marked him as a professional.

"Can I do anything for you, sir?" he asked, eyes scanning the room.

"Do you have any chips on you?"

He chuckled, reaching into his pocket. "I do. Was trying to blend in earlier." The chips clinked as they cascaded into my palm, cool and smooth against my skin.

"Thanks," I nodded, flexing my fingers around them.

"Anything else?"

"No, I can take it from here." I clapped his shoulder. "Good job."

"Of course," he said, melting back into the crowd.

I took another deep breath, feeling the tension coil in my muscles, and moved in the direction of the poker table.

There was an empty seat beside her, its red velvet cushion beckoning. I grasped the back of the chair and pulled it out swiftly, the legs scraping lightly against the polished wood floor.

"Mind if I join?" I asked, my voice cool and calm, a complete contrast to the storm brewing inside me.

Esme lifted her pretty green eyes, her gaze flickering with alarm for the slightest fraction of a second before the walls went back up. She lifted her chin, the perfect picture of power and control.

I almost laughed at the display.

She and I were anything but cool and calm, and we both knew it. But we mirrored each other, neither of us willing to let our guard down.

I threw the chips in the middle of the table and nodded to the dealer. My thigh brushed hers as I sat.

She didn't flinch, but her back straightened, her body stiffened, and her shoulders grew rigid and stoic.

When I glanced down, her knuckles had gone white around her cards, the veins in her wrists prominent.

I nodded to her, a gesture laden with unspoken tension and history.

"Good to see you again," I said, grabbing the cards the dealer slid toward me.

"Wish I could say the same," she muttered with a venom that cut sharper than a knife. "You always liked to make things as difficult as possible, didn't you, Aidon?"

A smile tugged at my lips, but I remained silent.

I could have thrown the accusation right back at her, for running off, for the betrayal, for this tangled web of deceit we now found ourselves ensnared within.

If it weren't for her treacherous ways, we wouldn't be locked in this relentless game of cat and mouse, each move more dangerous than the last.

We'd probably be in my bed fucking each other's brains out.

Instead, we were here, caught in a game with stakes higher than any poker match could ever hold.

My cards were strong, a trio of aces promising victory. I discarded two and raised the stakes, locking eyes with her.

Esme arched an eyebrow, silently accepting my challenge, her gaze a storm of defiance.

I leaned closer, bringing my mouth to her ear.

"Are you surprised to see me, little mouse?" I taunted. "You've made me a very happy cat."

The dealer slapped two more cards down in front of me, and I barely contained the triumphant grin threatening to spread across my face. With a dramatic sweep, I shoved all my remaining chips into the center of the table, the clatter echoing like a battle cry. The other players crumbled, folding under the pressure, leaving just us locked in this high-stakes duel.

Esme's jaw tightened, her beautiful features a battlefield of tension as she weighed her next move. My eyes drank in her face, each glance a punch to my gut, stealing the breath from my lungs. How could I ever articulate the seething fury she deserved?

She was worthy only of my unbridled wrath. Yet, a primal part of me yearned to offer her something entirely different. Every fiber of my being screamed to devour this woman whole.

The emotions tearing through me were maddening. I had come here with a singular purpose: vengeance. Not for carnal satisfaction, Not for the fleeting thrill of desire or lust. But my resolve was being challenged, and the turmoil was more than I had bargained for.

I forced myself to concentrate on the seething anger boiling inside me, trying to ignore the relentless pressure of my throbbing cock straining against the confines of my slacks. Esme laid down another card, her lips curling into a sly smile that vanished as fast as it appeared. Her jaw twitched when she glanced at her new card, a telltale sign of her confidence.

She thought she had me cornered, thought she could manipulate me like a puppet on her strings. She was so wrong. The anticipation of proving her mistaken, of shattering her illusion, sent a thrill coursing through my veins. If my instincts were right, Esme Theodorus was rarely confronted with her own errors.

The prospect of being the one to enlighten her was an exquisite pleasure I could hardly contain. With a defiant flair, she pushed her pile of chips to the center, matching my bet, exuding an arrogance that bordered on recklessness. A stray lock of hair fell across her face, and I fought the overwhelming urge to brush it aside.

I kept my cards close, leaning in closer to her, whispering with a dangerous proximity, my lips grazing her ear. She remained still, unfazed, her lack of retreat fueling my intrigue further.

Perhaps she wasn't afraid of me at all. Maybe she was just naive, teetering on the edge of a game she didn't yet understand.

"You've been running for too long, Esme," I snarled, grateful that my voice carried the fury I needed while sitting this close to her. "You knew I'd hunt you down, didn't you?"

Her gaze avoided mine, but the frustration blazing in her captivating emerald eyes was unmistakable.

I was struck by her beauty, those lips, those eyes, that

defiant tilt of her chin. It was a sight capable of unraveling even the most stalwart of men.

I prayed she couldn't see how she robbed me of breath. I needed to keep my emotions locked away, hidden from her perceptive gaze.

If she detected even a hint of weakness, she'd wield it like a weapon against me. With an air of defiance, she laid down her cards, revealing four of a kind. "Impressive," I murmured, my smile betraying none of the storm within as I showed my hand.

I couldn't suppress the triumphant grin that spread across my face, my royal flush gleaming back at her.

Her eyes widened, but she nodded with resolve, surrendering to her defeat.

I reached for the pile of winnings in the center of the table just as she stood and glided away, her movements a graceful taunt.

I smirked, shaking my head as I watched her sashay away with casual indifference.

"Thank you." I nodded to the dealer, abandoning the mound of chips on the table and slipping into the shadows of the casino, hot on the trail of my elusive prey.

Her hips swayed like a pendulum, counting down the seconds of my restraint. My jaw clenched so tight I tasted metal. Three strides and I'd have her.

Two. One. She veered down a hallway, dark and secluded.

Perfect.

The casino noise faded with each footfall until all I could

hear was my ragged breathing and the click of her heels against marble.

Jasmine and something darker, her scent filled my lungs as I lunged forward, fingers digging into the soft flesh of her shoulder.

She spun, a flash of emerald eyes widening before her back slammed against the wall. The impact knocked a small gasp from her lips.

She didn't cower. Didn't beg.

Instead, her palm pressed against my chest, the heat of it burning through my shirt like a brand. I felt her push, a butterfly trying to move a mountain.

The corner of my mouth twitched with an electric thrill as I leaned in, obliterating her resistance between us.

With a sardonic grin, I seized her wrist, yanking her arm up and pinning it above her head. She fought back with her other hand, trying to push me away, but I mirrored my actions, trapping her until she was forced to gaze up at me, both hands secured, her back arching, and her breasts pressing against my chest.

Being this close to her was like standing on the edge of a precipice; every nerve in my body screamed with urgency.

It was overwhelming, suffocating, an inferno of proximity. I struggled to draw breath as I held her captive. She squirmed against me, a defiant motion that sent shockwaves through my nervous system, igniting my fury, and stoking the inferno of desire roaring within me.

Yet, it was sheer astonishment that dominated my thoughts. How dare she challenge me now?

"Stop struggling," I ordered. "You're mine now. I've captured you. Time's up, Esme."

"Fine," she muttered defiantly, locking eyes with me, her gaze shimmering like stars in the dim light. "Now what?"

She bit her lip, her eyes flashing, her breasts pressing harder into me. A derisive laugh escaped me, sharp and mocking. Did she think her charade would deceive me?

"Now what?" I echoed, my eyes blazing with intensity. "What do you think?"

"I think," she purred, her words dripping from her lips like honey, "that you should let me go, Aidon."

"Is that so?" I snarled as I tightened my grip on her wrists with a force that could leave bruises. I forced myself to ignore the infuriating distraction of her breasts, her hardened nipples scraping against my chest sending a jolt of electricity through my spine.

She dared to bring her mouth close to mine, her breath a tantalizing whisper against my lips. My heart thundered in my chest, a wild drumbeat of rage and desire. She was playing with fire, toying with a predator without the slightest comprehension of the danger she was in.

Could she not see the destruction I was capable of? Did she not understand the peril of her reckless flirtation? With just a twist of my hands, I held the power to snuff out her life. Surely, she had to be aware of that.

I planned to obliterate this woman, and yet she treated this like some trivial game, a jest between us to laugh about. Very well; I could play along with her reckless charade.

I leaned in, my lips a hairsbreadth from hers. "You pretty

little mouse, do you believe I'll release you now that I've ensnared you in my trap?"

She lifted her chin, her lips brushing mine with a feather-light touch, a slow, provoking smile curving her lips. "Have you caught me, Aidon? Or have I caught you?"

She arched one perfect eyebrow, her silence stretching between us like a tripwire.

"Maybe I let you find me, Aidon." Her tongue caressed each syllable of my name. "Did you even consider that?"

My pulse hammered against my throat. The casino's neon lights caught in her hair as realization sliced through me. Las Vegas. She'd been here all along, moving through crowds I'd walked through, breathing air I'd breathed, watching me hunt for her while hiding in plain fucking sight.

"You're playing a very dangerous game, Esme." My fingers tightened around her wrists until I felt the delicate bones beneath her skin. Her pulse raced against my thumb, not from fear, but excitement.

She could have stopped me, but she chose not to. Her lifted chin was a response: a decision rather than a surrender.

She tilted her head, studying me like a scientist observing a particularly fascinating specimen. Those emerald eyes dissected me, cataloging every micro expression, every twitch of muscle. I'd seen her do this to others—strip them bare, with nothing but a glance before she went for the kill.

"A dangerous game?" She leaned forward until her lips brushed the shell of my ear. "How fun." Her whisper sent electricity down my spine. "Doesn't the thrill of it all turn you on, Aidon?"

She licked her bottom lip, driving me out of my mind. Her hands were still pinned above her head, and I knew that if I reached down just a bit, I could be under her skirt in seconds.

The thought of her thighs wrapping around me while I plunged deep into her pussy flashed in my head, tempting me, tantalizing me, driving me out of my fucking mind.

She knew what she was doing, too.

She fluttered her lashes with calculated precision, her tongue flicking over her lips before catching the bottom one between her teeth. She appeared every bit the damsel in distress, but beneath the façade lay a sinister villainess, poised to strike and obliterate her foe at the slightest opportunity. I would never yield to her.

This cunning vixen dared to toy with me, flaunting her audacity when she should have been quaking in terror. Her nerve was infuriating. Was she truly devoid of remorse? Did she not grasp the peril she faced? Not only from me but from countless others who sought her demise.

Esme had committed the ultimate betrayal by pilfering Zeno's cache of secrets. She ought to count herself fortunate that I found her first. Zeno would have shown no such restraint, no such mercy.

Still, despite my fury, her beauty was a relentless siren call. In the dimly lit corridor, she was a masterpiece in chiaroscuro, the hall's kaleidoscope of blues, greens, and reds painting her in a mesmerizing dance of shadows.

The compulsion to kiss her was overpowering. Her

breasts pressed against my chest, igniting a primal hunger within me.

Sensing my vulnerability, the dizziness in my mind, the involuntary twitch of my desire, she seized the fleeting moment of my hesitation. In a blur, she twisted free, slipping from my grasp with agile speed. She ducked beneath my arm and vanished down the hallway, dissolving into the throng of tourists like a phantom.

"You wicked little witch." My teeth clenched so hard my jaw ached as I stalked after her through the casino's labyrinth.

She moved forward with grace, each purposeful step a challenge. Not running and not even rushing.

My pulse hammered in my throat as she weaved through the crowd, the distance between us stretching and contracting like a living thing. The casino lights caught in her hair, turning each strand into a flame that beckoned me forward.

She glanced over her shoulder, her emerald eyes finding mine instantly in the crowd. The corner of her mouth curved upward before she tossed her hair, the scent of her perfume hitting me seconds later. Her laughter floated back, crystalline and mocking, piercing straight through my chest.

My fists clenched at my sides, nails digging half-moons into my palms. Blood roared in my ears.

Every muscle in my body strained toward her, a compass needle finding true north. I'd tear this fucking city apart brick by brick to reach her.

Each step I took burned with self-loathing, yet my feet kept moving, slave to her invisible leash.

Four

ESME

I zigzagged through the sea of bodies, ducking between slot machines and dodging cocktail servers until I spotted the swinging double doors marked EMPLOYEES ONLY. I shoved through them, the doors slapping shut behind me with a satisfying thwack.

My intuition told me Aidon couldn't be far behind. He'd never give up.

Not now that I'd managed to stir his fury, but I couldn't say that I felt any regret about that.

In fact, it was thrilling to know I could get so deep under his skin.

Behind the scenes, the casino was pure chaos.

Had I lost him?

The employee corridor erupted around me, a hive of white uniforms, shouted orders, and the metallic clatter of service carts.

A cook with a tray of champagne flutes glared as I shouldered past. My stilettos betrayed me on the slick floor, ankle twisting. I caught myself against the wall, leaving a sweaty handprint on the pristine paint.

"Hey! You can't be back here!" someone shouted.

I didn't look back. Just pushed off the wall and sprinted forward, the click-click-click of my heels like a time bomb counting down. Another set of doors loomed ahead.

I slammed through them and froze.

Flashing lights. Ringing machines. Another goddamn casino.

"Fuck!" The word hissed through my clenched teeth as my pulse hammered in my throat.

I'd find my way out of this one, too. I could do it.

I yanked my oversized sunglasses from my bag, fumbling them onto my face with trembling fingers, forcing myself to slow my steps even as every nerve screamed to run.

The tinted lenses turned the already dim casino into a murky underwater world where shadows morphed into Aidon's silhouette at every turn.

My phone vibrated with multiple texts from Selene:

SELENE: Where the fuck are you going?

SELENE: You're in Olympus. Are you crazy?

SELENE: You don't go from Olympus to the Underworld. Zeno's and Aidon's crews are everywhere.

SELENE: MULTIPLE EXITS COVERED. Aidon's and Zeno's. You're fucked.

SELENE: Let me know where to send the funeral flowers.

Sweat trickled between my shoulder blades as I weaved through the labyrinth of slot machines.

A man in a dark suit by the craps table touched his earpiece, eyes scanning the crowd.

One of Zeno's. I ducked behind a bachelorette party, their shrieks of laughter providing perfect cover.

Twenty feet to the side exit. Fifteen. Ten.

The taxi stand stood just beyond those doors. Then the airport. Then freedom.

My fingertips tingled with the phantom sensation of a boarding pass. The taste of champagne at thirty thousand feet. The sweet relief of disappearing.

A ghost in the wind.

A forgotten memory.

The Vegas casinos were designed to be a series of labyrinths that swallowed exits whole and made it almost impossible to leave.

The pathways twisted and turned like a monstrous snake, ensnaring me in a relentless loop, making me feel like a frantic rat trapped in a never-ending maze.

With every labored step, my frustration swelled, each breath more ragged than the last.

I stumbled to a halt by an elevator with a small map beside it, scanning the sea of faces in the glass reflection.

My heart thundered against my ribs as I spotted one of Aidon's men locking eyes with me, charging forward just as the elevator doors yawned open.

I dove inside, my fingers slamming the buttons with frenzied urgency to shut the doors. My luck teetered on the brink, but for some reason it held, and the doors slid shut mere seconds before the man reached them, sealing him out and propelling me skyward.

"God, thank you," I gasped.

I jabbed the top button, praying for a path to the roof, a sanctuary to lie low.

In moments, the elevator rocketed me to the top floor, revealing a vast, opulent, carpeted hallway.

Gold gilded mirrors adorned the walls, their frames cradled by rich red velvet damask wallpaper, imbuing the corridor with an air of extravagant luxury. At the far end loomed a pair of heavy, intricately carved wooden doors, flanked by gleaming gold sconces.

"Of course, the high rollers level," I muttered, my gaze darting all around.

I turned my head to the other end of the hallway and saw what I was looking for.

I bolted toward the roof access, my heels digging into the plush carpet with each frantic stride. Freedom waited just beyond that door.

All I needed was twenty minutes on that rooftop to disappear.

My fingertips brushed cold metal when the knob twisted. The door exploded inward, slamming against my shoulder.

Ares filled the doorframe, his scarred face twisting with recognition.

"You," he snarled, lunging forward. "You can't get away from us here."

His hands clamped around my biceps like steel traps, fingertips digging deep enough to leave bruises.

"Call the boss!" he barked over his shoulder, his breath hot against my ear. "NOW!"

I thrashed against him, my dress tearing at the shoulder. The second guard's phone glinted in the hallway light as he punched in numbers.

"Fuck you!" I screamed, dropping my weight all of a sudden.

As Ares adjusted his grip, I snapped my head forward, sinking my teeth into the meaty part of his forearm until I tasted copper.

His howl echoed down the hallway as my elbow cracked against his ribs. I stomped my stiletto straight down on his leather shoe.

Bone crunched. His grip slackened just enough that I twisted, tearing free.

Freedom. Twenty feet away. Ten. The elevator dinged.

The doors slid open, and there Aidon stood, blocking the light like a solar eclipse.

I slammed into his chest at full speed, the impact stealing my breath. His cologne hit me next, cedar and whiskey and something darker.

His fingers flexed at his sides. One heartbeat. Two. His lips curled upward, revealing teeth too white against his olive skin.

"You've always been a fighter, haven't you, Esme?" The words slid from his mouth like silk over steel. "It's one of the things I admire the most about you."

Despite the rage boiling in his eyes, he seemed to be in complete control of his emotions.

In contrast, my heart was racing a mile a minute, a thin sheen of sweat had beaded on my forehead, and my breasts were heaving.

Frustration mounted inside me.

How could he maintain such infuriating calm? Just being near him tossed me into a whirlpool of anxiety, my thoughts spinning.

I shot a glare up at him, struggling to regain my breath.

"You can't stand not being in control, can you?" I spat, a molten river of frustration matching his seething tension.

My gaze flickered downward, catching sight of the gun nestled beneath his suit jacket.

His men approached like a storm, their anger palpable, eager to demonstrate their loyalty to Aidon. Escaping their clutches would be a Herculean feat.

I edged back toward the penthouse doors, and he mirrored my movement with a predatory step forward. I retreated again, lifting my chin.

With a calculated stumble, I feigned clumsiness, aiming to catch him off guard. As he reached to steady me by the elbow, I lunged for his jacket, fingers brushing the cold, rigid steel of his gun.

"Fuck! Esme!" A primal growl tore from his throat as he seized my wrist, twisting it with merciless precision until the weapon clattered to the floor.

He shoved me against the wall with unyielding force, pinning my arm above my head in a vice grip.

He brought his face inches from mine, nostrils flaring, jaw clenched so tight a muscle twitched beneath his stubble.

I dropped my gaze to the floor, to his shoes, to anything but those eyes that burned like acetylene torches.

His fingers dug into my jawbone, wrenching my face upward. The pad of his thumb pressed against my pulse point, feeling it flutter like a trapped bird.

His pupils dilated until a thin ring of color remained. Something feral lived in that gaze, something that wanted to devour me whole. My knees weakened.

My mouth dried. The wall behind me was the one thing keeping me upright.

Sweat beaded at my hairline as his breath scorched my cheek. The scent of him, whiskey, cedar, and rage, filled my lungs until I couldn't remember how to exhale.

His chest rose and fell against mine, our heartbeats hammering in violent synchrony.

I clawed at the wallpaper behind me, desperate for purchase, for escape, for anything to ground me as the room tilted sideways.

"Do you think I'm going to let you get away from me again, Esme?"

Each syllable of my name vibrated through my sternum, down my spine, and between my thighs. My lips parted.

God help me, I wanted him to say it again.

How could I crave someone with such unbearable intensity while at the same time burning with the desperate urge to flee from him?

My lungs seized, refusing to pull in air. My mind was a chaotic void.

Above all, I could not allow Aidon to glimpse the power he wielded over me, the way he could unravel my very essence.

That would mean surrendering, and I was far from ready to concede.

I lifted my chin, a cocky smirk curling on my lips.

"You need me too much to hurt me," I taunted.

His eyes darkened, pupils expanding as if to swallow the light, a silent acknowledgment that I had struck a nerve. We both knew the undeniable truth in my words.

Aidon might not inflict pain, but he was resolute in his refusal to release me.

His grip on my chin tightened, a fleeting moment of possession before he withdrew, retreating and taking with him that intoxicating, searing heat that left me aching.

Damn it.

I stifled the whimper clawing at my throat at the loss. Something primal within me writhed in agony, a beast of longing and raw need.

But I would never let him see it.

My smirk widened, and I raised a brow, challenging him.

He gave no reply.

Well, not with words.

But his response was explosive, undeniable, and absolute.

He seized my hand with a grip of iron and yanked me toward the hidden wall panel with a force that brooked no resistance. I knew what it concealed: the elevator to his penthouse, a place of power and secrets.

With a swift swipe of his keycard, he thrust me inside. I stumbled, my heart racing, as the doors slammed shut. Silence reigned in the brief seconds it took to ascend to his domain.

In the entryway, he propelled me forward and secured the locks with a finality that echoed like a gavel.

He turned, fixing me with a gaze that was a tempest of fury, an unforgiving storm that sent shivers down my spine and ignited a fire of forbidden desire within me.

"You don't get to run from me again."

His words were a decree, devoid of hesitation, devoid of doubt.

He believed it with an intensity that shook the very air around us. But he was so damn wrong, whether he realized it or not.

There was no way in hell I wouldn't run again.

Maybe he'd claimed victory in this skirmish, but he hadn't won the war.

I smirked, defiant, shaking my head, daring him with every fiber of my being.

With a fierce scowl, he turned on his heel and walked away, leaving me alone to witness his retreat, every step a taunt, his form a testament to the maddening allure that made me question every choice that had brought me to this charged moment.

FIVE

ESME

Three hours and twenty-seven minutes. I counted every damn second on that Rolex clock Aidon had mounted on his wall, like he won it at a bloodsport.

My nails pressed half-moons in my palms.

I kept digging in, not sure if I was trying to keep myself anchored or just hoping I'd bleed.

I kicked off my heels. One of them hit the dresser, the expensive, shiny mahogany one, and made a crack that was a little satisfying.

He dragged me through that door, his hand tight on my arm. Hard enough to bruise, because, of course, that was his style.

Then he locked me in here, like some princess in a fairy tale, except the dragon was the goon outside the door. I paced the length of the room, back and forth, burning figure eights into the carpet.

Counting steps. Doors. Anything that looked like a weakness.

It figured. The bastard kept a penthouse in my brother's casino. Zeno and Aidon, circling each other, both waiting for the other to make a move. Two scorpions trapped in a glass. The idea of them sitting together, drinking, and talking, while I sat here, made my jaw ache.

I caught my reflection in the mirror. My cheeks were flushed, my hair wild. I slammed my fist into the wall again. The pain felt like something piercing, bright, and real.

"Fuck."

I pressed my forehead to the window, chilled glass against my skin, sixty stories above the Strip. Vegas glittered underneath.

And then my body betrayed me.

Ridiculous, but true. I remembered his hands, his mouth, the way he held me down. My thighs squeezed together. Instinct, or muscle memory, or just more proof I was the weak one.

I could see him in my mind, pinning me to the wall, breathing hot and rough against my neck. Just the thought sent a bolt of electricity straight through me. I hated him. I hated myself more.

What kind of woman gets wet for the man who locks her up?

The kind who'd spent years lying awake, imagining all the ways she'd hurt him.

Never like this. Not boredom. Not this soft, slow torture.

I thought I'd be ready for death. Or violence. But not for this. Not for him leaving me here, alone with these filthy thoughts, and the ghost of his hand on my throat, pressing just hard enough to make my pulse roar.

My skin still burned where he'd gripped me.

I paced the room, my thighs clenching with each step.

Not once had I thought Aidon would leave me alone.

My mind was spinning. I needed to escape. Aidon was dangerous. By now, he most likely considered me his enemy, despite our shared past, and hated me just as much as I loathed him, despite the sexual tension that pulsed between us like it had a life of its own.

But if we hated each other, why did I still feel my pussy quiver every single time I was near the man?

Maybe it wouldn't be so confusing, so complicated, if I'd never felt the firm caress of his touch, or the delicious slide of his cock entering me so smoothly.

Maybe if I'd never seen the look in his eyes while he exploded the searing heat of his desire deep inside my pussy...

This could have been much easier.

Maybe then, I'd have been long gone by now and had the strength to move on, not plagued with thoughts of Aidon that kept me lingering in places I should have left long ago.

Three a.m. hotel rooms, sheets ripped off the bed, my back nearly snapping in two, his name torn from my throat as I dug blood-red half-moons into his shoulders. That memory flashed behind my eyelids and made my thighs press together, my body clenching down on nothing.

I never believed Aidon would leave me alone.

My pulse pounded so loud I could barely think. Sweat prickled at my hairline, even with the AC blasting.

I kept circling my cage, brushing my fingertips over the cold wall, pretending it was the ice cube he once dragged down my spine.

He'd chased it with his tongue, slow, deliberate. I hated him. I hated how my body still reacted to the idea of him: nipples tightening, heart racing, that familiar heat rolling low in my belly.

I hated the way his eyes looked when he shoved me into this room. So dark they were almost black, pupils huge, wild with anger and something else I refused to name.

I slapped my palm against the wall. It stung, but the pain was nothing compared to the ache pulsing deep inside me.

I clenched my jaw so tight, I half expected to chip a molar.

Those dangerous little daydreams?

I forced them down, way down, into the coldest, deepest corner of my mind and slammed the steel vault shut.

There'd be time to indulge them later, when I wasn't worrying about Aidon sniffing around in my head, piecing it all together from a stray glance or a slip of focus.

Survival. That was it. Escape, or nothing.

Fuck Aidon. Fuck his predatory, hypnotic stare.

That animalistic growl should have terrified me, but instead sent a shiver straight through my bones.

Fuck his need to own me, to bend me to his will. Fuck the way my body remembered the heat of his hands, his mouth, every reckless, addictive second.

I almost started cursing myself aloud for letting him get to me, for hanging around long enough for all this to happen. I'd seen the warning signs. I wasn't new at this. But maybe there was something in me that craved the risk, that got off on seeing how close I could get to the fire before it burned me to ash.

Well, the flames had reached me now. Searing. Unforgiving.

Time to find my way to ice.

I stopped in front of the door, hand clamped around the knob, my whole body wound so tight I might snap. The plan was coming together, bit by bit, even though images of Aidon's body pinning me down kept slamming into my thoughts, refusing to be ignored.

Before he'd shoved me in here, he'd ripped my purse away. No phone. No weapons. Not even a nail file. Clean sweep.

But they'd missed the USB port stashed in my stiletto heel. My tiny beacon of hope. Somehow, Aidon and his goons hadn't found it.

So all I had?

My brain, my body, and combat training. Not comforting, considering the size of the guys I'd pissed off.

Ares had glared daggers at me when he'd limped down the hall earlier, promising payback.

I took one deep slow breath. Turned the knob. Threw the door open. The jolt of relief was so sharp, I almost laughed out loud.

No Aidon. No Ares. The coast was clear for now.

Instead, someone else was waiting.

A different guard hunched over his phone until he noticed me. His head snapped up. Surprise flickered in his eyes as I stepped forward, my "don't mess with me" face on full display.

Holy hell.

The guy was enormous. His biceps strained against his uniform sleeves, like they'd split the fabric if he so much as flexed.

When he stood, the chair beneath him groaned, as if grateful to be free. I swallowed because he started coming my way, and each of his thighs looked about the size of my entire torso.

His hands? They were big enough to snap my neck in two seconds flat.

I had to crane my neck to meet his eyes. He was looking down at me, like a bouncer sizing up someone who didn't belong.

I might be trained, but up against this guy, I'd be a hummingbird pecking at a grizzly bear.

My pulse spiked. A different tactic was in order.

So I relaxed my shoulders, softened up, and tilted my head just a little, the exact way I'd practiced in a hundred hotel-bar mirrors, watching men's eyes go wide every time.

"Hey," I said, mouth curving into a smile.

He blinked. His Adam's apple bobbed. "Ma'am," he managed.

"What's your name?" I took a step closer. Close enough to catch a whiff of his cologne.

"Seth," he said, staring at my neckline.

"Hey, Seth. I'm Esme."

"I know who you are, ma'am." His jaw flexed, arms bulging beneath the suit jacket like he was prepping for a bodybuilding contest.

Fabric straining, shoulders squared, posture so tense it bordered on cartoonish. If he was aiming for intimidation, it wasn't landing.

Not in this gilded, over-the-top hallway, all mirrors and candlesticks and money dripping off the walls.

But that little flick of his eyes, from my face to the door behind me and right back again, said he'd been warned. Probably more than once.

The whole thing amused me.

I didn't bother hiding it.

Instead, I stepped up so close I could feel the heat coming off him. Ran my fingers down his forearm, tracing up to his bicep. His muscle jerked under my touch, like he'd been shocked.

"Seth," I murmured in a low whisper. He had to lean in to hear me. "I need to use the bathroom."

Classic. His Adam's apple did a full bob, sweat popping up at his temple.

"I—" he tried, but the word fell apart when I circled his arm with fingers that were, yes, freezing.

"Sorry," I said, gliding my hand along the ridge of his forearm, right over a twitching vein. "Cold hands."

I added a shiver, making sure my nipples pressed against my blouse just so. His pupils dilated. The Adam's apple bobbed again, a real performance.

I leaned close, breath warming his ear. "I'd be so grateful."

He clenched his jaw, sweat beading at the edge of his hair.

"Can't," he managed.

The word fractured, then fell out in two rough syllables. His gaze darted to my chest, lingered for a split second, then snapped up to my face like he'd been caught with his hand in the cookie jar.

"Can't let you leave, ma'am."

I pressed against him until our bodies aligned like puzzle pieces, my hip bone sliding against his inner thigh. His skin burned through the fabric between us.

"Seth," I whispered, my lips so close to his ear my breath made him shiver.

His pupils swallowed his irises as I watched something crack behind them.

"Please? Just the bathroom. Five minutes."

He retreated half a step, but his body surged toward mine like a compass finding north. His gaze dropped to where my chest rose and fell, his fingers curling into fists then splaying wide, over and over.

I arched my neck in one fluid motion, exposing the pulse point where he couldn't help but stare. The corner of my mouth curled upward as I looked at him through a veil of lashes.

"Our little secret," I breathed, closing the space between us. My fingertip traced the vein running up his forearm, feeling it jump beneath my touch. "And afterward..." I let my nail scrape down his skin, watching goosebumps rise in its wake. "I'll make you forget your own name."

"Ma'am—" He leaned in, his breath hot on my face, pupils blown wide.

The word hit like a gunshot from down the hall. "Touch her and I'll cut off your fucking hands."

Seth jerked away from me like he'd touched a live wire. I whipped my head toward the noise.

Aidon's boots pounded down the marble hallway, every step a threat I could feel in my teeth. His jaw was clenched so hard I saw the muscle twitch, a vein showing at his temple.

I stumbled backward, slamming my shoulders into the wall.

Aidon never paused.

He grabbed Seth by the collar and tossed him aside like he weighed nothing. Seth crashed into a side table, glass shattering everywhere.

Before the sound even faded, Aidon's hands were on me, his grip like iron around my wrists, pinning them over my head. No way I wasn't going to have bruises tomorrow.

"What the fuck do you think you're doing?" His words broke in hot bursts against my face.

Seth's footsteps disappeared down the hall, leaving just the two of us.

Me.

Aidon. And Aidon's temper.

And, Jesus, the way my pussy clenched at the sound of his voice.

His grip was brutal this time, way harder than before, fingers digging into my wrists. If I didn't know better, I'd think he wanted to leave marks to prove a point.

His eyes locked onto mine, all wild and furious, like he was two seconds from snapping.

Whatever cool, controlled version of Aidon I had met before? Gone. The guy staring me down now looked like he wanted to tear the world apart.

He shoved his body against mine, heartbeat pounding so hard I felt it everywhere. His pupils were blown wide, hardly any color left.

Sweat beaded along his forehead, his cologne fighting with something raw and almost animal, and it hit me all at once.

He leaned in, close enough that his lips brushed my ear. It made my skin prickle, every nerve snapping awake.

"Did you think I wouldn't notice you trying to leave, Esme?"

My pulse tried to jump out of my throat, but I kept my face blank, even when it felt like lightning shot through me from every place he touched.

"You're playing dangerous games, woman."

I snorted, or tried to, but then his thigh shoved between mine, rough fabric scraping and dragging heat up my skin.

The wall was hard behind me. My shoulders ached from how he pinned my arms overhead, fingers tight enough that my hands tingled.

And right there, pressing against me, his cock pulsed against my clit, making it throb even harder.

I bit the inside of my cheek, trying and failing to act like I didn't care.

"Maybe you're scared I'll win, Aidon." His name pushed out on a dare, curled sweet and pointed on my tongue.

I leaned in, nipples grazing his chest, ignoring the warning in his eyes.

Something flickered there. Wild. Dangerous.

His knee drove upward, the pressure against my pussy. The jolt wrenched a gasp from me before I could pretend I didn't care.

"You lost the second I found you."

He didn't bother with the rest. His mouth crashed into mine, teeth catching, tongue everywhere. Unapologetic.

Hot. Unyielding. Starved.

His teeth caught my lip, sharp, and blood burst, copper tang mixing with the whiskey burn he carried. My vision blurred, my thoughts fuzzed, and still his mouth took more and more, until I was dizzy and shaking and boneless. He held me up anyway, hands sure and tight, like I was something rare and breakable.

Heat blossomed deep inside me, billowing into a bubble of desire that clouded my mind. His kiss was hard and painful and invasive, like a punishment that he'd been waiting for a very long time to unleash upon me.

All the anger, all the rage, all the fury that he'd hidden behind his cool demeanor seemed to rush to the surface and flow from his prodding mouth, stealing the breath straight from my lungs.

If I weren't careful, he'd know how much I wanted him, too.

"No!" The word ripped out of me as I jerked my head to the side.

The tendons in my arms screamed, wrists twisting, bones rubbing together under his grip. I shoved against him, every movement just grinding my hips tighter to his, my nipples hard and aching against his chest.

He was everywhere—the wall of muscle pinning me in place, the thick press of his thigh between mine, his cock hard and insistent against my stomach.

Wetness rushed between my legs, soaking through my underwear. My clit pulsed, greedy and desperate.

When he went for my mouth again, I bit him. Hard. Teeth sinking into his bottom lip until blood coated my tongue.

He jerked his head back, a drop of red beading at his lip and running down his jaw, bright and sharp. It hovered, then dripped onto his perfect white collar.

His pupils were blown wide, swallowing any color in his eyes.

I lifted my chin, still tasting him, teeth bared.

"Fuck!" The sound tore out of him, raw, rough, feral.

A vein pulsed at his temple as he pinned me harder against the wall, the pressure crushing the air from my lungs.

"You little—" His breath came in hot bursts against my face, each exhale carrying the scent of expensive whiskey and contained violence.

"Get. Off. Me." Each syllable dripped venom as I twisted against his grip. The bones in my wrists ground together beneath his fingers.

The corner of his mouth curled upward, revealing teeth stained pink with his blood.

"Look at you," he whispered, so close his lips grazed my ear, "fighting what we both know is inevitable."

"I'd rather die," I shot back.

It sounded tough, but the lie tasted like battery acid, especially when my body was betraying me so hard I wanted to punch myself.

I did the only thing I could think of and slammed my body forward.

For once, it worked.

Well, for a second.

His grip slipped, but then his hands locked down again, fingers digging in so hard I was pretty sure I'd be wearing his fingerprints for days.

He laughed.

Not just a regular laugh, either.

It was this dark, low sound, and I could feel it, the way our bodies were mashed together. His eyes looked a little bit insane and animal hungry.

"Bastard!" I jerked and twisted, but he just held on tighter, his whole body pressed against mine.

"Mine."

The friction was so electric, I had to bite back a moan.

"Never—" I tried to say, but it came out as a snarl.

He didn't care. He just kissed me. Hard. Like teeth and tongue and zero patience.

It was more like a fight than anything romantic, and he was winning.

I gasped, which was an engraved invitation for him to shove his tongue into my mouth. He went for it, rough and greedy.

And yeah.

I wanted to resist. I tried to claw his face off, or at least slap him. Would've tried if he wasn't pinning my wrists above my head.

I wanted to yell. Or scream. Or call him something even worse than bastard.

But all I could think about was his mouth. His tongue. And how much I wanted him, no matter how much I told myself I didn't.

My resolve started to slip. I whimpered into his mouth.

He knew.

God, he knew.

He could feel me teetering on the edge, ready to melt into him. If he pushed just a little more, my thighs would open wider and I'd let him in—no defenses, no hiding—just the dark, desperate want clawing at my insides.

And he saw it. I hated that he saw it. Hated it with every cell in my body, but I couldn't deny it.

No turning back now.

There was nothing I could do to stop the need that was bubbling up and spilling over, wild and uncontrollable, something with teeth and claws, something shadowy and fierce and impossible to ignore.

His kiss got rougher, deeper. My mouth went slack. I let him in, the fight draining out of me fast.

He tore his mouth from mine, eyes burning, searching my face like he had to confirm it.

Was he looking for a sign? Did he see that I wanted him just as bad? Had I given myself away already?

He must've found what he was looking for, because just like that, his mouth crashed back onto mine. This time, he was hungry. Confident. No hesitation.

Fuck.

The thing between us wasn't just a flicker anymore—it was wildfire, all heat and chaos and no room to breathe. I could barely gasp for air, let alone think straight.

Clarity? Gone.

All I could do was hang on and try not to get burned alive.

With every kiss, he dragged up shit I'd spent years shoving down. Wanting Aidon had never been safe. We'd done this before, twisted up together, and it never led anywhere good.

This was the same old routine: we'd dance, we'd burn, and it would all go to hell.

So I tried to bury the feelings. Let my body take over, shut everything else out.

Fine, I thought.

I'd fuck him, just once more.

Let him inside me. Watch him fall apart. See the look on his face when he came.

And then? I'd vanish.

Smoke, gone before the sheets even cooled. He'd wake up and wonder if I'd ever been there at all.

Like I always said I would.

Six

ESME

His mouth crashed over mine like a man who'd been waiting his whole life to do it, tongue hungry, lips hard, no hesitation. Each slide of his tongue felt like he was staking a claim, every press of his mouth another inch of ground taken.

I'd thought I'd put up a fight. Instead, my whole body just...melted. The heat pooled low in my core, spreading so fast it made my head spin.

Yeah, my hips were the first to betray me. I rolled up against him, right into the thick, demanding pressure of him, chasing friction I'd promised myself I wouldn't want.

Gravity? Gone. The world spun out. My lungs burned.

I needed air, but I needed him more.

He let go of my wrists, and I thought I'd be relieved, but nope. If anything, it just made the need worse, even more so when his arm clamped around my waist, like he couldn't trust me not to run.

Spoiler: I wasn't going anywhere.

I could have stopped this. I chose not to. It was about choice, not surrender.

So I kissed him back. Hard. My tongue met his, and there was blood, whiskey, and something else sharp and wild between us. His fingers found my hair, yanked hard at the nape until pain zapped right through my scalp, so strong my head snapped back.

My throat was wide open, and I made this sound that was half gasp, half moan, all desperation.

He refused to let up. His tongue dove deeper, taking everything, like he could own me from the inside. Every stroke was a jolt, lighting up nerves I never knew existed.

I clawed at his back, fingers curling through his shirt, nails digging down because I needed something solid or I was going to fall apart.

He let go of my hair and slid his hands down my body, palms rough on my thighs and fingers gripping my ass hard enough to bruise. He lifted me like I weighed nothing.

My stomach shot into my throat. I held on for dear life, but he couldn't have cared less; he carried me those last few steps and then tossed me onto the bed like it was the one place I belonged.

The impact knocked the breath straight out of me, mattress springs screeching like they were as startled as I was.

My dress twisted up, caught around my hips, leaving nothing but the lacy edge of my underwear.

He noticed, of course. His gaze flicked there and lingered, patient and predatory, like he was waiting for me to cave.

He was breathing hard, chest rising and falling, his shirt clinging to every muscle as he tensed up.

Dried blood streaked from his split lip, stark and red.

I should've been scared. That was the sane reaction, but my thighs were shaking for a whole different reason.

My body wanted anything but normal. Heat pooled between my legs, embarrassing and impossible to hide.

"I hate you," I whispered.

It sounded pathetic, all hoarse and shaky, since my hands reached for him anyway.

He gave no answer, just staring with eyes so dark that I couldn't tell where the blackness stopped and the rest of the eyes started.

When he leaned down, the bed dipped, and I slid just a little toward him, like the mattress wanted me closer, too. He was hot, close enough that I could smell him, a mix of blood, sweat, and expensive cologne.

My hands acted on their own, yanking at the pearl buttons and sending them flying across the floor. The ripping sound of fabric was loud, sharp, and satisfying, filling the space between our heavy breathing.

He growled, a real, honest-to-god growl, as I shoved his ruined shirt off his shoulders.

The first touch of skin to skin, it shouldn't have been any different than before, but somehow it was, a spark zapping straight up my arm and making me jolt.

My fingers skimmed over old scars, mapped the lines of

muscle I'd already learned by heart but somehow hadn't mastered.

Then he caught my wrist.

Hard.

Tomorrow, I'd see the marks.

He yanked my hand to his mouth, and his teeth scraped across my fingertips; his eyes never left mine, a dark dare set hard and challenging in the depths.

Copper flooded my tongue. I wasn't bleeding, not that I could tell, but my heart hammered so hard in my chest, I thought maybe it would break loose and smack him in the face.

Every single nerve ending I had screamed at me to run, now, but my body leaned in, desperate for the very thing it shouldn't want.

His other hand slid up, palm bracing against my throat, thumb pressing just hard enough that I remembered how easily he could snap it.

I swallowed.

He felt that, and his thumb pressed in a tiny bit more, tracking every movement. His mouth twitched up at the corner, not a smile, unless you could call something that wild a smile.

"You should be afraid of me," he said, and the way he said it made me want to laugh, or maybe scream, or perhaps melt into the bed and disappear.

He pressed his thumb to my throat. I could feel my pulse beating under his hand, fast, frantic, like a rabbit trying to escape a snare.

It was pointless to pretend I didn't like it. My body shivered, but not from fear.

It was something worse than fear, the way his hips locked me in place, holding me so I couldn't move. He was hard against my thigh, and I could feel every inch of him.

Then his teeth scraped my ear, and for a second, I forgot how to breathe.

"I can feel your heart racing," he said, hot against my neck. "Are you scared, Esme? Or is this something else?"

The mattress dipped under us.

He was a rock, and I was…I wasn't sure, perhaps a puddle?

I dug my nails into his shoulders, not caring if I left marks. If anything, I hoped I did.

He groaned, deep and guttural, and I tasted blood. Maybe I'd bitten my own lip.

"I hate you," I repeated, stoic in my resolve that he was the enemy, but my body wasn't getting the message. My thighs just opened for him.

"Liar," he said, and his mouth was on my neck, teeth scraping, biting down just enough to make my vision go bright and fuzzy around the edges.

My back arched up, pressing me against him, and he pinned me there like he was never going to let go.

His hand inched up my thigh, fingers digging in just enough to make me gasp as he shoved my dress up higher. His palm was rough, calluses dragging over my bare skin, each little scratch shooting sparks right between my legs.

God, I was already soaked, and he hadn't even gotten started.

When he grabbed my ass and squeezed, I couldn't even pretend to stay quiet. The moan was embarrassing and loud, and judging by the way his lips curled against my collarbone, he loved every second.

"That's it," he said, teeth scraping my skin. "Let me hear you."

He moved his hand, tracing along my panties, fingers light. Teasing. I squirmed, wanting more, needing it. When his fingers pressed into the damp fabric, I almost lost it.

My hips jerked up without warning. He just laughed, dark and smug, and slid a finger under the elastic, right against me.

"Jesus, you're soaked," he said, all but groaning.

He shoved the panties aside, rough but careful, and dragged a finger along my entrance.

It was torture.

He collected all that slickness, then slid inside, slow on purpose, making me clench and shudder and want more. I couldn't hold back. I made some desperate noise, but whatever.

"Look at you," he growled, hot breath against my neck.

He twisted his wrist, and somehow his finger landed right on that spot that made my whole body go tight and boneless.

My head spun. His teeth found my earlobe and bit down, just enough to hurt in the best way, and then there were two fingers stretching me, filling me up.

"Still want to tell me how much you hate me?"

I couldn't manage the words. My body arched into his hand, chasing friction, desperate. The mattress creaked under us as my hips jerked, helpless and greedy. He caught my mouth, swallowing my moans, his tongue matching the pace of his fingers until I could taste my need.

And then? Nothing.

Cold air rushed in where his warmth had been. I reached out, desperate, my hand closing on nothing. A broken sound slipped from my lips as I watched him get up, every inch of me aching at the loss.

He stopped at the end of the bed, the moonlight catching his chest and turning muscle into shadow and light. His hands went to his belt, the small metal click of the buckle deafening.

Then, slow and deliberate, he peeled away the last pieces of clothing, the soft sound of fabric brushing skin filling the room.

His cock sprang free, heavy and flushed dark with blood, a bead of moisture catching the dim light at its tip. My mouth went dry, pulse hammering so hard I could feel it between my legs.

I couldn't look away, couldn't pretend I wasn't memorizing every ridge, every vein, every inch that would soon be inside me. The thought alone made my inner walls clench.

I forced my gaze upward, past the taut ridges of his abdomen, the broad expanse of his chest, to find his eyes burning into mine with an intensity that stole what little breath I had left.

"I need you, Esme," he said, raw, primal. "Fuck, do you have any idea what you do to me?"

I couldn't speak. I flicked my gaze down to where he stood rigid and straining, then back up at him. The hunger on his face was savage, carved into every line. I cocked an eyebrow, let the corner of my mouth hitch up, a silent dare, even though my thighs were shaking so hard I thought I might collapse.

He looked at me, and something dangerous flashed in his eyes. Possession, obsession, some ancient, predatory thing. It should have scared me. Instead, it made my whole body flush hot, heat flooding between my legs.

He was on me in an instant, the mattress dipping like a sinkhole beneath his weight. His skin scorched mine where we touched, branding me.

My dress had twisted around my waist, the bunched fabric cutting into my flesh like barbed wire, leaving nothing but a scrap of ruined lace between his throbbing cock and my aching pussy.

His eyes darkened to obsidian as they fixed on the damp fabric.

"These are pretty," he growled, like gravel over velvet, "but they're in my fucking way."

His fingers hooked into the delicate lace, knuckles brushing against my hipbones. One savage twist and the sound of tearing fabric echoed through the room like a gunshot; the elastic bit into my skin for one sharp second before giving way.

I gasped as cool air hit exposed flesh, watching him toss

the shredded remains over his shoulder with casual dominance.

"Much better," he muttered, his gaze raking over me like a physical touch.

His nostrils flared as he inhaled. The mattress shifted as he sank to his knees between my thighs, his broad shoulders forcing them wider apart.

My pulse hammered in my throat as he lowered his face until I could feel his hot breath against my most intimate flesh. A visible shudder ran through his powerful frame.

"You're fucking beautiful, Esme," he whispered, the words vibrating against my inner thigh.

His fingertip traced a fiery path along sensitive skin, leaving goosebumps behind. I couldn't stop the violent tremor shaking through me, nor the way my hips tilted upward in silent offering.

My eyes locked onto his face, showing a predatory focus, with the muscle jumping in his jaw and his tongue darting out to wet his lower lip.

The same hands that had snapped men's necks now hovered millimeters from my core, capable of such violence yet trembling with restraint. My chest constricted with the contradiction of it all.

I held my breath until spots danced at the edges of my vision, suspended in that impossible moment between terror and surrender.

My thighs quivered with the effort to stay open when every survival instinct screamed to close them, to run. Yet deeper than fear ran a current of molten need, a hunger so primal it obliterated reason.

Sanity whispered in the back of my mind.

This man is dangerous, this man is your enemy, this man will destroy you, but it grew fainter with each ragged breath. I watched his eyes track the pulse point at the juncture of my thighs, felt the heat of his gaze like a physical caress against slick flesh.

I shouldn't want this. I shouldn't be here. I shouldn't arch my back, shouldn't dig my heels into the mattress, shouldn't expose my throat in ancient submission to the predator between my legs.

God help me, I did.

I surrendered everything—pride, power, and protection, spreading myself before him like a sacrifice on an altar.

The hunger in his eyes burned into me like a brand, reflecting the hollow ache I'd been running from across cities, across years. My chest constricted, throat tightening as the terrible truth crashed through me. This wasn't just want. It was a necessity, primal and inescapable as gravity.

I arched my spine, offering myself like a sacrifice, my body betraying every defense I'd built. The mattress creaked beneath us as I writhed, helpless against the magnetic pull between us.

His gaze swept over me, searching, hungry, assured. The moonlight caught the lines of his body, throwing sharp shadows across muscle and skin, making him look like something out of a fever dream, all edge, intent, and threat.

His cock was hard, no question, the veins standing out

and pulsing with every heartbeat, every second. Those hands looked like they could break granite, but as they moved closer, I saw them shake.

"Please," I whispered, the word torn from somewhere deep and hidden.

His fingertip traced fire along my inner thigh, leaving goosebumps in its wake. I bit down on my lip until I tasted copper, fighting the whimper building in my throat.

When he dipped between my folds, the contact was electric, a lightning strike of sensation that shot from my core to my fingertips. My vision blurred at the edges as he found my clit, circling it with devastating precision.

My thighs fell open wider, trembling with the effort to stay spread for him. He pressed harder, the pad of his finger slick with my arousal as he worked tight, merciless circles that sent shockwaves crashing through my system. Each touch was deliberate torture, calibrated to build pressure without release.

I clawed at the sheets until my knuckles blanched white. His thumb bore down on my clit with devastating precision, sending lightning strikes of sensation from my core to my fingertips. The room tilted and blurred, reality fracturing into shards of white-hot pleasure. My hips bucked against his hand with a will of their own, grinding for more friction, more pressure, more everything.

"Aidon," I cried out, his name torn from somewhere primal and ancient inside me.

The sound wasn't human, more animal than woman.

His eyes locked on mine as he dragged his middle finger

through my slickness, so slow I could feel each ridge of his fingerprint against hypersensitive flesh.

He circled my entrance once, twice, a third time, the pad of his finger collecting wetness but never breaching. My inner walls clenched around nothing, aching emptiness making me whimper.

My head shot up, muscles in my neck corded with tension. His lips curled into that infuriating half-smile, pupils blown wide with arousal but eyes glittering with something darker—control, power, triumph. A muscle ticked in my jaw as our gazes locked in a silent battle.

His finger pressed forward without warning, the thick digit parting my entrance and sinking into liquid heat. The invasion was both too much and still not enough.

"Oh, fuck!" The curse exploded from my lungs, my voice breaking on the second syllable.

My body jerked, hips twitching, as he worked his finger deeper. The muscles inside me clenched, tight and greedy, pulling him in like it was the one thing that mattered. Every little thrust sent heat slamming through my veins.

My vision blurred at the edges, with everything dimming. He watched, that stupid smirk spreading as I lost control right in front of him.

He slid a second finger alongside the first, stretching me further, the slight burn intensifying the pleasure. My greedy body accepted him, wet sounds filling the space between us as he began to move.

"Oh, Esme," he growled, dropping an octave, rough as gravel. "You're fucking drenched. Is that because of me?"

His fingers curled upward, finding that spot that made stars explode behind my eyelids.

He raised one dark eyebrow, looking up at me from between my trembling thighs, waiting. The power struggle between us crackled like electricity, even now, even with his fingers buried inside me and my body betraying every ounce of my hard-won composure.

"Yes," I hissed through clenched teeth, the admission burning my throat like acid. "You know it is."

The corner of his mouth lifted, that goddamn smirk as his chest expanded with a deep inhale of satisfaction.

Between my legs, his cock twitched, a bead of precum glistening at the tip.

This was Aidon Kosta, the man who'd ordered executions over breakfast, who'd built an empire on broken bodies, now watching me writhe beneath him with the raw hunger of a starving wolf.

His jaw clenched so tight I could see the muscle jumping beneath his stubbled skin. Triumph blazed across his face like a brand.

I let my thighs fall open wider, the cool air hitting my exposed flesh making me shiver.

"Fuck it," I whispered. "Just fuck me already."

I threw my head back against the pillow, neck arched, unable to bear the weight of his stare. The silk sheets twisted in my fists as I spread myself further, offering everything, surrendering. My heartbeat thundered in my ears, drowning out the voice of reason screaming at me to run.

His palm scorched a line down the inside of my thigh, his

fingers digging in hard and leaving marks. The pressure of his grip sent a jolt of electricity up my spine. He forced my legs wider, exposing me. He devoured me with his gaze. I was laid bare in ways that went way beyond just the physical.

Then...nothing.

The sudden absence of his touch left my skin burning cold. The fingers that had been buried inside me vanished, leaving an emptiness that made me clench around nothing but air.

My eyes snapped open to find him hovering above me, that infuriating smirk carved deeper into his face, his breathing controlled while mine came in desperate pants.

"Say. You're. Mine." Each word fell between us like a gauntlet thrown down, vibrating through my bones and making my inner walls clench around emptiness.

His pupils dilated, leaving a thin ring of amber, predatory and possessive. The muscle in his jaw twitched as he hovered above me, cock throbbing with each heartbeat, the veins standing out in stark relief against flushed skin.

A single bead of sweat traced the hollow of his throat, sliding down the carved planes of his chest.

I bit my lip hard enough to taste copper. My clit pulsed, abandoned and aching, my entrance slick and clenching around nothing. The silk sheets beneath me were soaked through.

"Make me," I replied, arching my back so my hardened nipples brushed against his chest, a jolt of electricity shooting straight to my core.

He growled, a primal sound that reverberated through

the room and seized my wrists in one hand, pinning them above my head with bruising force.

His other hand gripped my jaw, forcing me to look at him, his thumb pressing against my lower lip until my mouth parted.

"I told you this is a dangerous game, Esme," he whispered, his breath hot against my ear before he bit down on my earlobe, the sharp sting making me gasp.

"And I think you know I like danger, don't you, Aidon?" I rolled my hips upward, feeling the hot, heavy length of him slide against my wetness without entering.

"You never stop, do you?" His fingers tightened on my jaw, the pressure exquisite in its restraint.

"Do you?" I challenged, as the head of his cock nudged against my entrance, then retreated.

Our bodies trembled with the effort of restraint, skin slick with sweat, breath coming in ragged pants. His cock twitched against my inner thigh, leaving a wet trail of precum. I could feel my pulse hammering between my legs, my arousal dripping onto the sheets beneath us.

My eyes locked with his, pleading.

The air between us crackled with tension, thick enough to choke on. His expression softened for just a moment, a flash of vulnerability beneath the dominant mask before he inhaled deep, nostrils flaring as he caught the scent of my arousal.

He gave a single, almost imperceptible nod, the silent acknowledgment of a temporary truce in our endless war.

My eyes fell to his lips, full, parted, the lower one bearing the mark of his teeth. Something molten and primal surged through me, clenching in my pussy and between my thighs.

He bent his head with agonizing slowness, his hot breath ghosting over my skin seconds before contact. When his mouth descended, the first touch was a graze, a whisper, a promise. His lips brushed my clit with such deliberate lightness that I screamed in frustration.

Finally!

"Yesssssss," I hissed, my fingers diving into his thick hair, nails scraping his scalp as I anchored myself to him.

The first real stroke of his tongue sent lightning crackling up my spine, my back arching off the bed as if electrocuted. He growled against me, the vibration rippling through my swollen flesh, and my thighs began to tremble.

His tongue. God, his tongue traced maddening patterns, alternating between feather-light circles and firm, devastating strokes that had me seeing stars. He worked me like an instrument he'd spent years mastering, reading every twitch and gasp as if my body spoke a language he invented.

When his fingers slid up my inner thigh, leaving trails of fire in their wake, I sobbed with relief. He teased my entrance, gathering the embarrassing evidence of my arousal before pressing two thick fingers inside. The stretch and fullness made my inner walls clench around him, trying to draw him deeper.

"Aidon," I gasped, stripped raw with need. "Please—"

He moaned against me, the sound vibrating against my clit as I ground against his face.

My hips bucked beyond my control now, chasing the

pressure and maddening friction needed. His stubble scraped the tender skin of my inner thighs, the slight pain heightening every sensation.

He sealed his lips around my clit and sucked hard, rhythmic, relentless, while his fingers curled inside me, finding that spot that made coherent thought impossible.

The dual assault was too much. My vision blurred at the edges as pleasure built to an unbearable crescendo, my body coiling tighter and tighter like a spring about to snap.

My thighs clamped around his head, my heels digging into his back as I writhed beneath him, at his mercy yet somehow holding all the power.

My lungs burned for oxygen as the room tilted and spun, my universe collapsing to a single point between my thighs where his mouth devoured me. Stars burst behind my eyelids —constellations of pleasure I'd never charted before.

"Yes, harder, oh god, please don't stop, Aidon!" The words tore from my throat, raw and primal, bouncing off the walls and back to my ears.

My hips bucked against his face, my thighs trembling as they spread wider, the muscles burning with the strain.

His fingers curled inside me with devastating precision, the wet sounds of my arousal filling the room as he pumped faster, harder.

The calluses on his fingertips scraped against that spot that made lightning crack down my spine. Three fingers now, stretching, claiming, conquering. My inner walls clenched around him, trying to pull him deeper still.

"You're so fucking wet, Esme. You taste like fucking

heaven," his tongue flattened, licking a scorching path through my folds, gathering the slickness his fingers coaxed from me.

The sight of his dark head between my thighs, his shoulders bunching with effort as he worked me over, sent another flood of heat pulsing from my core.

My head thrashed against the pillow. Incoherent sounds spilled from my lips, half-sobs, desperate whimpers, his name like a broken prayer.

My fingers clawed at the sheets, at his hair, at anything I could reach as the pressure built to something terrifying in its intensity.

He sealed his mouth over my clit and sucked, hard, merciless, while his fingers drove deeper, curling forward in a command my body couldn't refuse.

The dual sensation shattered something fundamental inside me. My vision whited out as every muscle locked, suspended in that exquisite moment between agony and ecstasy.

Then the first wave hit, a violent contraction that wrenched a scream from my throat. My body convulsed around his fingers, clamping down with each pulsing wave, wetness gushing over his hand as he growled against me, drinking everything I gave him.

"Oh my god," I gasped when I could form words again. My entire body liquefied, boneless.

Aftershocks ripped through me like electrical currents, my back bowed with each one. My thighs shook as his tongue softened but refused to relent, lapping at my over-sensitized flesh until I clawed at the sheets, caught in that exquisite limbo where ecstasy becomes torment.

"Fuck—I can't—" My words dissolved into a broken moan as he dragged his tongue through my folds with devastating slowness, gathering the evidence of what he'd done to me.

The reverence in his movements made something crack open in my chest. His eyes never left mine as he pressed open-mouthed kisses up the valley between my breasts, across my collarbone, and the hollow of my throat.

When he claimed my mouth, I tasted myself on his lips, salt and musk and something primal that made me whimper against him.

His weight pressed me into the mattress, skin sliding against sweat-slicked skin.

My pulse hammered beneath his palm as it curved around my throat, not squeezing, just claiming. Between my thighs, I felt empty, aching, the muscles still fluttering around nothing.

"That was..." he breathed against my lips, pupils blown so wide his eyes looked black in the dim light.

A droplet of sweat rolled down his temple. His thumb traced my lower lip, swollen from his earlier assault.

I searched his face for answers to questions I wasn't sure how to ask. The air between us felt charged, dangerous in a way that had nothing to do with our history and everything to do with how his expression had softened into something I'd never seen before.

"I'm just getting started," he murmured, sending goose-bumps racing across my skin.

He shifted his weight, the movement dragging the hard length of him against my center. I gasped, fingers digging into the taut muscle of his ass.

"Then stop teasing me," I demanded, as I tilted my pelvis up, seeking more friction, more pressure, more him.

His lips curved into that infuriating smirk I both hated and craved as he positioned himself at my entrance, the blunt head of his cock parting me just enough to make my breath catch, then pulled away.

"Goddammit, Aidon!" I slammed my fist against the solid wall of his shoulder, my body arched off the bed, seeking him like a lightning rod seeks the storm. "Stop fucking toying with me!"

He wrapped his hand around his cock. The sight of him thick, flushed purple-red, a bead of moisture glistening at the tip, made my mouth flood with saliva. He dragged the velvet head through my folds, the contact electric, almost painful against my swollen flesh.

"You bastard," I hissed, as he circled my entrance, promising everything, delivering nothing.

My thighs quivered, spread so wide, the cool air hitting the slickness between them. I could hear how wet I was, that obscene, liquid sound as he glided through my folds, and the knowledge burned through me like wildfire.

I clawed at his forearm, leaving angry red trails. "I swear to god, if you don't—"

The threat died in my throat as he slammed forward in

one brutal thrust, and stars burst behind my eyelids. My body seized around him, inner walls clamping down on the intrusion, trying to pull him deeper still.

"Oh!" The sound that escaped me was primal, nowhere near human, half-pain, half-salvation.

"Is this what you wanted, Esme?" The cruel amusement had melted away, replaced by something almost vulnerable, a hunger that mirrored my own, raw and desperate.

He began to withdraw, the drag of him against my inner walls sending aftershocks through my pelvis. Panic clawed up my throat. I couldn't bear the emptiness, not now. My hands flew to his ass, fingers digging into the hard muscle, holding him inside me with desperate strength.

"Don't you fucking dare," I snarled.

I rolled my hips, taking him deeper, watching his pupils blow wide as I clenched around him.

His lips curled into that maddening half-smile, but it trembled at the edges.

"What the lady wants," he murmured, lowering his mouth to mine, "the lady gets."

The kiss was an invasion, his tongue mimicking the thrust of his cock as he drove back into me with enough force to shove me up the bed.

My head knocked against the headboard, pain blurring into pleasure as he at last gave me what I'd been clawing for, what I'd been dreaming about during those many nights when my fingers weren't enough.

He began, each stroke deliberate and devastating, the

ridge of his head dragging against that spot inside me that made my vision blur.

I bit down on his shoulder to muffle the sound tearing from my throat, my thighs trembling as they locked around his hips. My body clenched around him, greedy, desperate, a vise of need that had him hissing through clenched teeth.

"Look at me," he commanded, withdrawing.

The emptiness was unbearable, a hollow ache that had me clawing at his back.

When he thrust back in, the fullness bordered on pain, stretching me to my limits. Stars burst behind my eyelids. Sweat slicked between our bodies as we found a rhythm, my hips rising to meet each punishing drive of his. His teeth scraped my neck, my pulse hammering against his tongue.

The headboard slammed against the wall, each crack punctuating a thrust that drove me further up the mattress.

I tasted blood; his or mine, I couldn't tell.

The sheets twisted beneath us, damp with sweat and arousal. His hands gripped my thighs, spreading me wider, angling deeper, hitting places inside me that had tears leaking from the corners of my eyes.

"Fuck, Esme." I clenched around him. "You feel like—" He couldn't finish, his words dissolving into a groan that vibrated through my sternum.

The world beyond our tangled limbs ceased to exist. There was nothing but this—the slick slide of him inside me, the bruising grip of his fingers on my hips, the salt of his skin against my tongue.

The danger of what we were doing, of what we were to

each other, hovered at the edges of my consciousness, but I couldn't reach it through the haze of pleasure.

Something cracked open in my chest when he slowed, his forehead pressed to mine, our breath mingling in the scant space between us.

For a heartbeat, we weren't enemies or rivals or whatever twisted thing we'd become. We were just two people drowning in each other.

His eyes locked on mine as he moved inside me, pupils blown so wide the midnight blue was just a thin ring around bottomless black.

I couldn't look away even as something primal in me screamed to hide, to protect the raw, bleeding parts of myself his gaze was excavating with each brutal thrust. My chest constricted, lungs fighting for air that wouldn't come.

"What are you looking for?" I whispered, as he hit that spot deep inside that made my vision blur.

His answer was to grip my jaw, forcing my face up, denying me even the small mercy of turning away.

Let him look. Let him search. The truth was written in the tremble of my thighs, the desperate arch of my spine, the wetness coating his cock each time he withdrew, just to drive back in deeper.

For now, I would let him think he'd won.

I dug my heels into the mattress and arched up, taking him beyond deeper, my inner walls clenching around him like a vise.

His rhythm faltered, a choking sound escaping his throat.

The headboard slammed against the wall, each crack punctuating the wet, obscene sound of our bodies colliding.

"Fuck," he hissed, his fingers digging bruises into my hipbones as he yanked me down onto his cock.

The new angle sent lightning bolts of pleasure-pain up my spine, my body seizing around him.

Sweat dripped from his forehead onto my collarbone, sliding between my breasts. The salt of it stung the scratches on my skin.

Each thrust now knocked the air from my lungs in short, desperate pants. My nails carved crescents into his shoulders, drawing pinpricks of blood that smeared between us.

"Is this—" Each word punctuated by the snap of his hips "—what you—wanted?"

I couldn't answer as the pressure built low in my core and made me tremble.

The world beyond our tangled limbs ceased to exist, narrowing to the slick slide of him inside me, the bruising grip of his hands, the salt of his skin against my tongue.

My head thrashed against the pillow, hair wild and damp with sweat, as the first shockwaves of release threatened to tear me apart.

My spine arched with such violet force I thought it might snap, every nerve ending raw and exposed.

"Don't stop," I gasped. "Harder, Aidon. Please—" My plea dissolved into a broken moan.

He drove deeper, the thick ridge of him hitting that spot that made stars burst behind my eyelids.

His teeth scraped the shell of my ear, his breath coming in harsh pants that matched the brutal rhythm of his hips.

"Like this? Is this what you need, Esme?"

The headboard slammed against the wall, each crack echoing the wet, obscene sound of our bodies colliding. My fingernails drew pinpricks of blood into his shoulders, which smeared between us like war paint.

"Yes," I sobbed, beyond shame, beyond pride. "God, yes—" The rest of my words dissolved into incoherence.

He hitched my thigh higher, the new angle sending lightning bolts of pleasure-pain up my spine.

"Say you're mine now, little one." His rhythm faltered just enough to let me know this wasn't just dirty talk; this was the price of my pleasure.

The real surrender he demanded.

I knew it then. In the space between heartbeats, between the drag of his cock and the bruising grip of his hands on my hips, I knew.

He'd orchestrated this entire night— every touch, every kiss, every thrust to bring me to this precipice where pride and need collided.

He fucking knew what he was doing.

"I'm yours, Aidon," I gasped, the admission ripped from somewhere deep and primal as I opened my thighs wider, surrendering not just my body but something far more dangerous. "I'll be yours as long as you keep—" My voice shattered as he drove into me with renewed force, the confession he'd extracted rewarded with what I'd begged for.

He fucked me harder then, each thrust more punishing

than the last, the wet sound of our bodies meeting filling the room.

My vision blurred, tears leaking from the corners of my eyes, not from pain but from the overwhelming intensity.

Every nerve ending screamed for release, my body a live wire under his hands.

Deeper. The world beyond our tangled limbs ceased to exist.

Faster. My heartbeat thundered in my ears, drowning out everything but the slick slide of him inside me.

Until—

My orgasm hit like a tsunami, hot waves of pleasure rolling through my hips and radiating outward until even my fingertips tingled. My inner walls clenched and spasmed around him, milking his cock as I shattered.

I might have screamed his name, might have cursed, might have begged.

I couldn't tell through the roaring in my ears.

He continued fucking me through the aftershocks, not slowing, not stopping until I was trembling without any semblance of control, over-sensitized and delirious.

Right when I thought I might pass out, I felt him swell inside me, his rhythm turning erratic. His fingers dug bruises into my hipbones as he slammed into me one final time, his whole body going rigid as he came with a guttural groan that vibrated through my sternum.

The hot pulse of his release inside me triggered another wave of pleasure, smaller but no less intense.

"God, yes," I cried, my body still quaking with aftershocks, clenching around him as if trying to draw out every drop.

He collapsed half on top of me, his weight both crushing and comforting.

For long moments, all I heard was the sound of our ragged breathing slowing.

His lips found my neck, pressing lazy, open-mouthed kisses along the column of my throat. The gentleness was almost more devastating than the violence that had preceded it.

His mouth trailed up my cheek, finding my lips with surprising tenderness. The kiss was deep but unhurried, his tongue sliding against mine in a languid echo of our earlier frenzy.

Something in my chest cracked open at the contrast, the brutality of before against this almost reverent aftermath.

The tension that had defined us, predator and prey, hunter and hunted, seemed to dissipate like morning mist, leaving us suspended in a strange, unfamiliar territory.

His hands mapped my curves with possessive strokes, as if memorizing the landscape of my body now that he'd claimed it.

"You'll never run from me again, Esme," he whispered against my lips, each syllable burning into me like a brand.

His fingers traced the outline of a bruise blooming purple on my hip, his touch both reverent and possessive.

Goddamn him.

My heart slammed against my ribs as something primal and desperate clawed its way up my throat. I seized his face between my palms, my fingernails digging into the sharp edges of his jaw.

His pupils dilated, black swallowing gold until a thin ring remained.

"Then stop chasing me, Aidon. Please."

The corner of his mouth curved upward.

That fucking smirk that made my blood simmer and my thighs clench.

He rumbled in his chest as I tried to wrench away. His arm snaked around my waist like iron, crushing me against the hard planes of his body until I felt the thunderous beat of his heart against my spine.

"Goodnight, Esme," he murmured, his breath hot against the nape of my neck.

His teeth grazed my shoulder, not quite a bite, not quite a kiss, but a reminder that even in sleep, I was claimed.

Marked. His.

I let out a breath, all the fight sparking and guttering out in my muscles.

Holy fuck, I was done.

I'd been running forever, fighting by myself for even longer.

Way, way too long.

He curled in behind me, spooning close. His body heat pressed in and, for a second, I felt something almost like comfort. Like, real comfort.

With Aidon, it had always been a rough impact: fucking, snarling, and the second we were done? Back to being enemies.

But this...this soft tether of warmth felt dangerous and intoxicating.

And fuck, it felt good. Too good.

So damned good that I could get used to it, and I realized that would have been even more dangerous than sleeping with him.

I stared up at the ceiling, listening to him snore, caught in his tight, possessive grip, even in the depths of slumber.

My plan had been simple: ravish him once, then vanish and put miles between me and Aidon, this God-forsaken soulless city, chase any scrap of safety that wasn't here.

But the second he wrapped his arms around me, I caved.

Pathetic, right? Was I this weak? Did one night of freaky-hot sex wipe out every single conviction I'd ever fought for? If so, what did that say about me? What happened to the badass I'd spent years sculpting from pain and grit?

I lay there, wide awake, mind spinning like a blender set to "shred." Panic crawled up my throat and wrapped tight around my chest. My heart pounded like it wanted to punch a hole through my ribs and bolt.

Sleep tiptoed in, but it felt like sliding into quicksand, no clue if I'd come up for air on the other side.

Tomorrow? No idea what that would look like.

But none of it mattered with his arms around me.

In that silent tangle with Aidon, the entire world went dim, and for once, I felt safe.

Just safe.

Like maybe that was all anyone wanted all along.

SEVEN

ESME

Aidon's war room in the Underworld looked like a bomb had gone off in a stationery store. Maps flung everywhere, classified reports stacked in precarious towers across the table, a chaos of paper and half-scrawled notes. The only light came from the TV monitor's harsh glow, flickering surveillance feeds painting the clutter in cold, frantic color.

Every property in the city, probably.

That was just how he operated: total control, no exceptions.

And the tension and distrust?

Off the fucking charts.

They were a near living, breathing thing.

Now that we'd fucked (multiple times, thank you very much), both of us were back on high alert, like we'd never bothered to take our armor off in the first place.

That back-and-forth power struggle? Oh, it was alive and well, right alongside the inconvenient, can't-quit-you attraction that had gotten us into this mess to begin with.

Add all that together, and the air seemed to crackle, electric and hot and a little bit dangerous.

I should have been gone by now.

Slipped out of his arms hours ago, made my escape. It would've been a pain in the ass to get around the army of guards he kept parked outside the penthouse, but I could've done it. Easy.

But I hadn't even tried. Not once.

Curiosity, that's what I told myself. I wanted to see what happened next. What Aidon was planning. Stick around just long enough to grab the juiciest details, then vanish.

Except here I was, still here like a fucking idiot, waiting.

It wasn't because being naked with him, twisted up in his arms, was the nearest thing to heaven I'd ever tasted. No, that wasn't it. Not even close.

So here we were. Again. Caught in the middle of another goddamned tug-of-war.

My infuriating and sexy, pain-in-the-ass rival insisted I needed to shut up and do as he said, follow his every command.

I rolled my eyes and let out a derisive snort. Like that was ever going to fucking happen.

Nice try, Aidon.

He might have me dickmatized, but there was no way he'd ever control me.

"Not fucking happening," I replied, sharp, slicing

through the tension that filled the room, the fifth time now, each word colder, rougher than before.

Aidon's jaw flexed, the muscle ticking beneath the dark stubble across his face. His eyes went inky black, wild, dangerous, as if he was seconds from snapping.

"I'm not asking," he stated with a low rumble, the kind that sent warning chills and heat, all the way down my spine. "If you want that heart of yours to keep beating, in that goddamn sexy body"—his gaze swept over me, slow and deliberate, every inch intended to fluster, to conquer—"then you'll do what I say."

I clamped my arms tighter across my chest, nails digging into my skin, refusing to give ground.

"Esme, you don't have a choice."

"There's always a fucking choice."

He looked like he was about to snap. And then he did.

His hands slammed down on the desk so hard the whole thing shook, loose pens and paper flying. The wood split under his fist, splinters spraying everywhere.

"Rhea's men put three bullets in my guys last night. Three. You think they're fucking around? And you're standing here like this is a goddamn debate?"

I just lifted my chin, met his eyes. "No."

The silence was deafening, stretched so tight it could break.

He came around the desk, each step a threat—loud, angry, restrained. When he reached me, he didn't hesitate. He got right up in my face, so close I could feel his breath, hot and rough, brushing my lips.

"If you won't help me destroy Rhea," he breathed, "I'll lock you down so deep, even God won't find you."

He slid a single page across the desk. "Sign, or I will escort you to your brother so he can handle family law."

The terms were straightforward: two security escorts with me at all times, work in his war room until Rhea was bled dry, no outside communications, all external accounts frozen, and finally, an ankle monitor.

"Is this my punishment?" I asked.

"These are the consequences of your actions," he said. "You drew blood. You pay markers. Three of them. Sign."

I picked up the pen, hating the way it felt heavier than it should have. Thankfully, my hand remained steady as I scrolled my name across the line.

In the next moment, Ares crouched before me, placed a decorative silver band around my ankle, and fastened it. An LED then blinked green.

He didn't look at me, only past me, to the men at the door, before saying, "If it goes dark, trigger Team Five and Eight. Assume hostile interference."

"Copy," they said in unison.

I caught the look Aidon gave me. Message received.

"It's a leash," he said. "And you chose it."

My pulse hammered, but I refused to so much as flinch.

I wouldn't blink or swallow. I wasn't about to let him see a single goddamn crack in my armor. I held his stare, refusing to look away.

Fuck him.

He thought he owned me now.

As if letting him between my thighs somehow meant I belonged to him? That fucking delusion would be his undoing.

His hand shot up before I could move, fingers skimming over my throat, a touch so gentle it burned.

He took a deliberate step forward, eyes locked with mine, and my instincts did the only thing they could.

I backed away. He followed. I retreated again. Over and over, until my shoulder blades hit the cold, unyielding plaster.

Nowhere left to go.

Then his hand tightened around my throat, not enough to hurt, just enough to remind me he could.

A perfect move. Textbook.

I set my jaw, gave him my best "don't fuck with me" glare, even as heat crawled like a traitorous serpent beneath my skin.

My body, the betrayer. Always.

"You want to pretend this is a game, Esme?" His voice was a low, rough caress, rasping over my skin.

It stretched between us, thick and consuming, filling up the tiny space where our bodies hovered, almost touching.

His hold softened, and one finger traced a slow, deliberate path from my shoulder to my wrist, leaving a burning line that made my nerves tingle. Goosebumps erupted across my skin wherever he touched.

His mouth hovered just above mine, so close I could taste the scotch on his breath, sharp, smoky, and dizzying.

"Fine. But you don't get to walk away," he murmured, the words a promise and a threat, a dare and a surrender.

My chest squeezed tight, lungs refusing to work as the pounding in my throat matched the relentless ache gathering between my thighs.

If I moved even a fraction, our mouths would crash together. I could see it play out, the heat and the wildness: his tongue forcing its way into my mouth, my nails clawing his shoulder, clothes tearing, neither of us stopping, both of us frantic, pressed to the wall until nothing existed but this until all my patched-up pride went up in flames, scattered and ruined at our feet.

No. I bit the inside of my cheek until the sharp taste of blood cut through the haze.

Never again. I couldn't let it happen again.

My eyes darted over the room, tallying every potential weapon within reach. Two weighty lamps. The iron poker by the hearth. If I timed it, caught him off guard, maybe I'd have a chance, a sliver of leverage.

But I wasn't naive.

Aidon was strength and danger, all honed muscle and ruthless instinct.

He'd disarm me in a heartbeat if I faltered, and I didn't forget the loyal men posted just beyond the door.

If I were going to beat Aidon, it wouldn't be by brute force. I'd have to outmaneuver him some other way.

Outsmart him. Outlast him. I just had to accept it would take longer than I wanted.

He moved in, fast and deliberate, and I jerked my head aside before our mouths could meet, wrenching myself free.

"What do you want from me, Aidon?" I asked, my resolve refusing to bend.

His eyes snapped with a wild, hungry light.

"There it is." He rocked back on his heels, like I'd just delivered him a fistful of gold, the keys to a kingdom or a candy shop. "Knew you'd come around."

He prowled over to the teetering stack of paperwork crowding his desk, flipping through the pages with quick, impatient flicks, each movement taut with restless energy.

"Start with these. There's something buried in here; I know it. Dig hard enough, and we'll find the dirt on Rhea. We make her squirm, back her into a corner. While she's too busy cleaning up, we slip beneath her guard and rip the real secrets out from under her."

"That's the plan?" My eyebrow arched, skepticism I couldn't hide. "You just want me to...read these reports?"

He shot me a look, already tapping his watch. "For now. I have a meeting in five. But this is what I need from you. Can you handle it?"

I shrugged, the answer already carved into my bones as if any of it could be simple.

No, nothing about this would be simple. That much was written in stone.

"So what do I get out of it?" I fired back, folding my arms tight across my chest, refusing to give an inch.

He glared at me, irritation etched into those sharp eyes, and spat a single word, "Protection."

I didn't even hesitate. "From whom?"

The idea that I needed him for anything, let alone protection, was so absurd it almost made me laugh. I could handle my own shit.

I always had.

His answer was a low growl, "Me."

The word hit like a punch, hanging between us, heavy and undeniable. I arched an eyebrow, silent, daring him to keep going.

"And everyone else who's looking for you." The way he said it, so casual, like there weren't a dozen people desperate to see me dead. Like it was just another day, another threat.

I let out a slow breath, collapsing into the chair next to the pile of papers, rifling through them to give my hands something to do.

Let him think he'd won this round.

Let him have his moment. Bastard.

But the truth was, I already had leverage on Rhea. Maybe not enough to end her, not yet, but what I'd found in Zeno's little treasure chest was enough to set the whole thing in motion. Enough to put a little fear in her, at least. No way in hell I was sharing that with Aidon.

Trusting him was never in the cards. Digging up dirt on enemies was his entire reason for existing.

Why would I hand him everything when he always had the upper hand?

I didn't need his protection. Not ever.

What I needed was my freedom.

He thought he owned me, that he controlled me. That I'd bend, break, snap to his will.

He was so goddamn wrong. But if playing his little game got me out of here? Away from Aidon?

Fine. I'd play.

I gave no reaction to the threat he tossed over his shoulder.

Instead, I said as he started to walk away, "I need my phone back, Aidon."

"Why?" he demanded, his tone all rough edges and warning.

"So I can tell the people who'll come looking if I disappear that I'm safe. Unless you want someone tearing down your precious penthouse doors?"

He muttered something, annoyance evident as he flicked his wrist, dug my phone from his jacket, and let it drop onto the desk.

The gesture was pure calculated control.

"I probably shouldn't, but I'm trusting you, Esme." All of a sudden, he was behind me, his presence a searing heat at my back, his breath hot on my neck.

He leaned in. God, the way it made my skin prickle and my pulse race. It was pure torment.

I hated it. I loved it. I couldn't untangle the two.

His lips grazed my ear, scorching me. "You're under my protection, but it lasts as long as I trust you. Don't give me a reason to change my mind."

I let myself smile, just a little. "You think you're in control of me, Aidon. That's adorable."

If he wanted a war of wills, I'd make damn sure he never saw me surrender.

He growled again, sharp and deep, then stalked out, the sound of his departure echoing in my chest. A slow, wicked grin crept across my lips. I drove him out of his mind, made him lose control, and the truth of it sent a shiver of dark delight through me.

The second he disappeared, I shot to my feet, heart pounding. I closed the door, fingers trembling, and grabbed my phone.

I texted Selene without hesitation.

ESME: He thinks he owns me. Watch my back.

Eight

AIDON

From the window of my office, I narrowed my eyes into the darkness, gaze trained on my club below. Plumes of cigar smoke curled thick in the air, catching the pulsing, electric flashes of the dance floor and swirling in the sudden bursts of colored light. The effect was disorienting. Ominous.

Something was off.

A cold shiver traced down my spine, the unmistakable sense of trouble stalking the edges of my thoughts. My gaze swept the room, cataloging the faces of those gathered, the regulars, the newcomers, the veterans of The Underworld.

I read every twitch, every sideways glance, the silent language of men who knew how to hide secrets and hold grudges.

Nights like this made me wonder why I'd ever created this place at all.

I knew the reasons, of course, but stress had a way of clouding even the sharpest motivations, of making old certainties dissolve into smoke.

My mind drifted, lost for a moment in those same blue-gray clouds, back through the years and the city streets that led me here.

Chicago seemed like another planet, a different life altogether. I was nothing like the boy I'd been then, though maybe the roots had always been there, waiting.

It made sense now, in a way. Of course, I ended up here.

A sudden rush of memory hit me, sharp and cruel: my parents, flickering through my mind like a reel from an old film.

My mother's face, barely remembered, brought a familiar ache twisting deep inside me. She'd vanished when I was a kid, leaving behind fragmented moments, impressions that faded every year.

And yet, here I was.

My father was a different story. A different kind of gravity, pulling me off kilter, shaping the man I'd become.

The life he led. The life he surrendered to was etched into me, whether I liked it or not.

Sometimes I wondered who I might have been if he'd been a different man. If he'd wanted more than the next hand of cards, if he'd been stronger, present. If he'd been a father instead of just a man in the same house.

After my mother left, he was a husk. Hollowed out, haunted by memories I was never part of. He fought every day, but not for us, not for family. He fought for escape. For the bottle. For the flash of cash we never had.

For me? Maybe. On the good days, I told myself it was possible. But I couldn't pretend he'd tried his best. Anyone's best would have been better than what he gave me.

Gambling was his obsession. Not me, not his family, not even himself. That was obvious. It always had been.

I lost count of the nights he staggered home, bloodied and unsteady, black eyes and broken ribs and a terror in his eyes I'd never seen anywhere else. He was scared of the people he owed, the debts he couldn't pay, the life he'd dragged us both into.

By the time I hit my teens, he was gone, gone, circling rock bottom and taking me with him into every pit he found.

Raising myself was brutal. But near the end, parenting him, caring for him, left marks on me no one could see. Ones that never faded.

Then, one afternoon, I came home and found him in the garage. Beaten. Bleeding. Almost unrecognizable, except for the shape of his regret.

After he died, nothing was the same. The world quieted, as if it were grieving with me, every echo of him lingering in the hollow of our rooms.

The emptiness was suffocating, but the chaos he'd left behind clung to the walls, a gnawing shadow that never let up.

The path I spiraled down after that felt inevitable. What else was there when you had nothing, when every day was a challenge and survival was a game no one won? I would have done anything in those days. Anything at all.

And I had.

It helped that I'd grown into an imposing force. I was tall, broad-shouldered, a presence that filled every doorway.

I learned how to use it—every inch of muscle, every ounce of strength, every bit of fury that burned through my veins.

Fearless. Dangerous. I wore my anger like armor, and it made me unstoppable.

Turning to crime? It wasn't a choice.

It was a pull, a gravity I never could have resisted. The first steps were effortless, a couple of jobs for a friend's uncle, hands dirty before I'd even realized what I was doing.

And then word spread.

People said I could get things done, that I was good at making others see reason, good at putting the right kind of fear in them.

The truth?

I rarely had to do much.

One look at me and they'd shrink, eyes wide, reading the violence I promised. They handed over cash, signed whatever paper my bosses wanted, and begged me not to come back.

Sometimes, breaking bones was necessary. Rare, but not impossible. When I had to do it, I never hesitated.

Pain was a promise, and I kept mine.

After a while, my reputation worked for me.

I'd walk in and see my mark go pale, trembling, scrambling for their wallet without a word from me. That was when I started learning the real game, the way fear worked, the way power meant more than fists.

I had power. Not just brute force, though that was always there, simmering under the surface. But something sharper.

Influence. Reputation. The threat of what I might do was more potent than the memory of what I'd already done.

I watched the true players. The men who never raised their voices, who ran empires from smoke-filled back rooms, settling scores with a look or a whispered word.

I watched their every move, every calculated silence, every glance that meant more than a shout. And I learned. Lesson by lesson. Threat by threat.

That's how you survive.

It was a game, nothing more.

At first, I was the quiet observer, listening in on those shadowy meetings, absorbing every calculated move and razor-sharp strategy the mafia bosses revealed.

I learned fast.

This was about power, yes, but more than that, it was about secrets.

Leverage.

Blackmail was the currency, and they traded it like kings.

If you had dirt on someone, you owned them.

I watched men sit on secrets for years, never showing their hand until the perfect moment. They collected information like gold coins, stashing it away, hoarding it, biding their time.

When the CEO of the local bank was fucking someone's wife? One filed it away.

That was leverage when you needed a loan, or a favor, or a little of both. Or if you caught wind of a politician squeezing a developer for cash? You tucked that away, too. That kind of knowledge was dangerous, priceless, and it glimmered in the dark like a sharpened blade.

So I listened. I collected. I waited. And, in time, I became one of them. The kind of man I'd spent my whole life watching from the shadows.

When I was twenty-two, I made it to Vegas with a couple of buddies, and the place got under my skin in an instant.

The lights, the nightlife, they were the obvious draw. But damn, the women. Everywhere you turned, gorgeous girls in barely-there dresses, hips and legs and laughter in every direction, and for a kid in his early twenties, it was like something out of a fever dream.

But I wasn't just wide-eyed and wasted, even if the liquor, sex, and drugs had done their best to drown out everything else.

I was always watching and learning. It hadn't taken long to see where the real game was being played.

Vegas was a city in motion, always building and expanding. Casinos and chain restaurants fought for space with local dives and little tourist traps.

The possibilities felt endless, and the rules? They bent for anyone with the nerve and the bankroll to make things happen.

With the right connections and the right cash, you could do just about anything. And make a killing doing it.

All those casinos, strippers, and showgirls were smoke and mirrors for the tourists. The real deals happened out of sight, in back rooms and smoky lounges, where fortunes changed hands and nothing was ever as simple as it looked.

Vegas was a wild city. And I wanted to own it.

I'd earned my reputation in this city the hard way, every promise kept, every threat delivered. Sometimes that meant showing my hand, brutal and fast, making sure no one ever doubted the violence I was capable of.

It was important, and they needed to see it, remember it, let it haunt them.

For the most part, I pulled my strings from the shadows.

Blackmail. Hidden surveillance. Alliances forged in fire and blood, all of it mine.

I was almost untouchable now, even by law enforcement.

Almost, but not always, and right now that razor edge of possibility had my nerves humming, alive and burning with adrenaline.

The apprehension in my veins was real, raw.

Not fear. A warning from instincts sharpened on the streets of Chicago, where hesitation meant death.

I'd learned to trust my gut above all else. And tonight, my gut screamed danger.

Ares waited at his post, a silent sentinel at the top of the stairs just outside my open door. His presence gave me a thin thread of comfort, but it wasn't enough, not tonight.

My fingers tightened around the snifter of whiskey, knuckles white, as I scanned the swirling sea of Las Vegas's elite below me. Faces blurred together, polished and hungry. None of them looked out of place, but that only made the tension coil tighter inside me.

Maybe it was just Esme winding me up, making me restless. Or maybe, beneath the surface, something darker waited to strike. Either way, I was ready, always ready, to answer violence with violence. No hesitation. Never again.

She was only a few feet away from me, just past the wall in the war room that adjoined my office, and I was still rattled from our last encounter.

Having her leave me raw, nerves exposed, my mind in chaos. Being near her was like injecting poison and adrenaline, a rush of hate, lust, and confusion so sharp it almost took me to my knees.

If I didn't fucking need her as much as I did, maybe I would have regretted ever finding her at all.

The burner phone buzzed in my pocket, insistent. I slid it out. Ares shot me a look, brows raised.

RHEA: You can't protect what doesn't belong to you.

I stared down at the screen, turning her words over, trying to pin down what the hell she meant.

There was a lot I was protecting these days, and whether any of it belonged to me was debatable.

It could have been a message about anything.

"What is it, boss?"

I looked up at Ares, my pulse pounding, fingers tightening around the phone. "Another threat from Rhea."

He nodded, shrugged, opened his mouth to speak, and then, just as I'd dreaded, chaos detonated.

The doors to the private club exploded open at the bottom of the stairs.

Two of my men were already down, sprawled in pools of crimson, bleeding out in sick, glossy puddles on the marble.

Masked men flooded inside, a small unit, but armed and trained, their movements sharp and merciless as they swept through the threshold.

Ares and I reached for our guns at the exact same time.

Shouts and screams erupted, a discordant symphony as the masked men unleashed bullets into the crowd. Glass shattered, wood splintered, bodies dove for cover, panic rippling through the room like shockwaves.

People scrambled behind chairs, bolted through side doors, vanished into the back rooms, desperate to escape the slaughter.

"Where's Aidon?" one of the men shouted.

At the sound of my name, Ares closed the distance, stepping in front of me, a living barricade, as the masked men lunged up the stairs toward my office.

They hit the landing, and gunfire tore through the air again, deafening and relentless.

Ares and I fired back, the strobe of muzzle flashes illuminating the insanity as bullets ricocheted off walls, chewed through furniture, and sent paper snowing from shelves.

We ducked behind my desk, pressed close, but there were too many of them. The odds were ugly and getting worse by the second.

Then I heard it, the pounding boots, the shouts from my guards. Hope clawed its way up my throat.

I risked a glance, catching the epic clash erupting in the hall: my men versus theirs, both sides ruthless, both sides bleeding, neither side willing to yield.

Whoever these fuckers worked for, they had been trained for this. My men fought hard, but they were holding the line.

My mind spun.

I worried about Ares, about whether I could protect myself.

But above all, I worried about Esme. She was right on the other side of this wall.

My reason for every move, every breath.

And I would die before I let anyone touch her.

I searched through the deafening chaos. "I need to get Esme."

"I'll cover you," Ares never hesitated, rising to his feet and unleashing hell in the direction of the men charging our way.

Bullets tore through the air, slamming into two of them.

They dropped, dead weight, but it wasn't enough. The rest kept coming, relentless, spraying round after round like they had eternity in their magazines.

Ares's shout ripped through the room, raw and desperate, as he collapsed behind my desk.

Shit.

I was back at his side in an instant, dropping down and meeting his gaze.

Blood soaked through his shirt, blooming fast, dark and ominous. That wound was bad. Really fucking bad.

"Ares! Fuck!" I ripped off my shirt and pressed it hard to his chest.

He grabbed my wrist, shoving the fabric tighter against his wound and shaking his head.

"Go get Esme!" His words were sharp, cutting through the haze. "Go! I'm fine!"

My eyes flicked to the room behind me, the panic, the noise, the violence.

Esme was fighting for her life, locked in brutal combat with a linebacker-sized bastard who hadn't a clue death was breathing down his neck.

"Fuck," I spat, pushing off the floor and leaving Ares behind, everything in me surging toward Esme and the man stupid enough to lay hands on her.

I came up behind the man, my hands finding his head with brutal efficiency.

The crack of his neck snapping reverberated through my fingers, a sickeningly familiar jolt.

He dropped to the floor, a dead weight, and there she was.

Esme. Blood smeared across her face, eyes wild as a cornered animal.

"I could have taken him," she muttered, defiant even in defeat.

"No time to argue," I ground out, grabbing her hand. "We need to get the fuck out of here."

Pulling her after me, I leapt over overturned tables and broken furniture.

The bedlam from the floor below faded with every frantic step we took.

My mind spun, rage coursing through my veins, hotter than anything I'd ever felt.

How the fuck had this happened? Was this Rhea's handiwork? Whoever it was, they wanted to make a statement.

A bloody one.

But whatever message they were sending, I couldn't give a damn, not right now.

All that mattered was Esme.

Getting her out. Keeping her alive.

We burst out of the office, and I yanked her down a narrow hallway, fury boiling inside me, uncontrollable, volcanic.

I found the hidden door and shoved her through, slamming it behind us. The heavy bulletproof lock clicked into place, sealing us off from the hell outside.

"What the fuck?" she muttered, eyes darting as she scanned the room.

"I like to be prepared," I said, and before she could react, my hands gripped her shoulders.

One hard shove and she hit the wall with a gasp, wide-eyed, her fear bleeding through.

Let her be scared.

If my gut was right, all of this was her fault anyway.

"You tipped them off," I accused, slicing through the space between us.

No mercy, no doubt.

Her green eyes narrowed for a fraction of a second, and her lips twisted into a savage little grin, blood painting her mouth like warpaint, and something inside me snapped.

She was fucked up from the fight, her mouth split, swollen, and seeping red, but worry was the last thing I felt.

She deserved every second of it.

Let her hurt.

She laughed, low and bitter, a sound that scraped along my nerves. "If I wanted to betray you, then you'd already be dead."

The fury inside me turned molten, burning away reason, burning everything.

She kept needling, pushing, tempting fate like she had no fear at all.

Maybe she just liked the battle.

How could she be this way? Reckless, fearless, taunting me even when all I wanted to do was keep her safe.

My anger was a live current, crackling between us, the words unspoken but sharp enough to draw blood.

My fingers dug into her arms, torn between wanting to shake her until her teeth rattled or crush my mouth to hers so she stopped laughing.

The urge to do both warred inside me, raw and primal.

Maddening.

I growled, the sound rough and guttural, before shoving her away so hard she staggered.

She just laughed again, mean and broken, dragging the

back of her hand across her bleeding mouth and smearing red across her cheek.

That bloody smirk of hers was enough to drive a man mad.

"Aidon," she drawled, velvet and venom, "you should be asking yourself why they only came for you."

NINE

E SME
Every step I took across Aidon's office was a risk. The creak of the floorboards beneath my feet echoed in the darkness, loud enough to make me wince. I hesitated, my heart hammering, praying he wouldn't hear me.

Beyond the glass walls, the city pulsed with neon and electricity, Las Vegas Boulevard lit up in a perpetual flash of color, all garish and alive.

Even at this hour, tourists crawled the Strip like ants, a shameless procession of laughter, slurred voices, and cash burning in their pockets.

My gaze snagged on a woman in stilettos that defied logic. She staggered, friends gripping her elbows, keeping her upright as she tottered close to the curb and a dangerous outcome.

A groan slipped out, low and irritated. People here never

changed. No matter how blinding the lights, the darkness beneath always found a way to seep through.

I tore my attention away from the window, focusing on Aidon's massive desk.

Before making any moves, I shot a nervous glance at the doorway, needing to know I was alone.

Most of his drawers were shut tight, locked, as I'd expected.

Of course. I gritted my teeth.

"Dammit," I whispered, turning to the credenza behind me instead, refusing to give up.

There was something Aidon was hiding.

I felt it to my bones. But what? That was the question.

After the ambush, he'd left in a rush, straight to the hospital to check on Ares.

He'd locked me in the penthouse, a guard keeping me from leaving, but that hadn't stopped me from searching for answers.

If Aidon thought isolation would keep me from snooping, he was dead wrong.

Anticipation surged through me, making my fingers tremble as I tried another drawer on the credenza.

I held in a sigh of relief when it slid open.

I knelt, rifling through the files, but the thrill faded just as fast.

Just paperwork, dull and ordinary. Beverage receipts, food orders for Underworld. Typical for Aidon, locking up the good stuff and leaving the rest to rot.

Pushing to my feet, I faced the desk again, determination

sharpening inside me. If I wanted real answers, I'd have to pick those locks.

My pulse spiked when footsteps sounded outside, each one closer, heavier, unmistakable.

Aidon.

He appeared in the doorway, rage sharpened the lines of his face.

His eyes locked on me, hard and unflinching, cold with accusation. "Looking for something, you little thief?"

That anger, I knew it well.

Aidon always seemed angry with me, always ready to catch me in the act.

And now he had.

There was no point denying I'd been snooping, so I wouldn't bother.

I smirked, shrugged, and leaned my hip against his desk, forcing myself to look easy, careless, as if his presence wasn't making my pulse stutter out of control every time he turned that furious gaze on me.

"Just wanted to see what the great Aidon kept hidden," I tossed back.

He closed the distance, his presence becoming overwhelming, and he brought his face inches from mine. "You realize you're playing with fire, Esme?"

He took a step closer, and I matched it, retreating backward, edging toward the windows, both of us locked in this old, dangerous dance.

I lifted my chin, refusing to give him the satisfaction of looking away, meeting that heat in his eyes head-on.

"Maybe," I said. I wasn't about to let him see how much he affected me.

He advanced again, closing the space, until my back hit the glass. Neon lights bled across the city below, but all I could feel was the heat of Aidon's body crowding mine.

"Why do you keep testing me, Esme? Do you want to see what happens when you push me too far?"

A slow, twisted smile curled my lips right before I whispered, husky, taunting, seductive, "Maybe I do, Aidon."

And he played right into my hands.

His hand cut through the space between us and gripped my hip, jerking me in, pressing me flush against the hard line of his erection.

His other hand tangled in my hair at the base of my skull, yanking my head back until I gasped. Then his mouth crashed down on mine, hot and hungry, lips parting me open with a force that left no room for resistance.

This was my choice, my passion, my desire, and nobody else's.

I whimpered into the kiss, lost to the heat and need, his tongue sliding deep, tangling with mine until I couldn't tell where I ended and he began.

We kissed like two animals starved for the same thing, fighting for control, neither of us giving in, neither of us willing to lose.

My arms wound around his neck, dragging him down, demanding more, and the electricity between us only burned hotter, stinging and wilder.

My hands clutched at his shirt, fists twisting, desperate to pull him closer, to dissolve the last inch of space between us.

Inside, my thoughts fought a war all their own. I should have pulled away.

I told myself to stop. To break free.

But I only wanted more. I melted into him, opened myself wider, and let him in deeper.

When he released my hair, his hands found my hips, gripping tight and lifting me up.

Without a second thought, I wrapped my legs around his waist, clinging to him as he pinned me against the window.

The hem of my dress rode up high, baring me completely, leaving nothing between us but a fever neither of us wanted to cure.

He groaned, low and rough, as his fingers found my pussy.

Calloused fingertips slid through my slick folds, dipping into me. I gasped, arching despite myself, my body betraying every lie I wanted to tell. There was no hiding the wetness or the need, not with him.

His mouth tore from mine, breath hot, searching my face.

I blinked, hard, desperate not to look at him, not to let him see the want in my eyes, the hunger in my body, the way every part of me burned for him.

If he looked, he'd find the war inside me—raw and exposed, tangled up in want and shame.

But he could feel it, all of it, in the way my body moved against his hand.

"Mmm, you're so wet," he groaned, the words dark velvet in my ear, his mouth dragging molten, hungry kisses down the slope of my neck.

His finger pressed deeper, and I spread my thighs wider, greedy for more of him, desperate for every inch.

A second finger plunged inside.

God, I was so slick, so ready, and the feeling made me quiver around his hand as he fucked me relentlessly, his palm grinding just right.

My hips jerked up to meet each delicious thrust, needing him harder, faster, as pleasure crackled and bloomed sharp and wild inside me.

"Say it, Esme," he growled, thick, rough, and barely held together by lust.

Fuck.

Aidon had me cornered, right where he wanted me, and he knew it.

He expected me to break for him, to admit that I belonged to him, that I was his, body and soul.

But no. Not a chance. Nobody would ever own me. I'd never give him that satisfaction.

Even if my body was a traitor, shuddering under the assault of his hand, clenching around his fingers, every nerve ending screaming for surrender, for him, for more.

I wasn't giving in. Not yet.

Breath hissed out of me, tight and defiant.

I pressed my mouth to his, lips gentle at first, then teeth sinking into his lower lip, a silent refusal to back down.

He groaned, the sound torn between hunger and frustration, and I knew I wasn't the only one caught up in this war.

The question was always how much he could take before he lost control, before this little game of ours spun into something dangerous.

Aidon's patience was infamous, a legend whispered in wary tones.

He was calculating, cool, always in control, right up until you pushed him past the breaking point. And I had a feeling we were standing on the razor's edge of that moment, right here, right now.

He tried to pull away, but I bit down again, my teeth sinking into his lush bottom lip until it gave beneath the pressure.

"Esme!" he barked, hand flying to his mouth.

When he drew his fingers away, I caught the smear of blood on his cheek and felt a wicked satisfaction twist inside me.

"I told you not to do that again!" His eyes went black, pupils blown wide with a furious, almost decadent hunger.

But the pain only drove him wilder. He crashed his mouth back to mine, rougher this time, his kiss bruising and wild.

His hand plunged between my thighs, fingers slamming inside me, fucking me hard and fast against the window.

Angry now, he lost all restraint. And I let him.

I reveled in it, the ferocity, the raw, violent pleasure that only Aidon could rip from me.

Every thrust, every punishing flick of his fingers, sent jolts of ecstasy ricocheting through my body, fracturing me in the best way.

Pleasure built, ruthless and hot, cresting inside me with every ragged breath. My thighs fell open, mouth open wider, surrendering completely as he pushed me closer and closer to the edge of oblivion.

"Yes," I whimpered, letting my head fall to his shoulder as he poured every bit of energy and focus into the relentless rhythm of his fingers, pushing my desire to a fever pitch.

His mouth hovered at my ear, his breath ragged and hot.

"Goddammit, Esme," he growled, voice raw, "you're so fucking sexy. Your pussy feels so good...so fucking wet and hot."

A shiver raced down my spine.

"Please don't stop," I gasped, the words tumbling out between shallow breaths. "I need you to keep going."

He kept the pace steady, holding me right on the precipice.

"Still pretending this doesn't mean anything?" The question was a blade, sharp and impossible to ignore.

My eyes snapped open at his words, the cold shock of reality slicing through the haze.

I was letting this go too far, letting him inside in ways I'd promised myself I never would.

I jerked my head back, fighting to meet his eyes, even as his fingers thrust relentlessly inside my desperate, clenching heat.

"I don't belong to you, Aidon," I bit out, through trembling lips and praying he wouldn't stop, not until I shattered.

Anger flared in his eyes, dark and electric. He increased his speed, fucked me harder, punishing and perfect, just like I wanted.

I ground down onto his hand, chasing that desperate pleasure, moaning as the pressure built.

I was seconds from coming undone, teetering at the edge, when out of nowhere, he pulled his hand away.

The loss hit me like a slap.

I whimpered, aching, every nerve ending burning for him.

I searched his face, wild and pleading, needing him to finish what he started.

Then I saw it. The twisted, triumphant grin he wore made my stomach drop.

He'd won, and he knew it.

"You will belong to me, Esme," he hissed, letting my legs slip down and stepping back, leaving me open and wanting.

I glared at him, letting him see pure rage in my stare, even as my body screamed with unsatisfied need.

He spun on his heel and strode out of his office, abandoning me there, skirt shoved up, thighs slick, pulse thundering with frustration.

"You bastard," I snarled into the darkness, yanking my skirt down with shaking hands.

His laughter echoed down the hall, taunting and victorious.

In that moment, I wanted to hate him more than I'd ever hated anyone.

But all I could taste was the bitter hunger he left behind.

TEN

ESME
Aidon had fallen right into my trap, letting me pore over the intelligence he'd gathered on Rhea's syndicate.

Now I had twice the leverage. The scales tipped in my favor, though he would never admit it.

He was beginning to trust me again. The process was a slow one, but I could work with it.

Not that he'd ever say as much. But he let me leave alone, as long as I kept in touch, kept him updated on where I was and what I was doing.

It was a leash, sure, but looser than before.

After slipping back to my rental, showering off the sweat and grime, and changing into dark clothes, I set my plan in motion.

If Aidon discovered what I was up to, he'd think I was betraying him all over again.

Maybe I was in a sense, but not really. I'd deal with that later.

For now, I moved through the shadows of Rhea's warehouse on the city's edge, my nerves stretched tight as piano wire.

The darkness pressed in, broken only by overhead lights that flickered on and off, drenching the concrete floor in jagged, shifting shadows.

After all this time, I found out where she kept her servers, a secret I'd hunted for weeks.

If I could get to them, I'd have the last piece. Enough to ruin her, to force her out of the city forever.

The air tasted of oil and rust, the ghosts of old machinery haunting every breath.

I could hear, somewhere distant, the faint drone of another warehouse.

My heart pounded a manic rhythm as I darted from one patch of darkness to the next, the tiny, encrypted flash drive in my pocket thumping against my thigh with every step.

My mission was brutal and simple: find Rhea's servers and download everything I could.

Aidon, in his arrogance, had handed me the intel I needed.

Now I knew the exact place to look. If I reached them, I could gut her operation from the inside.

Every second was borrowed time. Every breath was a risk. I slipped deeper into the dark, adrenaline lighting me up from the inside. All I had to do was get in, get out, and not look back.

The clang of metal split the silence, sharp and sudden, and I snapped rigid behind a pillar, praying the shroud of darkness would be enough to hide me.

My heart hammered as I strained to listen, every shallow breath burning in my chest, while footsteps and muffled voices crept closer and closer.

I crouched low, muscles coiled tight, ducking behind a battered crate just in time to watch two men slip past me.

I risked a glance, peering around the splintered edge.

Recognition hit me. They were Rhea's men.

A slow, secret smile curled my lips. At least I wasn't lost; I was where I needed to be.

I held my breath, lungs aching, not daring to let even the softest exhale betray me.

"Did we get the information we needed?" one of them murmured, tension in every syllable.

"I think so," the other replied. "The deliveries are funneled out of a small warehouse near the airport. We obtained the schedule and are planning the best way to attack it. Aidon will never know what hit him. It'll be fucking glorious to pay that bastard back."

"Good, fuck him. He thinks he's untouchable because he owns The Underworld. He's sorely mistaken."

"Rhea wants it to hurt. Bad."

"I can make that happen," the other laughed, low and rough, their voices dissolving into the darkness as their footsteps faded away.

Fuck.

They planned to hit Aidon. The realization slammed

into me, leaving me reeling and driving a new sense of urgency through my veins.

I needed those files, but now a warning burned at my tongue.

My loyalties twisted and tore inside me, piercing as a blade scraping bone.

I pressed my back tight to the cold concrete, barely daring to breathe until those footsteps faded into nothing. Then I moved, silent and low, fingertips grazing the gritty floor as I slipped between shadows. The server room couldn't be far.

I found it. A closet-sized cave washed in the eerie, pulsing blue of machine-light. I almost sagged to my knees. Empty. For now.

The USB slid into the port with a loud click that made me flinch.

My fingers flew desperately over the keyboard.

The progress bar crawled agonizingly slow. Sweat prickled beneath my clothes, sliding down my back and pooling at my waistband.

"Move," I whispered, nails beating a staccato on the desk.

47%... 48%... The hum of the servers pressed in from all sides, louder and louder. It was the only thing I could hear besides my ragged breathing.

The air behind me shifted. A slow, deliberate exhale.

Goosebumps prickled along my skin, every nerve suddenly on edge.

"You never can help yourself, can you, Esme?"

I spun at the sound of Aidon's voice, my veins turning to ice.

He filled the doorway, broad shoulders eclipsing the only escape, predatory and dark. The harsh fluorescent light carved shadows across his face, illuminating that lethal glint in his eyes I knew too well. His jaw flexed, muscle jumping beneath stubble, as if he was holding back a snarl.

"Aidon—" His name cracked as I edged away, the unforgiving metal of the server biting into my spine.

He prowled toward me, each step deliberate and deadly. The room felt smaller, colder, every inch of air between us charged with tension so thick it was hard to breathe.

"We don't have time for this," I hissed, but my hands shook, betraying me. "I just saved your fucking empire, but you'll never—"

His hand clamped around my arm, brutal and uncompromising, dragging me into his orbit. The heat rolling off him was dizzying, intoxicating, tinged with whiskey and sharp mint.

"I knew I shouldn't have fucking trusted you." The words came low and rough, scraped raw from his throat.

I jerked in his grip. "You don't understand—"

He leaned in, lips curling just enough to reveal teeth. "I let you go." He tugged me closer, inches from my face. "And now you're here, feeding intel to my enemy?"

Something inside me broke.

I shoved him hard, catching him off guard so he staggered a step.

"I would never work for her!" The shout scorched my throat. "You're a goddamned fool if that's what you think!"

Behind me, the computer chimed. Done. Heart hammering, I snatched the USB free and shoved it deep into my pocket.

"We need to leave, Aidon. Now!"

The first gunshot shattered the air, exploding concrete from the doorframe.

"Fuck!" Aidon ducked, his arm reaching for me, but I was already lunging for the exit, adrenaline burning through me.

I risked a glance over my shoulder. It was a mistake. Arms like iron bands seized me around the waist, hauling me off my feet.

Hot breath ghosted against my neck as I thrashed, clawing at the vice crushing my ribs, panic turning my vision white at the edges.

My body jerked like a live wire as iron fingers dug into my skin.

Instinct took over. First, I thrashed, and next, I snapped my head down, teeth sinking through fabric, through flesh, until I knew I'd pierced through skin and drawn blood.

"You fucking bitch!" The man's roar rattled my ear, his fist slamming into my ribs.

Something cracked. White-hot pain flared, ripping away my breath.

Concrete slammed against my cheek, grit grinding into my skin. I gasped and clawed for air that just wouldn't come.

Everything seized inside me.

"ESME! NO!" Aidon's shout tore through the chaos, raw and desperate.

Boots thundered around us, black tactical gear surging

from every shadow. Two men wrestled Aidon back, straining to hold him.

His face twisted, something wild in his eyes, a terror I'd never seen before.

The wall of men at the doorway split down the center.

Rhea glided in, heels clicking sharp and cold against the concrete. Her suit was midnight-dark, swallowing the light, so her pale face hovered in the gloom like a ghost.

"Well, well, well," Rhea said from across the room, every word sugar-coated poison.

Crimson lips curled as she paced around me, a predator savoring the moment.

"Look who we have here." She knelt, one manicured nail tracing along my jaw, ice trailing in her wake. "Take her away, boys."

Hands like steel clamps hooked under my arms, dragging me upright.

A flash of silver at my ankle, then the crinkle of mylar as it cinched tight. The green light on my monitor went out.

Across the aisle, another anklet blinked to life on a runner's boot, same casing, same pulse, already sprinting toward the service door.

Panic surged hot and choking.

"Move," someone barked. Zip ties bit into my wrists as cloth hit my mouth.

The world shrank to boots, tiles, and the sound of the decoy feet running away in the wrong direction.

My legs wouldn't move. I hung limp like a rag doll, pain raging through my chest as they carried me over a shoulder.

My ribs ground together, the agony so excruciating, I couldn't help but scream.

I clawed at the fucker's back, nails tearing into anything I could reach. Digging in, I scored fabric, skin. But the pain won out, cut deeper, shooting lightning through my shattered ribs.

The world spun, black spots dancing at the edges of my vision. All I could hear was my frantic heartbeat and Aidon's broken shout.

"Let her go!" His plea cracked, as if something in him shattered wide open.

Rhea's laughter sliced through it all, a sound like glass breaking. "You should choose your allies more wisely, Aidon."

She dragged a finger along his cheek, painting a smear of my blood across his skin.

His eyes found mine, just once. "I should have let you burn!"

His voice was ruined, grief and rage twisted together, chasing me as I was carried away.

Every step sent splinters of pain through my chest until even screaming became impossible, my lungs locked in a useless, frantic search for air.

Eleven

Esme

Venomous rage burned through me, hotter than any fire. It wasn't a simple pulse. It tore through my veins, leaving nothing but raw hunger and the acid bite of desperation.

The ropes cut deeper with every movement, digging into my wrists and ankles until blood slipped warm and slick across my palm.

I should have surrendered, let despair swallow me whole in this windowless cell, but instead I pulled harder, the need for freedom clawing at my insides.

The faint hum of television monitors droned on, mixing with the ragged edge of my breathing.

Beyond the walls, the rhythmic stomp of Rhea's armed guards was a constant reminder of how I was never alone, not even for a second.

A thin wall separated us. Just that much between me and the taste of freedom I ached for.

I allowed the pain to anchor me, forced myself to breathe, to focus.

The air was heavy with the copper tang of blood and the electric charge of panic.

I told myself over and over again not to panic.

To breathe. To calm my mind.

But the fury pounded like a war drum, wild and relentless, and logic whispered encouragements that I could take those guards down if I were given the chance.

I gritted my teeth as the rope sliced deeper, my mind a whirlwind of pain and determination.

I wasn't giving up. Not yet. Not ever.

If Rhea wanted me dead, I'd be dead.

I knew that.

Instead, her men had tied me up, wrists burning, and dumped me in this tiny room. Claustrophobic, yeah, but also...lavish in a strange way.

Like a hotel suite shrunk to the size of a jail cell, and all I could do was wait, breathing through shallow breaths and every muscle aching from the ropes.

For what, though? That was the question.

Why was she keeping me alive? What was Rhea planning?

I let my head fall back, chest heaving, sweat sticking my shirt to my back.

The monitors in front of me flickered with restless, shifting images.

I recognized them now. They were live surveillance feeds of Rhea's casinos, her resorts, and a handful of dull, gray warehouses scattered across the city.

Her whole empire, mapped out in grainy color, just for me.

I was trapped in the heart of everything she owned, and there was nothing I could do but watch and wait.

She was a fucking force in Vegas.

Over the last few years, she'd scooped up property after property, carving out her territory like a wolf starved and seeing prey.

If she weren't such a ruthless bitch, I might've respected her for it.

However, I couldn't be impressed.

Not by her.

Not when I knew just how far she'd gone to claw her way to the top, how many people she'd stepped on, crushed, ruined.

Rhea was dirty. She was sly. And nothing but cold, hard ice pumped through her veins.

Everyone knew it, too. If you crossed her, your days were numbered. She wasn't just playing the game. She hunted. She was a fucking predator who had no problems cheating.

And as my luck had it, I was the latest prey trapped in her net.

The question wasn't if, but how long she'd toyed with me before tearing me apart, piece by piece.

My time was running out, and if I was going to survive

whatever she had planned for me, I needed to keep my focus razor-sharp, attuned to every minute detail.

For what felt like the hundredth time, I scanned the small room, memorizing every nook, cranny, and object.

If I somehow managed to get free, I'd need every scrap of an advantage I could find.

My gaze caught on the doorknob. Locked from the outside. Once these ropes were dealt with, my next move would be straight for that door.

I wasn't leaving my fate up to her. I was getting the fuck out, no matter what it took.

Every lock had a key. I'd find mine.

That was when it clicked. My heart stuttered in my chest, eyes wide as the door swung open.

Rhea strutted in like the queen of the universe, all attitude and malice.

Her hair was wild, a tangle of ginger curls that made her look like some modern Medusa.

She grinned, but it was the kind of grin that never touched her eyes. Those eyes, by the way, were bright blue and mean as hell.

She wore a black dress so tight it looked painted on, plus these red stilettos that had to be six inches high. Every step made a sharp click on the marble, like a countdown.

She circled me, slow and silent, checking me out like I was on display at the zoo.

I knew what she wanted. She wanted me to beg. Maybe she thought I'd cry, or start bargaining. Honestly, if that was her plan, she was in for a disappointment.

I kept my mouth shut, not even looking at her when she stopped right in front of me, her finger tapping her chin, nails perfect.

"I knew Aidon would come for you," she said. "The question is, will he arrive fast enough?"

There it was, a challenge, floating between us.

I refused to give her the satisfaction.

I expected her to threaten me. Maybe rough me up, or try to mess with my head. I was ready for all of it.

But there was no way I'd let her win. I looked her right in the eye, to make sure she got the message: I wasn't scared. She could try whatever she wanted. She wouldn't break me.

"You think you have control, Esme, but the truth is that you're just a pawn."

She arched a brow, waiting, but the reply she expected would never come.

With an exasperated exhale, she reached for a remote resting on the desk beside the monitors. A single click and the screens fizzed, shifting to a different feed.

My attention caught on the central monitor, and my breath hitched.

Aidon.

Alone in his Underworld office, hemmed in by maps, disordered stacks of paper, and the clutter of empty whiskey bottles.

He stalked back and forth like a caged predator, his designer suit jacket discarded, sleeves rolled to the elbows, knuckles white around a tumbler of amber liquid. The king of Vegas had vanished, and in his place prowled a man consumed by something primal, something desperate.

"Look at him," Rhea said, chuckling. "It's quite delicious. Seeing him like this? Mr. Cool, Calm, and Collected was losing his shit and looking like a mad scientist or something. It's good to know he's human, right?"

She knew I wasn't going to answer. Even if I could, I wouldn't. Seeing Aidon like that, unraveling, knocked the breath right out of me.

None of that bothered Rhea. She was loving every minute, her laughter swelling until it filled the whole cramped room, thick and poisonous.

"He's losing himself for you, Esme. Isn't that what you wanted all along?"

Still, I wouldn't say a word. Screw her. I just glared up, wishing my eyes could burn holes straight through her. I set my jaw. If she wanted a reaction, she'd have to keep waiting.

I promised to make her pay for this. That was a vow.

Her time would come, and I would be the one to deliver it.

She rolled her eyes, lips twisting with frustration, and shook her head at my stubborn silence.

Then, without ceremony, she reached right into her ridiculous cleavage and fished out a USB stick.

It thunked onto the table between us.

I knew it instantly: mine.

Her goons must've picked my pocket before dumping me in this room. It had been wiped clean when I arrived.

Now the only thing it held was the data I'd ripped from her servers.

"You thought I wouldn't find out?" She arched a brow, watching me.

I broke eye contact, staring back at the monitors.

Aidon was losing it at Ares, flipping through the maps like a maniac.

I couldn't hear a thing, but wow, his body language said it all. He looked like he wanted to shatter the whole place.

I wanted to take every ounce of his frustration and just, I wasn't sure, erase it.

It was on me, all of it.

He was losing his mind because I'd managed to get myself abducted by this absolute psycho, and it was all my fault.

I should've bailed a long time ago. Instead, I got cocky, screwed around, and now this was my mess to deal with.

Rhea, now more than pissed at my silent treatment, stalked over until she was right in front of me.

She leaned down, got all up in my face, and grabbed my chin, forcing my head up so I had to look at her.

I clenched my teeth and met her gaze, making sure to glare at her with every ounce of loathing I had. I might not have said a word, but I wanted her to know just how much I hated her right now.

She curled her lips into a slow, wicked grin, then dragged her fingernail along my jaw, taking her sweet time. Standing, she leveled a look at me, gaze sharp as a knife.

"Aidon might be ruthless, but even he has weaknesses.

And you, pretty little Esme? You are his greatest weakness of all."

I rolled my eyes, shaking my head. She was so sure of herself.

She seriously underestimated Aidon, and yeah, she was going to regret that.

Big time. Probably soon.

I was almost tempted to feel bad for her.

Almost.

The storm brewing inside me threatened to crack me open.

The fury I wanted to let loose on Rhea was at a full rolling boil now.

Whatever pain Aidon would inflict on her, she'd brought it on herself. I almost wanted to laugh at her stupidity. Challenging him so openly, leaving breadcrumbs like she was daring him to follow.

She had a death wish. That was the only rational reason for all of this.

Rhea hadn't the faintest clue of what kind of monster she'd poked, what sort of cold violence was tucked behind all those designer suits. He was going to destroy her. Rip her into pieces.

The craziest thing? She thought she would be the one to win. Even better, she seemed to think I'd be right there, helping her do it.

Talk about delusional.

How had she honestly survived this long being so clueless?

"If you think I'm going to help you destroy Aidon, you don't know me at all," I finally said.

Rhea's smile stretched wider, her crimson-stained lips parting to reveal perfect teeth as she threw her head back. The laugh that erupted from her throat bounced off the walls, harsh, grating, unhinged, the kind that made the hair on your arms stand up and your fight-or-flight instinct kick into overdrive.

My stomach twisted up.

"Oh, Esme," she said, breathless and shaking her head like I'd told the world's funniest joke. "You've got me all wrong, darling. I don't need your help. Least of all to destroy Aidon."

She looked down at me, clicked her tongue, then bent down again, way too close, staring hard into my eyes.

"I just need you to be his downfall."

She pushed off the wall and marched for the door, but halfway there she stopped, spun back around, and fixed those wild eyes on me like a pair of angry wings.

I'd faced down the worst Vegas had to offer. Men who'd buried bodies in the desert without blinking. Women who'd smile while slipping poison in your drink. But something crawled behind Rhea's eyes that made those others look like amateurs, something rabid and unhinged that hadn't been there moments before.

"When I'm finished, pretty Esme, Aidon will look at what's left of you and see a stranger."

With that, she yanked the door open and slammed it

behind her hard enough to shake the frame, and then she was gone.

The silence after felt like a punch. I was left standing there, bones shaking, every nerve lit with a cold, crawling dread.

On the monitors, Aidon stalked back and forth like a caged predator, hands raking through his dark hair, muscles coiled tight enough to snap. My throat closed around his name, swallowing back the urge to cry out.

I swallowed hard and locked my eyes on his image, letting his rage feed mine, transforming my terror into something I could use. This wasn't over. Not by a long shot. Whatever nightmare Rhea had scripted for us, I was about to rewrite the ending.

Twelve

AIDON

Empty whiskey bottles littered the floor of my office. I kicked one, hard, and it clanked against the wall, rattling across the mess.

Three weeks... three weeks of searching, planning, waiting. I was so damn close. I could feel it. Any second now, I was going to find out where they'd taken Esme.

After she'd been dragged away, I'd managed to get out of Rhea's compound in one piece. There was no way I could have taken on all her men by myself, so I slipped into the woods behind the place and called Ares's team for backup.

While I waited, there wasn't a damn thing I could do except watch. Two of Rhea's goons hauled Esme toward a black SUV. She fought like hell, kicking and twisting, until one of them smacked her across the face. The slap echoed in the night air. They shoved her into the backseat and sped off, taillights vanishing around the bend. My hands curled into fists. I was too far from my own car to do anything but curse and glare into the dark.

I'd been drowning in information for days and still had nothing. My office was a disaster zone: walls, desk, floor, every inch buried under satellite images, property records, informant reports. A paper war, and I was losing. I stared until the words blurred and my eyes ached, hoping for one thread, one slip, that would unravel Rhea's whole operation and lead me straight to Esme.

I needed that last piece in the puzzle: a name, a stray rumor, any scrap of a place that could get me to Esme and to the throats I'd have to cut to reach her.

My reflection in the window stared back at me, some stranger with bloodshot eyes, stubble crawling up his jaw, and a shirt splattered with proof of what I'd done tonight.

The skin over my knuckles was split, raw flesh peeking through clotted blood, and I'd circled my office at least a hundred damn times already.

Vegas was my calling card: bartenders with their jaws wired shut, bouncers hobbling on broken knees, informants spitting out teeth, and still, nothing.

Not a damn thing to show for it.

I'd left a trail of broken men across the city. Every single one of them swore up and down that they didn't know where Esme was. It didn't matter. I knew they were lying. I could tell, just by the sound of their bones snapping under my hands. There was still blood on my face, not even mine, from some guy who thought he could hold out longer than the others.

He couldn't. None of them could.

My knuckles were wrecked, throbbing with every beat of my heart, but in truth, I liked it. It kept me sharp.

I would have set myself on fire if it meant getting Esme back. I wasn't stopping, not for anything.

She belonged next to me. Safe. No marks on her unless I put them there.

The next idiot who got in my way, he'd find out I could do a whole lot more with a knife than just threaten. I had patience for days, and I was just getting started.

One of Rhea's men slumped in the corner chair, wrists zip-tied, blood dripping in slow, ugly dots onto my twelve-thousand-dollar Aubusson.

Every drop, a new blemish. I couldn't even bother caring.

His face was a mess, all shifting colors and swollen flesh, one eye sealed shut, the other a slit open. Only the spasming vein in his neck told me Ares and I hadn't pushed him over the edge.

Not yet. Not that it mattered. He hadn't told us a damn thing.

I pulled my attention back to the surveillance wall, screens flickering with feeds from Rhea's properties. Estate after estate, all sterile, all quiet.

No Esme. No flash of dark hair, no stubborn tilt of her chin.

Rhea wouldn't slip up so easily. She'd hide Esme some-where off the map, somewhere only she knew. Personal.

The clue was out there. In someone's memory, or some

small thing we'd missed. I just had to get to it before the clock ran out.

Ares and Helena watched me from the plush red velvet couch, eyes glued to my every twitch like I was about to explode and take half the room with me.

Maybe they weren't wrong. My hands wouldn't quit shaking. I kept glancing at my watch, then the clock on the wall, over and over, like maybe if I stared hard enough the minutes would reshuffle themselves and give back what I'd lost.

Every second made the anger in my veins twist tighter, heavier, colder.

I slammed my fist against the desk, not caring about the jolt of pain burning up my arm. Pain was easier than this... this gnawing emptiness hollowing me out.

Somewhere, Esme was breathing, bleeding, screaming.

Or maybe not breathing at all.

Rhea wouldn't blink before hurting Esme. That was the whole damn point of it all.

Taking Esme was the perfect revenge play.

Rhea had sniffed out my weakness, the one thing sharp enough to cut through everything else and bring me flat on my face.

But I was still breathing. And unless I saw a body, Esme was too.

The clock was running. I spun around to face Ares and Helena, both of them staring at me like I might go off at any second.

"Your men find anything?" I snapped.

Ares pressed his lips into a tight line. "They placed her anklet in a Faraday bag in under two seconds and attached a tracker to a courier. We monitored the broadcast for thirty minutes before realizing the signal wasn't coming from her. We've checked the band's internal log up to the moment just before the kidnapping; after that, it was silent until they removed the tracker sleeve."

"Fuck." The word just blew out of me, loud and ugly.

I stalked over to the balcony, grabbing the rail and squeezing until my knuckles ached.

Down below, the Underworld was dead quiet, the dance floor a black sea.

Hours earlier, this place had been packed with the city's finest, laughing and plotting, not a clue there was a war brewing right above them.

My fingers clenched tighter around the balcony rail. I could practically see Rhea's body flying out into the dark, limbs flapping, dress riding up, her scream cut short before she slammed straight through one of those stupid glass tables.

That sound, that last disgusting wet crunch, would be the payoff for every miserable hour I'd wasted tracking her down.

I shut my eyes, grinning at the thought like some junkie who could finally taste water. If it weren't for the promise of her death, I'd have torched this city a long time ago.

"We're missing something," I gritted out, nails biting hard into my palms.

Helena cut in, no patience in her tone. "Aidon, you need

to get your head on straight. Running around like a rabid animal isn't helping. You'll get yourself killed. You'll get Esme killed. You know how Rhea thinks. She didn't take Esme just to kill time."

The door swung open, and an Olympus courier in a charcoal suit stepped in, holding a cream-colored card in his palm like a summons. He placed it on the desk and waited.

"From Zeno Theodorus," he said. "Interdict: Esme is black booked at all Olympus properties. Access revoked. Accounts frozen. Associates flagged. A bounty is authorized for the device and any copies. Not for her life."

I kept my face expressionless.

"To reverse the Interdict," he continued, "return the original hardware and a verified full copy. Or cut one of Rhea's arteries and bring proof. Until then, no Olympus, no favors, no name."

He handed me a receipt pad, and I signed my name. The courier took the pad and headed out the door.

Helena's eyes stayed firm, her voice steady. "Protection isn't absolution." The sound of the door shutting behind him echoed like a gavel, final and unyielding.

Her words barely dented the pounding in my skull. I kept pacing toward the map wall, the same maze of streets and alleys blending together as I traced them for what had to be the thousandth time.

The trail ended at Rhea's compound. I'd tailed her there, watched her sweep in with her people.

I pressed my forehead against the cold glass, trying to breathe, feeling every inhale as if it might break me in two. I'd torn through this city for days, leaving a wreck behind me, and still had nothing. Not even a whisper.

The maps blurred in front of me, Rhea's territory splattered over the city in red circles like bloodstains.

Zero.

We'd ripped through every property, nothing left but dust and disappointment.

The paper crumpled in my fist, veins popping along my forearm as I tried not to shred it into confetti.

"Fuck!" The shout cracked out of me, bouncing off the walls.

Over in the corner, our guest twitched, coming around like someone who'd overslept for a job interview he never wanted.

I crossed the room in three long steps, dropping my shadow over him before his brain could catch up.

My hand knotted in his filthy hair, dragging his head back. His right eye was swollen shut, purple-black and ugly, and fresh blood snaked down from the split in his bottom lip, painting his chin bright red.

"Last chance," I said, my voice dropping to a register I hardly recognized. "Where is Esme?"

My fist met his cheekbone, a sharp, clean hit. I felt the jolt run all the way to my shoulder. A fine red mist peppered the wall behind him, almost pretty if you ignored the context.

He spat a tooth onto the filthy floor. "Doesn't matter now. Rhea's got her stashed someplace you'll never find."

Something in me snapped. Before I blinked, my knuckles

crashed into his face again, caving in what was left of his left eye socket. Ugly, purple, swollen.

I leaned in, so close the blood-tinged copper stung my tongue. "Then Rhea better start saying her goodbyes."

I shoved him away, hard, sending him crashing into the wall. My boot caught the edge of a table and flipped it. Glass decanters shattered on the marble floor. Bourbon splashed everywhere, soaking the maps and bleeding the ink into a giant mess. The smell of liquor flooded the room, thick and sweet, like perfume at a funeral.

Something cracked in my chest.

Not pain.

More like the sound of ice splitting on a frozen lake.

Dangerous. Final.

Every time I blinked, I saw Esme's face. The sharp eyes. That stubborn, impossible mouth.

The idiot. The gorgeous, reckless idiot.

Just waltzing straight into Rhea's trap like it was nothing.

What the hell had she been thinking? I wanted to be mad, but something worse took over, a cold, clawing panic.

Because Rhea wouldn't just kill her, death would be the easy way out.

My hands curled into fists at my sides.

What if that bastard was right? What if I was too late? What if I'd already lost her?

The thought was too much. Just imagining it made my chest tight. Because if I let that nightmare happen, I'd never be the same man. Losing her would rip me apart. The anger would eat me alive, day after day, until there was nothing left.

Desperation took over, winding through me like poison. I stopped fighting it. I let it in.

I grabbed the nearest table and flipped it, wood splintering, my control slipping, my rage turning into something black and ugly, so much so that it almost scared me.

I turned on my heel and stalked toward the door. I needed to get the hell out of this room. I needed air. Space. Time to think.

"Boss, where are you going?" Ares called out.

Not slowing down, I said, as I passed him, "No one takes what's mine and lives."

If Rhea Konstantinou wanted a war, I'd make damned sure she got one.

Thirteen

AIDON

It took hours before I finally broke, driving nowhere, hands welded to the wheel, jaw locked so tight my teeth felt ready to shatter.

The office, the silence, those still walls, they'd been suffocating. Out here, at least, the engine's roar gave me something to focus on besides the endless, gnawing images of what Rhea might be doing to Esme.

I blew straight through a red light. Horns blared, distant and muted. I-15 was wide open, just a hot ribbon of asphalt slicing through the city haze, when my phone buzzed against the console.

Ares.

My heart damn near jumped out of my chest. I answered.

He wasted no time. "We found her."

That was all it took. I yanked the wheel hard left and

crossed three lanes without blinking. A semi's horn screamed at me.

Not caring, the needle shot past the I-215 Beltway. The engine howled, and I realized I was making the same animal noise low in my throat.

Every second counted. Every red light I ran, every car I whipped around, it blurred.

I saw nothing but her. Just Esme. Her face, her eyes, the way she smiled. The way she might never smile again if I didn't get there fast enough.

Rhea was smart. She'd found my soft spot, the one crack I'd always denied having.

She was counting on it.

Forty-seven minutes, start to finish.

Then I was in front of a mansion in Henderson, shirt clinging, sweat soaking me despite the desert air.

Ares at my right, twelve of our best behind us, every one of them loaded for war.

My pulse pounded so loud it nearly drowned out the world.

Those ornate doors in front of me were the only thing between me and Esme.

"You sure this is it?"

Ares checked his phone. "Confirmed. East wing, second floor. Our guy's inside."

I chambered a round. The metallic sound was sharp and final. "I'll paint these fucking walls with anyone in my way."

Ares met my eyes, his face hard. "We're with you, boss."

The weight of my Glock pressed against my palm, safety off, finger hovering outside the trigger guard. Kevlar hugged my torso like a second skin.

All around me, you could hear the metallic click of safeties coming off. No one bothered with words. Just a bunch of silent nods. We all knew there was a pretty good chance we'd be dead in the next five minutes.

I stared at the mansion. It was ridiculous, honestly. Like something out of a fever dream. Blinding white stucco, palm trees sagging in the dead heat, sun so bright you wanted to claw your eyes out.

Whoever built it had more money than sense. Not a single blade of grass or anything alive, rocks everywhere, shimmering in the heat like coals.

And then there were the gates. Eight feet tall, crowned in metal spikes that screamed "don't even think about it."

Security cameras everywhere, I counted twelve.

Each little red light blinked like the whole place was waiting to bite.

Two Escalades, black as sin and probably bulletproof, parked out front. The air above their hoods was so hot it shimmered. Marble lions by the door, looking like they'd eat you if you got too close. Real subtle.

My pulse? Steady. Hands? Rock solid.

The cameras already had my face, beaming it to monitors where assholes with guns would see me and freak out. I hoped they were running around like headless chickens, grabbing rifles and barking orders.

Good. Let them get ready. Let them know who was coming to ruin their day.

I checked my watch.

Ares wouldn't have dragged me here unless he was sure. The entire mansion screamed Rhea's taste, all that white marble pretending it was pure, when everyone knew the kind of dirty business that went down in places like this.

I jerked my chin once. "Now."

Boots hit the top of the iron fence. Metal spikes grazed my calf as I vaulted over. The landing rattled my knees, but I was already moving, Glock slick in my palm.

Behind me, the solid thuds of my crew hitting ground came like a heartbeat, the war kind.

The flash-bang didn't just take the door off; it exploded it. The boom rattled my teeth, and smoke rolled out in thick sheets. My ears rang, but there were already shouts from inside.

A shadow moved in the haze.

I double tapped his chest before his gun cleared the holster. Another guy rushed from the left, but Ares was faster.

A bullet tore the man's throat out, spraying the pristine foyer wall with red, modern art courtesy of Ares.

"Three o'clock!" someone yelled.

I pivoted and dropped low. A bullet whizzed past where my head had just been.

I fired back twice. The guy dropped like soggy cardboard.

We pushed forward. Boots crunched on broken glass.

The scent of copper and cordite filled the air, signaling violence. Four more of Rhea's men showed up at the living room entrance. They seemed more competent. The first shot scraped Dmitri's shoulder, causing him to cry out and fall. I ducked behind a marble column as bullets shattered it, stone splinters hitting my cheek.

Twenty seconds. That was all it was. But it felt longer.

When the shooting stopped, I was panting, ears ringing, blood trickling warm down my neck, bodies everywhere, tangled on imported tile.

One of Rhea's men was still making noises, gurgling over a chest wound. Ares finished him off.

"You hit?" Ares asked, giving me a look. His face had someone else's blood on it.

I pressed the side of my neck. "Scratch. Stairs?"

"Left wing." He jerked his chin toward the hall. "Second floor, east end."

I slammed in a fresh mag, the sound loud in the sudden quiet. Every second counted. Esme was in this house, in Rhea's hands. I refused to let myself picture what that meant.

"Let's go," I said, already running.

She was all I could focus on. The thought of Esme burned so hot, I nearly saw her every time I blinked. We hit the landing, boots pounding, and there was another group of men storming down the hall straight at us. I dropped them.

No hesitation, no wasted shots. Each body that hit the floor was a little victory, every spill of blood a step closer to her. Esme.

We tore through the top floor, ripping open doors, one after another, nothing but empty rooms staring back at us. Ares glanced at me, tension buzzing. We were both thinking it now.

What if it was a setup?

What if the intel was shit?

Walking into an ambush was a real possibility.

But we kept moving. No way in hell we'd stop now, not with this much at stake, not with her name echoing in my skull. I wouldn't let myself think about coming up empty—not when I'd been obsessed with finding Esme. Failure wasn't possible. Not for me.

Not ever.

The hallway opened up into a sunken living room the size of a small nightclub, all white marble and glass.

My boots stuttered to a stop.

Rhea lounged against a white leather sofa, champagne flute dangling from two perfect fingers, bubbles catching the light like tiny gold bullets. Her red lips curved upward as she took a deliberate sip, eyes fixed on me, unblinking.

Six men in black suits formed a wall around her, hands resting on visible holsters, faces carved from stone. The only sound was her soft chuckle echoing off marble.

The tallest one—a shaved head, neck wider than my thigh—cracked his knuckles on purpose, slow and loud.

Behind me, boots scuffed to a stop. The weight of a dozen stares pressed against my back, waiting.

I felt Ares tense up at my shoulder. The air between both sides felt like it could snap.

"Well, well, well. You do love a dramatic entrance, don't you, Aidon?"

Rhea's voice cut through the room, thin as wire.

My finger twitched on the trigger. Every muscle wanted to see her pretty smile splattered across the wall. She raised her champagne in my direction, the gold liquid catching the light, glass shaking just enough to betray her nerves.

Blood rushed in my ears. All I could see was Esme, somewhere in this fortress. Maybe bleeding and maybe screaming. Maybe already dead.

I counted the men flanking Rhea, their holsters, the way they stood, the time it would take to drop each one.

Six men. Six bullets. Nothing complicated.

Rhea was still talking, smooth and full of herself, but I stopped listening. It was just noise. The only thing that mattered was the pulse in my throat, steady and counting down.

I shifted, weight on my toes. Ares caught it, tensing up next to me. We both recognized this. The hush before everything blew apart.

Not blinking or breathing, I let the silence speak as my finger curled tighter on the trigger.

"How's this for dramatic, bitch?" I squeezed the trigger, and the world exploded.

Glass shattered. Marble chipped. The air went thick with gunfire, every shot pounding in my ears. My men opened up beside me, and the sound became one constant, punishing roar.

I dove behind an overturned table. Bullets chewed

through the wood, sending splinters across my face and hands. Across the room, Ares pressed himself flat behind a column.

Our eyes met for a split second.

No fear, just focus.

One of Rhea's men popped up, his pistol aimed right at Ares' head. I put two in his chest. He folded like someone had cut his strings. Another guy tried to swing around on the left. I got him under the jaw.

Blood hit the ceiling in a bright red spray.

Through the mess, I saw a flash of Rhea's crimson dress vanishing down the hallway. She was gone, leaving her men with us.

"Cover me!" I yelled, though I could barely hear myself over the bullets.

I pushed off, staying low, zigzagging between furniture. A bullet skimmed past my ear, so close I felt the heat. Another one punched through the space where my head was a second before.

Then something hit my side, a brutal, white-hot spike between my ribs.

I staggered and caught myself against the wall. My hand came away red with blood.

The pain was sharp, ugly, but underneath it, something hotter burned.

Rage. Focus. Desperation.

Rhea's heels hammered the marble floor, echoing down the corridor. She was running, but I was closing in. Every labored breath edged me closer. Each step was Esme's name ringing in my chest.

Blood dripped down my side, leaving a trail. I ignored it, jaw clenched so tight my teeth hurt.

Somewhere ahead, Esme waited. And nothing—not bullets, not blood, not Rhea's entire army—was going to keep me from her.

Fourteen

Esme

Gunfire. Like the world's angriest drum line pounding against the walls, and then my heart, then everywhere.

I jerked, hard, the zip ties biting deeper into my wrists, panic in my mouth. I twisted, shoving the chair legs across concrete, ignoring the pain screaming up my back.

Sweat dripped into my eye, the one Rhea's ring had gotten up close and personal with, leaving it all puffy and split.

Sweet flaming hell, it burned. I squirmed, shoulders howling, and reached for my stiletto.

The heels had seen better days. I was going to see another one, if I could just...

Yes. Got it. My fingers fumbled the tiny catch, and the heel's secret compartment snapped open.

In a room this small, the click might as well have been a gunshot.

"Fuck yes." It came out in a wet croak, my split lip stinging as I sucked in a breath.

Razor blade pinched between fingers, hands shaking so bad I almost dropped it.

Blood on my chin, sweat everywhere, ribs on fire, all thanks to Rhea's goons.

The memory flashed, ugly and full of Rhea's smeared lipstick and laughter. She'd watched her guards work me over. Laughed harder every time someone's fist smacked into my face.

The plastic ties would not go. The razor was dull, and my hands were slippery. I sawed anyway, frantic, while gunshots kept count in the halls.

Each cut, closer. Each heartbeat, faster. Finally, the zip ties gave, my arms flopping forward like they'd died.

Pins and needles, stars behind my eyes, and I nearly screamed, but bit down instead, tasting blood.

Outside, boots stomped. Rhea's guy was clueless. The gunfire rolled away, deeper into the building. Bought me a minute, maybe two.

Not much, but I could work with it.

Something in my head snapped into survival mode. The zip ties had left angry red welts on my wrists, and as I pressed my ear against the door, my heart pounded so loud I couldn't hear anything else. One breath. Two. Nothing. Absolute silence beyond.

Fuck it.

My fingers were shaking as I gripped the cold metal knob, turning it millimeter by excruciating millimeter. The hinges whined—a whisper, but enough to make me freeze. A sliver of light. Then a little more.

One guard. Broad shoulders, back toward me. Pistol on his hip, black and gleaming under the washed-out fluorescents. Holster strap open. Sloppy. He shifted his weight, keys jingling on his belt. Scratched the side of his neck. No clue I was even there.

The razor felt pathetically fragile between my fingers as I stepped into the room. Three careful steps. Bare feet against freezing concrete. I kept my breathing shallow, steady. Close enough now to catch the cheap, pine-scented aftershave.

I rose on my toes. One arm wrapped around him for balance. The blade drew across his throat, deep and clean, opening him ear to ear. Hot blood sprayed, covering my hand, my wrist, dotting my face, warm and wet.

He convulsed, grabbing at the wound as he collapsed to his knees. He turned his head to the side, his eyes were wide, disbelieving. Then empty. The gurgle as he tried to talk. The way the light vanished as he fell forward.

I wiped my hand on my dress and grabbed the pistol from his holster. The weight of it was grounding. I ejected the magazine. Full. Popped it back in, racked the slide, safety off.

Another door. More captivity. Like Russian nesting dolls, just layers of locked rooms. I pressed my ear to the next door.

This time: voices. And then, his.

"Where the fuck is Esme, Rhea?" Aidon's asked, clipped, cold, furious.

A jolt went through me. He came. He came for me.

I cracked the door, ready to spring out, but stopped cold at what I saw. Aidon and Rhea were in each other's faces, and Rhea was grinning that nasty, twisted grin of hers.

Two of her men stood behind her, both of them looking pissed, blood all over their clothes, guns pointed at Aidon. His hands were up.

My heart pounded so loud I thought they'd hear it.

I had to move. Fast.

If I hesitated, Aidon and I were dead. This was one of those situations where you didn't get a second chance.

I slid the door open and crept behind them. One shot. Then another. Both bullets went straight through the backs of their heads. They dropped like rocks.

That was all it took for Rhea to snap. She launched herself at Aidon, punching him hard as she closed in. Time practically froze as the two of them went at it.

Aidon shook off her punch, blocked the next, then slammed his elbow into her face. Her nose gushed blood, but she kept going, landing another punch on him.

They were both fighting like they'd been waiting for this.

Rhea stepped back, wiped her mouth with the back of her hand, and then gave him this bloody, twisted sneer. And she laughed.

Aidon's face twisted, all sharp lines and fury. "You think you can just take what's mine?"

Rhea grinned, blood staining her lips. "Darling, I already did."

"She was never yours to take," he snapped, low and dangerous.

Rhea dove at him again. He knocked her fist aside, but she spun on her heel, and her boot slammed into his thigh. She landed lightly, and suddenly there was a knife in her hand, pulled from her boot like she'd done it a thousand times.

The blade caught the fluorescent light. It sliced, ripping cloth and nicking his skin; a thin red line appeared on Aidon's thigh.

The gun felt steady in my grip. I squeezed the trigger. Rhea screamed, grabbing at her arm, blood pouring between her fingers where my bullet tore through.

I stepped forward, gun aimed right at her, finger tight on the trigger and ready to finish it.

Aidon's broad shoulders slid in front of me, blocking the shot. I cursed under my breath.

Rhea staggered back, blood dripping. Her laughter echoed off the concrete as she slipped away.

"Enjoy your prize while you can, Aidon," she called out. "We both know this isn't over."

Her words bounced off the concrete, sharp and ringing. I slid past Aidon, gun steady, tracking her every move as she darted for the exit.

Rhea's hand disappeared into her pocket. Something small and black flashed under the ugly fluorescent lights. Her thumb slammed down.

And then everything blew apart. It was like getting punched in the face by the sun; heat roared over my skin, concrete rained down, and I hit the ground so hard the air left my lungs. My head was buzzing, my eyes stung, and smoke filled the space where Rhea had been.

Strong arms caught me, crushing me tight against a solid chest.

"Jesus, Esme." Aidon's voice was thick, barely making it through the ringing in my ears.

I reached for him, fingers coming back red and wet.

"You're bleeding," I said, trying to see how bad it was.

He gripped me tighter, his heart beating wild against my cheek. "Doesn't matter." He sounded wrecked. "Tell me you're okay."

"It'll take more than this to knock me down," I managed, even though my face was throbbing.

His jaw was set. "She's dead. Next time I see her, she's fucking dead." He hauled me upright. "Ares and the rest are waiting. We've gotta move."

"Move where?" I blurted without thinking.

Something flickered across his face, quick and hard. "Where else? I'm taking you home."

His hand clamped over mine, dragging me forward, straight into hell. Where were we headed?

No matter. All that mattered was not dying.

The walls moved, alive with fire, flames crawling up and spitting embers like dying stars. Smoke clawed at my throat with every breath.

I coughed, yanked my sleeve up, and tried to keep breathing. Gunfire didn't stop. It hammered, constant, growing louder with each step as we tore through the burning house.

Aidon stopped and backed against the wall with a slam. The click and slide as he reloaded echoed between shots.

"Ares is pinned with my crew," he said, eyes burning orange in the firelight. "We go in hot."

I checked my gun. It felt heavy. Real. The only thing that was.

"Behind you," I said. "I'm ready."

Aidon snarled and lunged, leaving a messy trail of blood on the floor and up the wall. I wanted to stop him, or at least slow him down, but it was pointless. He wasn't going to listen, and honestly, I'd die before letting anything happen to him. For now, we just had to keep moving.

We rounded the corner, guns raised and firing.

Ares and his men were completely outnumbered, doing a shit job of holding their ground. We came just in time and, from behind, picked off most of Rhea's crew.

The only thing that mattered was getting out of there. So we booked it for the exit, shooting as we ran, lighting up the perfect target for the last few guys left.

They emptied their magazines, bullets screaming past us and pinging off the walls as we sprinted for safety.

The zing of pain as a bullet ripped open my side almost dropped me. My hand flew to my ribs, and I hissed, fighting the urge to stop.

Blood oozed out, hot and sticky, but I didn't slow down. I just clenched my fists and kept running, sweat popping on my forehead.

Breathe, Esme. Just breathe.

My jaw locked as I dove behind a couch to get out of the line of fire. Aidon dropped to the floor next to me, his eyes going straight to my bloody hand. He didn't even have to say anything.

"You've been shot!" His eyes were wide and wild. "Fuck."

"I'm fine," I said, my tone flat, determined.

He practically vibrated with anger, scanning me up and down as he considered his next move. "Stay here. I'll come back after I kill these fuckers!"

He was seething, on another level of pissed, maybe even crazy. But there was no way I was going to sit tight.

"I don't take orders from you, Aidon."

He glared at me, jaw tight. He might have actually growled, all annoyed and exasperated.

Two quick shots from him, and somewhere in the house, then bodies hit the floor. He didn't even blink, just shot me a look.

"You're fucking stubborn, you know that?" The way he spat it out almost made me laugh if I wasn't in so much pain.

Then he grabbed me around the waist, hoisted me up, and tossed me over his shoulder like I weighed nothing. I screamed—the pain rocketed through me, white-hot and blinding.

Aidon didn't let up. He held on, carrying me out of there while Ares, covered in blood, cleared the way, and more bloodied bodies crashed down as we barreled to the front door.

The whole house reeked of smoke, fire eating everything in its path. It was loud, chaotic, but we kept moving.

Outside, Aidon didn't slow down. He took me straight to his car, hands digging into my side like he was afraid I'd disappear if he let go.

FIFTEEN

AIDON

I should have felt better. Esme was alive, back under my protection, and according to my doctor, she was on the road to recovery. Thank god for small favors.

Except...every time she so much as winced, guilt sucker-punched me all over again. Logic told me it was bullshit to blame myself.

She was the one who'd decided to go to Rhea's in the first place, without bothering to so much as send me a damn text.

She was the one who refused to stay put and let me handle the resistance. She was the one who decided to play kamikaze with Rhea's guards.

If she'd just stayed in the room I'd locked her in, she wouldn't have been shot. If she'd never gone to Rhea's ware-house at all, she wouldn't have gotten herself locked up. But she had.

Every step of the way, she'd done the opposite of what I'd told her to do.

Which meant, of course, I got to be the lucky bastard who dragged her through the firestorm. And that was where I'd fucked up.

She got shot. Right in front of me. On my watch.

Now, she was in pain, thanks to me.

I was so pissed off, I couldn't see straight. Furious at her for making my life difficult, angry at myself for not keeping her safe, and just pissed in general at the universe for serving up this particular brand of hell.

I kept leaving the room to get my shit together because there was no way I'd let her see how much she got under my skin.

Not after everything. Not even now.

Most of all, though? I was just fucking furious.

So, there I was, pacing in and out of the room she was resting in like some rabid yo-yo, totally failing to bottle my temper and ignoring every other feeling clawing its way up from the pit of my stomach.

Knowing I needed to get my shit together, I decided to walk around the perimeter of the building and inspect the security.

When I stepped back into Esme's room, she jumped and sent the book she was reading tumbling to the floor.

She tried to reach it and then yelped and winced like an injured puppy.

"Stop," I grumbled, squatting to grab the book and dumping it back in her lap.

Her eyes locked on mine, and for a second, I forgot how to breathe. There was a whole hurricane of emotion in her stare, and all of it was directed right at me.

I hadn't even considered how she might feel.

I'd been so wrapped up in my own mess, staggering under the weight of it, that I never paused to think about what she was dealing with.

Now, we were locked in this silent standoff, both of us stubborn as hell, both refusing to blink first. But underneath all that attitude, some part of us was just relieved.

We were safe.

At least for now.

Not that I'd put it past her to pull some reckless stunt and drag us right back into a shitstorm.

I didn't trust her one bit.

And judging by the suspicion and hostility lurking behind her eyes, she didn't trust me either.

A flicker of guilt stabbed through my chest.

Still, she'd screwed up, and she needed to hear it.

"You could have died," I snapped, the words sharp, my tone as cold as I could make it.

I wanted her to understand just how close it had been. Inches, maybe less, between her and being gone forever. And I wanted her to know what that would have done to me.

She neither flinched nor blinked, giving no indication whether she heard the accusation in my voice.

"So could you," she said, with a shrug, like we weren't talking about life and death. Like it was nothing.

That just pissed me off even more, a rush of anger burning in my chest.

"Do you think you're invincible?" I shot back, not bothering to hide the fury anymore.

She looked at me, chin up, eyes stubborn.

"You don't get to decide when I fight," she said, another shrug, full of attitude.

I stared at her, shaking my head.

This was what I was up against.

A woman-child, stubborn, impossible, convinced she already knew it all.

A brat who refused to listen to reason.

I closed the distance, leaned in, and stared into those defiant, flashing eyes. "You disobeyed me, Esme."

"You don't own me."

I shook my head and exhaled hard. The whole mess inside me—the worries, the anger, the urge to shake her, hug her, lock her away.

All of it started to drain out, like maybe I remembered it didn't matter. She thought she knew everything. And maybe, in her mind, she did. It wouldn't matter how much I argued or yelled, Esme Theodorus would always do what she wanted.

Endless battle of wills. Tiring as hell.

I let my forehead fall against hers and exhaled a long sigh.

She froze. Her body was still, like a deer caught cold in headlights.

She probably figured all I had left was rage. Then, her shoulders dropped. She inhaled a shaky breath.

I took her face, making sure to remain gentle and careful of the fresh bruises, the swelling, the angry red cuts.

Rhea was going to pay for every single mark on Esme. That much was certain.

I ran my thumb over the cut on her cheek and shook my head again.

"I almost lost you," I said. "But you're mine, Esme."

She melted beneath my touch, caving in, pressing closer, letting go.

Something in me snapped, wide open, right there, all raw and exposed by her softness.

My thing for Esme went deep. Way deeper than I liked. I had no clue what to do about it, but just for a second, I stopped fighting it. I let it hit me.

All of it.

My lips crashed into hers, hungry.

The heat of it slammed into me. There was nothing soft about it.

It soared through us, all that we wanted, like a freight train. By the time our mouths met, there was no space for tenderness, only gasping breaths, raw and jagged.

The kiss turned frantic, desperate, alive, like it was the only thing left in the world. Underneath, the anger festered, simmered, just hidden under the push and pull of our lips.

I tore my mouth from hers, chest heaving, pulse roaring in my ears.

Her eyes, wild and dark, locked onto mine, pupils blown wide.

There was something electric simmering between us,

something nameless and hungry, and it threatened to swallow both of us whole.

My fingers gripped her hips, hard, maybe hard enough to bruise, but I couldn't let go.

"Fuck this," I stated. My hands shook against her skin. "Fuck the games. Fuck the lies."

She arched an eyebrow, lips curling into that maddening, defiant smirk even now, even as her mouth was red and swollen from how hard I'd kissed her.

She was daring me, always daring me.

My blood pounded hot as I crashed my mouth onto hers, teeth clashing, copper sharp on my tongue.

She bit back, nails raking down my neck, and I hissed, the sound torn from somewhere deep.

I broke away, gasping, lungs burning.

"I can't fucking sleep. Can't think. Can't breathe when you're not—" I couldn't finish, because she rolled her hips against mine, silencing me with that single motion.

With a surge, I lifted her, her legs wrapping around my waist, as if she'd always belonged there.

The weight of her was fire and absolution and every kind of sin. I kicked open the bedroom door, the slam echoing as it shut behind us.

The mattress groaned as I lay her down, hovering above, every inch of me hyper-aware of the bruises and cuts scattered across her skin.

My hands froze, suspended, caught between wanting and restraint.

Her eyes, fierce and unyielding in the half-light, never left mine.

She grabbed my wrist, fingers digging into my pulse, and yanked me down until our foreheads touched.

"Don't you dare hold back now," she whispered. "Not after everything. Not when I need to feel alive."

She reached for me with trembling fingers, nails raking over my shoulders as she dragged me down to her.

Our lips collided, brutal and hungry, not a trace of gentleness between us. The metallic taste of blood mingled with the whiskey on her tongue, and I felt her thighs clamp around my waist, hot and unyielding, her core burning through the fabric.

The groan that tore from my chest was raw, desperate, my cock straining helplessly toward her heat.

Without warning, she twisted, using every ounce of strength to flip us in one fluid, violent motion.

The room spun, and all of a sudden, she was straddling me, wild-eyed and triumphant, her hair streaming around us like a veil.

The lamplight threw the bruises on her cheekbone into stark relief, the split in her lower lip vivid and fresh, but her eyes, they blazed with hunger, with something feral that made my pulse roar in my ears.

She brushed her swollen mouth over mine, a feather-light touch that somehow scorched worse than the kiss before.

Then she moved, sliding down my body, inch by torturous inch, her breasts dragging over my chest, her teeth grazing my collarbone, ribs, the jut of my hip.

I propped myself up on my elbows, legs hanging off the mattress, as she dropped to her knees on the hardwood between them.

The sight of her there, looking up through lush, emerald eyes, lips swollen, and cheeks flushed. It stole the breath right out of my lungs.

"Esme..." Her name broke from me, hoarse and reverent, half a plea and half a curse I couldn't swallow.

The world ground to a halt when her fingers found the buttons of my jeans.

One by one, they surrendered with sharp, distinct pops that sounded in my skull like gunshots.

Her eyes never left mine. If anything, her gaze grew more intense, a silent challenge, daring me to stop her.

It was the last thing I wanted to do.

She hooked her fingers into my waistband and waited.

There was no mistaking the silent command.

My breath stuttered, caught somewhere between lungs and throat, as I lifted my hips in surrender.

The rough denim scraped down my thighs, stripping me bare, followed by the softer slide of cotton.

She settled between my legs, her breath warm against my inner thigh, close enough to make my heart stutter but still not where I needed her.

When her tongue flicked out to wet her lips, leaving them glistening in the half-light, my cock jerked, helpless and eager for whatever she planned.

Then her fingers, the same nimble, dangerous fingers that

had once stolen from me, fought me, now wrapped around my shaft with deliberate, exquisite slowness.

The pressure had me throwing my head back, pleasure spiked so hard it was almost pain. A ragged sound ripped from my throat, raw and desperate.

Her hair spilled over my thighs, dark silk against pale skin, stark and startling. It made me draw a ragged breath. She glanced up at me through thick lashes, pupils blown wide so her eyes looked almost black with rings of green, all hunger and intent. Something primal clawed at my chest, breaking loose and leaving me raw.

The first brush of her lips was fire.

Heat scorched through me, vision blurring at the edges until the world narrowed to just her wet mouth on me. I made a strangled sound, low and rough, barely recognizing it as my own.

My hands fisted the sheets, knuckles aching white with the effort it took to keep from grabbing her, from burying myself deeper.

She never looked away, not once. Her tongue traced patterns that made my thighs tremble under her steady palms, as it followed the bob of the wet, slick heat of her mouth surrounding me.

She knew how to work me—a glancing scrape of teeth, a tease, a threat, pleasure, and pain balanced to perfection.

It was merciless. Devastating. Every nerve in my body seemed to converge, drawn tight around the place where her lips stretched over me.

She was a fucking goddess.

The room spun, heartbeat pounding, as she hollowed her cheeks and pulled back so the suction made my hips jerk off the mattress.

"Fuck," I gritted out.

The word was a guttural sound, just air forced past my teeth as I watched a thin thread of slickness connect her swollen lips to my cock.

Then she was back again, sinking lower, going deeper until I felt the back of her throat, over and over.

The vibration of her moan sent lightning up my spine, shattering whatever control I had left. I was unraveling for her, every defense stripped away, at her mercy and wanting nothing else.

A grating sound ripped from my chest as my fingers dove into her hair, letting the silk slip and tangle tight around my knuckles.

I lost myself to her rhythm, surrendering as she took me deeper, heat and pressure compressing the whole world to a single, blinding point.

All I saw was her: the hollow of her cheeks, lashes fluttering against flushed skin, lips swollen, stretched wide, and slick with want, drawing gasps from both of us.

"Fuck—Esme—" Her name tore out in a broken gasp, my jaw clenched tight.

My spine snapped off the mattress, electricity spiking through me when she swallowed around me; the muscles of her throat flexed around the head of my cock, so hot and tight it made my balls draw up.

Her nails scored my thighs, holding me right where she wanted me as she pulled back, a tease, a promise, and the suction forced my hips to jerk, helpless to her ministration.

Then her tongue traced over the ridge, followed the vein underneath in a perfect, lethal pattern. The moan she breathed around me vibrated all the way up my spine, a live wire. My grip locked harder in her hair, the other hand losing the fight to take over the tempo.

"Slow down—" The warning locked itself in my throat as her mouth drove me past every threshold of restraint. My thighs quaked under her palms, my whole body wound so tight I felt like I might shatter. "Esme, I can't—"

And then, just as the pressure built to a blistering edge, she broke away.

The sudden absence left me raw, gasping, my hips thrusting upward into empty air.

My eyes snapped open to find her standing over me, breathless, eyes blazing, lips swollen and wet. The only thing left between us was a thin strand of saliva that trembled and snapped.

"What the—" The words caught, half-choked, as she locked eyes with me.

Her chest rose and fell hard, and the slow, dangerous smile on her mouth promised both heaven and hell.

She reached under her skirt, moving so deliberately it was almost cruel, inch by inch exposing the pale length of her thighs.

Her fingers found the black lace, dragging it down with agonizing patience. The fabric clung to the curve of her hips, then surrendered and slid to the floor, pooling at her feet, a dark, delicate scrap abandoned on the hardwood.

She stood there, still in her clothes but somehow more naked than if she'd stripped bare, and every primitive instinct inside me howled to the surface.

My blood pounded, drowning out everything but the drumbeat of raw, animalistic need.

"I need you inside me," she whispered. Her eyes blazing, wild and dark. "Please, Aidon. Can I fuck you?"

The sound of her begging almost undid me.

My cock jerked so hard it hurt, a slick bead already forming at the tip. I gripped myself tight, fighting for any scrap of control as it threatened to slip away in its entirety.

"You know you don't have to ask," I growled, my words savage and unsteady. Every muscle in my body was straining, pulled tight as a wire. "Take what you want."

Her lips curled with something feral and triumphant, twisting her features until she wasn't the woman who'd stolen from me or the one who'd begged a moment before. She was something elemental now, a goddess of ruin, nothing less.

My lungs locked up as she stalked forward, each step deliberate, thighs parting just enough to bare the swollen, glistening flesh between them. Every muscle in my body went rigid, jaw clenched until I tasted the sharp tang of copper.

Then she straddled me, heat radiating off her in waves that hit my skin before her body did.

Her thighs caged mine, her weight settling over me with

the inevitability of conquest. The scent of her arousal wrapped around me, thick and heady, salt and musk and something pure Esme. My cock twitched, smearing wetness across my stomach as I struggled for breath.

"Esme," I choked out, her name shattering in my throat when she held herself above me, hand wrapped around my base, lining me up with her entrance.

She sank down, slow and merciless, an inch at first, just the head breaching her, the tight heat stretching to take me in.

Then she lifted off, leaving me cold and desperate for her, only to drop again in a brutal stroke that tore a raw, broken sound from both of us. Her inner muscles clamped around me, pulsing, trembling, squeezing so tight I saw bursts of white behind my eyelids.

She rose above me, wild and vengeful, like something untamed and immortal.

Her head fell back, throat bared and slick with sweat, her spine arching in a perfect, impossible curve as she rocked down onto me with relentless force.

Every motion sent a surge of sensation through my body, her weight crashing against my hips, the searing heat of her body clenching around me so tight it was almost agony.

Her hair tumbled loose and feral, each savage thrust lashing it across my chest, scorching a path down to my bones.

The sound she made was raw, inhuman, a guttural, wordless cry that vibrated from her chest and straight into mine.

She moved with a ruthless precision, hips rolling in a punishing, endless rhythm, drawing me deeper, her muscles tightening around me until the world narrowed to nothing but the black edges of my vision and the desperate need clawing at my spine.

I tried to hold on.

"Not yet," I ground out between my teeth, hands digging into her thighs, desperate to anchor myself, to leave something of me on her skin.

I couldn't give in, not with her like this, feral and perfect, her skin flushed and gleaming, nipples hard and red from our earlier battle, lips swollen and parted, her whole body a living memory I never wanted to let go.

Then she slowed, the change in pace so sharp it nearly broke me. Every inch of her slid against me, torturously slow, sending bolts of raw electricity through my nerves.

Her eyes met mine, pupils blown wide and hungry, and she bent low until our chests were pressed together, heartbeats racing wild and uneven.

She caught my bottom lip between her teeth, biting down, sharp and perfect, and the pain shot straight through me.

That was it. I snapped.

I flipped her beneath me in one rough, unyielding motion. Her gasp shattered the silence, but I was already driving into her, hard and deep, the force of it making her body arch up beneath mine, legs snapping tight around my waist and hauling me impossibly closer.

I sank into her until it felt like I was lost inside her, pleasure and pain twisting together, so sharp it left me trembling.

Her eyes flew open, wide with shock and need, her lips parted around a breathless, silent cry.

I caught her wrists and pinned them above her head, holding her there, helpless and shuddering, every muscle quivering under my control.

"Oh, god!" she moaned, the sound breaking from her throat, cheeks flushed a desperate crimson.

Her pussy clenched and fluttered around my cock, and I let my thumb press down on her clit, rubbing slow, punishing circles until she was writhing and gasping my name.

"Yes, fuck yes, Aidon! I'm gonna come!" she cried, head tossing side to side, her body tightening and milking me as she shattered beneath me.

"Me, too," I groaned, thrusting harder, faster, chasing that final surge until it swallowed me whole, my release pulsing deep inside her as I lost myself in the raw, consuming pleasure.

Her thighs locked around me, muscles trembling like a trap sprung tight, holding me captive in her impossible heat.

Release tore through me in violent, shuddering pulses, each one dragging a ragged, primal sound from deep in my chest.

For a moment, the world narrowed to white, blinding and absolute, before color bled back in, the flush of her skin, sweat shining along her collarbone, the wild tangle of her hair fanned across my pillow.

I couldn't move. It was the last thing I wanted.

Every nerve ending screamed with oversensitivity; still, I stayed buried inside her, feeling her pulse around me in aftershocks sharp enough to make my jaw clench.

Her lips found my throat, teeth grazing the thundering pulse there, the sting instantly soothed by the drag of her tongue. Pain and pleasure crashed together, sending another jolt of electricity down my spine.

"Fuck," I breathed into her hair.

But then I felt it, the impossible hardening, hunger surging again through my veins, wild and insistent even as release still cooled on our skin.

Her eyes went wide, pupils black and blown when she felt me swell hard inside her.

"Already?" she whispered, a wicked smile curving her lips.

She squeezed around me with a deliberate flex, drawing a hiss from between my teeth.

This time, everything changed.

I caught her mouth, swallowing her gasp as I drove into her with slow, ruthless precision.

Every thrust was measured, deliberate, finding the spot that made her back arch off the bed, her nails digging into my shoulders.

The frantic desperation had faded, replaced by something deeper, hungrier, and rawer. Her gaze locked onto mine, and I couldn't look away.

I was held fast, not just by her body but by something else neither of us could name. Something inside me cracked open, terrifying in its intensity, as I watched pleasure transform her face and felt her surrender, not just her body, but something far more dangerous.

We were tangled together, bodies fused, and I remained buried inside her slow and deep, refusing to let go.

My lips found hers, desperate and hungry, savoring her heat and softness as I sank into the impossible liquid warmth of her.

She was wet and yielding, swallowing me whole, and I couldn't pull away even if I tried.

Time stopped. The world faded.

All that remained was this frantic need, the friction of skin on skin, and the quiet darkness that wrapped around us.

We took our pleasure again and again, neither of us willing to stop, not when we'd finally carved out this pocket of safety in the middle of chaos.

There were no promises here, no declarations. We both knew better. This was all we had, all we could have—a secret space stripped bare and honest in its hunger.

We chased that high until we were delirious, until the lines between our bodies blurred, until we were nothing but need and pleasure and exhaustion.

Hours later, she lay sprawled across my chest, her breathing soft against my skin.

"What now?" she whispered.

"Now we finish this," I said. "Tomorrow, we cut Rhea's airport feeder. You lead it—manifests, faces, burns. You bring it home."

She lifted her head, eyes steady. "And that buys me what?"

"One marker retired," I said. "Not your name. Not Olympus. Progress."

A beat passed, then she nodded. "Then we start at dawn."

I pressed my mouth to her hair, breathing her in. "Sleep. The world will still be waiting when the sun comes up."

Sixteen

ESME

Dawn hit hard.

The band on my ankle blinked green, a quiet accusation and a reminder of the contract I'd signed. Two escorts waited outside the door like punctuation marks.

Aidon was already in the war room. Maps covered the table. Camera feeds transformed the walls into a city of screens.

Ares slid a glossy print into my hand. "East-side warehouse to the airport feeder. Manifest window puts the next run inside two hours. We cut it here." His finger tapped a narrow choke point—one road in, one road out.

I looked from the route to Aidon. "I lead."

"You lead," he said without hesitation.

"Debt-for-deed. You bring the proof home; I retire a marker."

"One," I said. "Not my name. Not Olympus."

"Progress," he agreed.

"Two-guard rule stands," Ares added.

"Side by side," I said. "Or I walk."

Aidon swallowed the argument I saw forming and gave a sharp nod. "Side by side."

While Ares ran drivers like a drill sergeant, I let the briefing wash over me and did the only thing that steadied my hands before a job. I ran Rhea's file in my head.

Vegas resembled an organism, with its neon veins pulsating, arteries humming. Rhea didn't just sustain it. She constructed it. As the youngest of three, a Greek American raised in The Underworld and groomed as an heir, her father focused on stability with his sandbags and sermons, while she targeted fault lines, tearing them asunder.

After gutter punks shot him in the head, she moved quickly to restore order. She sliced throats, broke alliances, and electrified his walls with razor wire. The Shadow Syndicate was resurrected from the dead, with her name resonating from Moscow to Macau.

Gunrunners were the first to call her. Politicians memorized her contact. Hackers competed for her paydays. Vegas remained her prized possession—her desert fortress she was willing to die for. Her communication was direct and relentless: the lesson preceded the headshot. She didn't merely win; she imparted knowledge.

Rhea was like a glacier, slow yet unstoppable. Zeno preferred to strike with the sudden power of lightning. She crafted landscapes over many years. I spent weeks in her servers, still marveling at how she planted a seed in January that blossomed into a flower three Decembers later.

Every smile seemed like a trap, every toast a countdown, and every so-called 'random" encounter was part of a web woven across the Strip. I saw her condemn a man with a drink in her hand and a plan already underway across town.

Today, I cut a vein. Make her feel it.

The screens refocused—route, timing, proof.

"Ninety minutes," Ares said. "Gear up and brief the drivers."

I put the photo in my jacket and headed to the hall.

Aidon caught up beside me. "Rhea's not getting near you again."

"It was too easy," I said. The words felt wrong. "She let us walk. Rhea never backs down unless there's something behind it."

"Maybe," he said, mouth a hard line. "But we'll still cut her feeder."

I didn't answer. The strip burned beneath the windows like an open circuit. Somewhere in that neon, Rhea was preparing her next move.

A sharp knock shattered the silence. I saw Aidon tighten his jaw before slowly walking to the door, each step purposeful toward whatever waited beyond our temporary refuge.

Now someone stood on the other side of that door with a pin. I watched the muscles in his back tighten beneath his shirt as he crossed the room, each step bringing us closer to whatever hell waited outside our borrowed paradise.

Seventeen

AIDON

Esme had carved her way into me like shrapnel, sharp and impossible to dig out. For days now, her presence burned under my skin, a constant ache I couldn't shake.

When we fucked, it was a collision, the kind born of people who'd tried to destroy each other and hadn't quite managed. Her teeth sank into my shoulder hard enough to break skin. My hands left bruises along the insides of her thighs.

When it was over, neither of us could bear to let go. We'd collapse, limbs tangled in the aftermath, her breath hot and ragged against my neck.

I never pulled away first. Neither did she. Even when we were supposed to be strategizing, planning our next move, all it took was a look across the room, and we were on each other again.

Maps abandoned, scattered underfoot. Her back pressed to the wall. My name ripped from her throat, raw and desperate as a confession.

This morning, I woke to find her watching me and calculating, always.

Even in the half-light, those obsidian eyes burned with something dangerous. She traced the scar on my collarbone with a single finger, slow, thoughtful.

My pulse kicked up. I didn't dare breathe.

Then, a knock.

Three sharp raps, so precise they echoed like gunfire.

Ares. The spell shattered, reality roaring back in.

I yanked the door open, hinges shrieking like wounded animals.

"Fucking finally," I spat, stepping aside.

Ares strode in with the cold grace of a blade, all edges and purpose, every move coiled and lethal.

The sickly hallway light slashed over the scar at his temple, jagged and ugly, a gift from Rhea, burned into flesh.

His eyes, hard and empty as spent shell casings, flicked past me, locking on Esme.

She stood by the windows, the city sprawling beneath her like something conquered. The silk robe clung to the body I had worshipped with my mouth not an hour ago, Vegas neon painting her in colors too wild for this world.

Goddess and demon, temptation and threat, all tangled together.

Ares' jaw worked, muscles tight beneath skin, but he didn't flinch. He was used to this by now, to finding Esme here, the woman who nearly burned my entire world down, standing in my sanctuary like she belonged.

Esme didn't look away. Her chin tipped up, a silent dare. Ares stared back, eyes narrowed, his hand drifting close to the weapon at his side, a habit, or maybe just instinct.

"There's news," he said.

The pneumatic door hissed shut behind us, sealing us in.

"Let's hear it." I stepped between them, shoulders stiff, heart pounding so hard it rattled my chest.

The weight of my Glock pressed firm against my lower back, a bitter comfort in a place that should have been safe.

Ares's face stayed blank, unreadable, but the way he shifted his weight told me everything.

This was it.

Either Rhea had slipped away for good, or we had her dead to rights.

Blood was coming, one way or another.

I felt Esme move in behind me, her presence igniting the air, close enough to raise the hairs on my neck.

The three of us hung there, caught in the split-second before the world changed, tension crackling, waiting for what came next.

"We have movement at Rhea's last known location."

The words hit me hard, adrenaline spiking in my veins and making my pulse roar in my ears.

Esme was already on the move before I had time to process the information, a blur of silk and hunger, her robe fanning out behind her as she lunged for the table, a woman possessed by need and fury.

"Finally." The sound ripped from her, a demand, rough, raw, and desperate.

Her nails tore over the scattered maps, frantic, the scrape of a hiss of violence in the hush.

Neon from the Vegas Strip caught her green eyes, making them burn with something feral, something honed enough to cut straight through me.

She slammed her palm onto a spot, the force rattling the table and sending papers shivering.

"Was she here?" The question was a challenge, a weapon, and I could feel the expectation coiled inside her, ready to detonate.

Ares stalked forward, the weight of his boots grinding against the cheap floor.

"That's it." He leaned in, scar at his temple seemed to throb, his battered knuckles just a breath from Esme's hand on the map.

Neither one flinched, their intensity vibrating in the scant space between them. Two predators. Two guns cocked and waiting for an excuse.

"No movement since?" Esme's gaze narrowed, blazing emeralds ready to fire.

I felt the ruthlessness gathering in her, the anticipation of the hunt, and the promise of blood behind her eyes, the air thick with want and violence.

The softness vanished from her in an instant, gone as if burned off by desert sun.

Her spine snapped straight, shoulders locked, jaw set in a line that meant nothing, and no one would stand in her way.

This was the Esme who had stolen from me, outplayed me, survived things I'd rather forget.

Her fingers glided over the map, each nail clicking against paper as she pinpointed entry after entry. My blood rushed south so fast it was almost dizzying. The rough scrape of denim against my cock forced me to shift, to ground myself as she leaned in, calculating vengeance with a precision that was almost surgical.

Her teeth caught on her bottom lip, her eyes narrowing as she weighed timelines, risks, casualties.

I couldn't stop staring at her mouth, remembering how it felt pressed to my throat just hours before. Sweat pricked at my hairline.

When she planted both hands on the table, the muscles in her arms taut and bracing, I nearly let out a groan.

Power pulsed from her, not the counterfeit kind you bought with money or threats, but the kind you earned when you survived everything.

Vegas neon caught in her hair, reflecting a sheet of electric fire on the black strands.

Christ, I wanted to grab it, yank her head back, taste her again right here, right now.

Maps, plans, whatever she was plotting could wait. I wanted her intelligence scraping against my skin, her rage on my tongue, both of us burning hotter than the city outside.

She prowled, lethal and elegant, every movement a taut promise. The way her fingers traced the map was the same way she'd traced my scars hours before, with a kind of reverence edged in danger.

I saw it then, something buried beneath the silk clinging to her skin, deeper than the curve of her spine: a reflection of my own darkness, sharp and hungry.

When she looked at me, her pupils were blown wide, emerald, just a thin ring around black. The kind of gaze that devoured. The kind I recognized in the mirror.

"This means we can move, right?"

I stepped in, close enough to feel her heat, close enough that when my fingers brushed hers, a jolt shot straight through me, wild and electrifying.

"Fuck yes." The words scraped out, raw. "And this time, we end it on our terms."

She didn't smile, not a true smile. Her lips parted, teeth flashing, a predator's promise. Blood thundered in my veins as she leaned in, gunpowder and expensive perfume swirling around me, dizzying.

"Then let's get to work."

She bent back over the table, neck exposed, skin begging for teeth or protection.

Both.

The urge hit so hard it ached: to guard her, to devour her, to build her an empire or tear the world down for her.

Whatever tangled, savage thing thrashed between us, it was here to stay. And so was she.

Eighteen

ESME

My skin buzzed, like I'd been plugged into a socket, every nerve on. My fingers wouldn't stop drumming on the window.

Tap-tap-tap.

Like they had somewhere to go but nowhere to be.

But my lungs? Crushed.

Like someone poured concrete in my chest, breaths came short and fast.

Rhea's voice ran circles in my skull. "I'll peel the skin from your pretty face."

And then there was Aidon, with his stare, all sharp edges and want.

This war we were about to start... Vegas would be picking up bodies for days.

I paced Aidon's bedroom, back and forth, five steps, turn, five steps back.

I'd worn a path in the carpet by now. Forty stories down, the Strip threw neon everywhere, a river of lights and trouble under our feet.

Cars crawled. People scurried around, clueless. No one had a clue about the blood that was coming.

"Fuck this waiting," I muttered, leaning into the window.

The glass was cold against my skin. My reflection stared back at me, eyes gone dark, face all angles. I didn't even look like myself. I needed to move. Hunt. Get my hands around Rhea's throat.

And after? When Rhea was dead, and Zeno was dealt with? What then?

I'd slept in Aidon's bed, plotted with him, tangled up in every way possible. Hatred and lust. That was what we had. But when our enemies were gone, what the hell would be left?

The air changed behind me. Sandalwood and gunmetal. The sound of expensive shoes on marble. I didn't turn. I already knew who it was.

Aidon's reflection lined up beside mine in the glass. His jaw set so hard I could practically hear the crack. "You haven't said a word since last night."

I pivoted, shoulder blades digging into the icy window. That muscle in his jaw wouldn't quit. His eyes were all steel, but under it, something flickered—a split-second of doubt he'd never admit to.

"What's to say?" It came out rough, like I'd swallowed gravel. "We both know what comes next."

He closed the gap in two steps, hands on my upper arms, before I could blink. His grip was punishing, but his chest was warm against mine. I inhaled him: sandalwood, whiskey, and some dark, coppery note that screamed violence. His heart pounded, way too fast for a guy trying to play it cool.

"Esme." My name, low and strained. Almost reverent, almost damning. He touched the cut on my cheek, thumb gentle. "You don't have to fight this battle. Ares and I can handle it."

I jerked back. "You're wrong, Aidon." My hands curled into fists, nails biting skin. "If I don't fight, she wins. That's not going to happen. Not ever."

He clenched his teeth so hard the scar above his eyebrow stood out, white and angry. He shoved a hand through his hair, wrecking the neat look he always went for.

"Why won't you let me protect you?" He just stood there, staring, like the answer might write itself in thin air.

I laughed, I couldn't help the brittleness of the sound. "Who said that was your job?"

I kept moving until we were nose to nose, chin up, daring him to flinch. His breath was hot, and I could feel it on my lips.

"If I'm remembering right, last time I asked who you were protecting me from, you said it was you."

"Goddammit," he snapped. His eyes went dark and stormy, all that anger wrapped up in a painfully handsome package. "You know I would never hurt you. Even if there were times I thought about it."

"Sure you did," I said, smirking. "I buy that."

"You can't blame me." He looked like he wanted to punch a wall. "Every time I think I can trust you, you pull something like stealing Zeno's box."

"And yet, you still want to play bodyguard? Who's the threat now, Aidon?"

"Fucking everyone, Esme!" His voice ricocheted off the walls, way too loud for the space between us. "Don't you get it?"

"I'm not sure I do," I said, chin up again. "Do you get that I can protect myself?"

"Oh? Is that what you were doing when Rhea abducted you, and I had to show up and bail you out?"

That stung. I hated that he was right, that I'd needed saving at all.

If Aidon hadn't shown up, Rhea would have kept going.

I knew it. He knew it. Still, I wasn't about to say it out loud.

"Rhea used me as bait. What she wants is you," I said, refusing to give him the satisfaction of being right.

"I disagree with that fact. You're the one stealing everyone's fucking secrets, Esme." He took a step closer, close enough that I caught the whiskey on his breath. "Maybe if you cut that shit out, they wouldn't be hunting you like a prize deer."

"Oh, that's rich!" My palm hit his chest, hard, moving him not even a fraction. "Collecting secrets is your fucking business, Aidon! Your entire empire is built on blackmail and threats!" My voice cracked at the end, damn it. "Don't you dare try to blame me for all this shit."

"I'm not blaming you, Christ, Esme!" He caught my wrist, fingers digging in, tight enough to bruise. "But if you didn't stick your nose where it doesn't belong, maybe we wouldn't be in this fucking mess with bodies dropping all over Vegas!"

"My nose?" I tore my arm away, skin hot and burning where his hand had been. "I was only trying to help you, you ungrateful bastard!"

"Help me?" He slammed his fist into the wall next to my head, hard enough to crack the plaster. "I don't need your fucking help with that."

I stuck my finger into his chest, jabbing hard. "If it wasn't for me," I hissed, "you'd never have known about Zeno's vault or how to get in. You'd be dead in a ditch somewhere."

His face was all of a sudden right in mine, so close I could count the flecks in his eyes. "You came to me for help!" he shot back. "You were running scared when you crashed through my door!"

His breath was hot on my lips. The air between us buzzed, a mess of anger and something way more complicated.

Rage and want, all tangled up, and I couldn't tell where one started or ended. My heart hammered so hard it hurt.

"Fuck!" He turned, stalking over to the glass like he was about to burst through. His reflection broke up across the window, multiplying the fury on his face.

I watched his shoulders knot up beneath his shirt as he pressed his hands against the window frame.

His knuckles turned white. There was a thin, bright line of blood trailing down from where he'd torn his hand open on the wall. Seeing it made my stomach twist, not satisfaction, not even close.

It was something worse.

My throat tightened, like I was being choked.

I'd seen Aidon angry plenty of times before. I'd watched him shoot a man in the head and not blink. But this wasn't the usual. This wasn't even close.

This was raw. And it was about me.

No way would I ever let him know how my pulse hammered when he looked at me like that, like he couldn't decide if he wanted to strangle me or rip my clothes off.

Even now, with Vegas about to burn to the ground, I was thinking about the weight of him pinning me to his bed, his teeth sinking into my neck, his hands moving everywhere, all at once.

He stared down at the Strip, shoulders shifting with every rough, uneven breath.

Neon glare from the casino signs painted red and blue shadows across his face, turning him into...I wasn't sure... something carved from stone.

A statue, unmoving. He wouldn't look at me. Maybe he just couldn't.

I wondered if he saw in himself what I saw in the mirror.

Someone drowning. Someone fighting the current and losing, arms flailing to stay above water. Someone was afraid of what would happen if they stopped struggling and let themselves sink.

Whatever the hell this was, neither of us had the nerve to be honest or vulnerable about it.

The back-and-forth, the weird little dance, was wearing me out.

If I was honest with myself, I couldn't even tell who was the cat and who was the mouse anymore.

I'd had more than enough chances to walk away from this mess, but here I was, tangled up in it, neck-deep and nowhere else to go.

I let out a sigh of relief when I heard footsteps coming up behind us.

We both turned, and Ares was standing in the doorway.

He looked at us, and the tension in the room must have been obvious because he hesitated, shifting his weight like he was thinking about turning around and going right back out.

"Boss?" he asked. "You got a second? There's been another development."

"Come in," Aidon said, waving him over and moving away from the window. "What's up?"

"We got word that Rhea relocated."

Aidon looked like he was about to lose it. "Again? We were finalizing the plans to invade."

Ares nodded, his mouth a grim line. "Yeah, I know."

"Fuck!" Aidon snapped. "Now we have to start over? Is this the worst game of whack-a-mole ever?"

"I know," Ares said again, like he was agreeing with every word. "But if we move fast, we can still catch up to her."

"So where is she now?" Aidon asked, and this time he sounded bone-weary.

"She and a small army of men are holed up in Blue Diamond."

Aidon blinked. "What the fuck is in Blue Diamond?"

"Exactly." Ares nodded, a faint smirk on his face. "Nothing. That's why it's perfect for her and her minions to lay low."

I darted over to the table, where we'd laid out a mess of state maps.

"I know it." My finger traced the lines on the map. "There's what. There are fewer than three hundred people in Blue Diamond. Only a few buildings. It shouldn't be hard to find her."

"We've got her. She's holed up in one of the tiny compounds on the west side of town." Ares stated.

"That's perfect! Let's go!" My pulse jumped. If we could get to Rhea and take her out, we could finally move on with our lives.

Aidon made a low, irritated sound at my excitement, immediately shaking his head.

"No fucking way, Esme," he snapped. "You're not going anywhere near that compound. Ares and I can handle it."

My mood did a complete 180, from thrilled to pissed in two seconds flat.

"That's ridiculous," I fired back, crossing my arms and digging my heel into the floor.

Aidon's eyes narrowed. He stalked over, closing the gap between us in about two steps, glaring down at me.

"Why do you think she moved somewhere so rural, Esme?"

"You seem to know everything," I shot back, tilting my chin up. "Go ahead. Explain."

He rolled his eyes, all attitude. "So she can see anyone coming. No surprises in a place like that."

"Which means it's even more dangerous," Ares tossed in.

Aidon glanced at Ares, nodded once. "Go get everything set up, Ares. I'll be right behind you. You're right, we need to move fast."

"On it, boss," Ares said, already heading out of the room.

Aidon wheeled around, stubbornness written all over him. Only one of us was going to win this. I wasn't about to let it be him. We squared off, neither willing to budge even a fraction.

"Esme," he started. "I get that you want revenge. But you can't go. I'm not going to let you throw yourself into danger again."

"Try and stop me." I raised a brow, daring him.

"Goddammit, woman!" He flung his head back, spun on his heel, and stalked away, muttering curses under his breath. "Why are you so fucking hard-headed?"

The space he put between us gave me a second to breathe, but it didn't do a damn thing for the tension strung tight between us.

I shrugged, matching his energy. "Right back at you."

He drifted over to the window, raking a hand through his hair.

I watched him, careful and deliberate, my gaze roved over the broad set of his shoulders, the muscles pulled tight under his shirt, bunched and restless.

I knew I was driving him up the wall. He only wanted to protect me.

But when was he going to figure out that was never his job? Why did he think that just because we'd had a little fun, it meant he was suddenly responsible for me?

He sucked in a ragged breath. Steam curled from his mouth, fogging up the glass. He stared down at the street, but I could see he wasn't looking at anything.

I wanted to ask him what he was thinking, but I already knew I wouldn't like the answer. Most likely, I'd get an earful of angry words and protests, because I wouldn't just fall in line and let him boss me around.

So instead, I stayed silent. Waited for him to speak.

When he finally did, he turned back to me. His eyes were raw, full of something that looked a lot like pain.

"Esme," he said, steady now, even if nothing about it sounded calm. "You don't get it. Rhea controls almost every channel for getting guns into this city. She has access to weapons you've never even heard of. If she wanted, she could wipe you out, just like that."

"And yet she hasn't. Why do you think that is, Aidon?"

He stepped back, shaking his head like he couldn't believe what he was hearing.

"Oh, come on, are you that dense?" I threw my hands up. "She used me as a pawn to get to you. She pretty much told me that herself. If she wanted me dead, if what I knew was a true threat to her little empire, she'd have offed me without a second thought. Instead? She locked me up. That's it.

Waiting for you to show up. Don't you see, Aidon? It was always about you. It still is."

He didn't say anything right away, just stared at me, eyes narrowed, searching my face for...what, a lie? I didn't flinch. I wanted him to know I meant every word.

"You're playing a dangerous game, Esme," he said at last.

I grinned, the edges sharp. "Danger makes life interesting, don't you think?"

He just shook his head again, more frustrated than ever. "I don't like this. Not any of it."

"That's not my problem, Aidon. Your problem is Rhea." I met his eyes. "Let me help you. We can take her down together. For good this time."

He growled like he couldn't decide whether to punch a wall or give in.

"You're not going to accept no as an answer, are you?"

"Not from you," I said, grinning. Maybe a little smug. I closed the distance between us, and I could tell he was done fighting. It was all over his face. I put my hand on his cheek and looked up at him.

"We can do this, Aidon. But it's going to take all of us. Working together. As a team."

He exhaled like he'd just finished a marathon. "I think you're right, Esme."

"What was that?" I laughed. "Sorry, couldn't hear you. Can you say it a little louder?"

He laughed back, shaking his head. "You were right. We end this. Together."

He leaned in, forehead to mine, and there it was: the

spark, the fire, the thing that happened every damn time he got close. I could almost taste it on my tongue.

Well, look at that, he was on my side.

"Together," I whispered.

It was a win, and the jolt of victory zinged through my brain. I kissed him, just a brush, just enough to feel the heat, and then his arms came around me, pulling me in.

The kiss deepened, and I melted.

My heart did that thing. The swelling thing.

Soon, it would be us against the world, a mission that could kill either of us, or both.

But for now? Right now? In his arms, I let it all drop.

The danger. The dread. The million questions and the constant gnawing fear.

Gone. Just gone.

All that was left was this, the quiet, the warmth, the weird comfort of letting go for a second. And in that calm, all the unhinged edges in me smoothed out.

Peace. At least for a little while.

Nineteen

ESME

My fingertips gripped the edge of the marble counter so hard my knuckles turned white.

The chill from the stone bit into my skin. I stared at my reflection, hoping for some miracle.

No such luck.

The bruises were the first thing you saw, spreading over my face in disgusting splotches. The reds and purples had started to fade, but the new colors weren't any better, a gross, sickly green melting into yellow.

The cuts on my cheek had gone crusty, the scabs making everything look even more dramatic. Basically, I looked like something out of a horror movie, no makeup department required.

"Lovely," I muttered, yanking my black hair back and twisting it up into a pathetic French knot.

I'd thought about trying to cover the bruises, but that would only make it worse. As for my go-to red lipstick?

Not a chance. I'd look like a fucking corpse.

Everything hurt. Not the sharp, sudden pain that makes you gasp, but something heavier. Duller.

It was a slow, pounding ache that throbbed through every nerve, every second, like it was trying to remind me I was still alive.

I should be used to it by now. I wasn't. I could've complained, but I didn't. What was the point?

I had to remember: I'd fought back. I was still breathing. That had to count for something.

Rhea was going to pay for this. No question. Honestly, I wanted front row seats for when it happened.

The shower was running. Steaming, loud, practically vibrating with Aidon inside. Like I needed any extra reminders of him.

I mean, the man had been glued to me for days. Couldn't even cross a room without him practically shadowing my every step.

And the crazy thing?

I didn't even mind. Not really. Yeah, I was supposed to be staying in the guest room, technically, but somehow I woke up in his bed every morning.

Every single time.

Half the time, I wanted to sneak into the shower with him.

But I knew better. The hot water would torch my skin.

Every time we had sex, I tried to ignore the pain. I focused on how good he made me feel.

Because Aidon naked was the best painkiller I'd ever had.

I spun away from the mirror, unable to stomach another second of my reflection. The bruises mocked me in shades of decay.

However, whenever I caught Aidon staring, his eyes never lingered on the damage. Instead, they burned into mine with that intensity that made my stomach flip.

"Beautiful," he'd whisper, sometimes when I was naked beneath him, sometimes when I was passing him in the hallway.

Each time, something inside me unclenched just a little, a momentary reprieve. Like morphine hitting the bloodstream, not healing anything, but making existence bearable until my face matched my driver's license photo again.

My skin was knitting itself back together. My mind was another story.

Aidon's moods whiplashed between extremes, volcanic one moment, arctic the next, with no warning between eruptions and freezes.

Even when his hands burned against my skin, I could feel the underlying current, that electric charge waiting to shock us both.

I'd catch myself staring at him while he slept, wondering if we'd ever escape this power struggle or if we were destined to keep circling each other like predators, neither willing to yield first.

Could we ever exist together without keeping score?

I knew why he'd turned into a human ice sculpture; the whole Zeno's box situation and my vanishing act afterward.

The betrayal lived rent-free in his mind, filed away with all his other grievances, preserved like precious artifacts in a museum of resentments. Yet for all his emotional frigidity, his body had different ideas. The second we were alone, those hands would find me, contradicting every icy glare from earlier in the day.

Then, as soon as the moaning and panting died down and the night got bulldozed by the sunrise, he slid right back into his usual cold, distant routine. It was clockwork, every single time.

Daylight was starting to piss me off.

Every morning, it woke me up, all smug and bright, to rub it in: body satisfied, bed empty.

Like clockwork, when I saw Aidon after, he'd pretend nothing had happened between us. No glances. No words. No mention of how the night had ended.

It was like bodily fluids and feelings, especially feelings, never existed.

Last night? Same story.

We fought, fell into bed, and by the time daylight crept back in, he was gone like a ghost.

I spent the entire day dodging him because every time his eyes landed on me, I wanted to scream in his face.

Now here we were, tucked away in his ensuite bathroom, getting ready for bed all over again.

The air was thick enough to choke on, tension crackling between us.

I knew how this would play out: the second he stepped out of the shower, we'd fight, then we'd fuck, then we'd sleep, and then tomorrow morning we'd both pretend none of it ever happened.

Classic.

I also knew I wouldn't say a word tonight, even as the silence between us grew thick enough to cut.

We'd dance around it like always. Aidon would sooner walk naked through the Vegas Strip than volunteer his feelings first. The man kept his emotions under triple-encrypted lockdown.

I'd need a team of professional hackers to access a smile.

The only message that came through loud and clear was his iron-clad conviction that my safety belonged to him, like he'd signed some cosmic contract with my name on it that I never got to read.

I couldn't keep lying to myself about this. Every day felt like another round in a boxing match where neither of us would tap out.

My muscles ached from the constant tension, my mind exhausted from calculating my next move. I leaned against the counter, listening to the shower run, trying to summon whatever energy I had left.

This thing between us had an expiration date. Once Rhea was handled and the dust settled, I'd slip away.

Right now, we were useful to each other.

I wasn't stupid enough to deny that, but his constant hovering, the way his eyes tracked me across rooms?

That would have to end. His protection came with too

high of a price tag. Only a fool would mistake this intensity for something sustainable, something real.

Whatever this was between us. This collision of bodies, this addiction, it had an expiration date stamped on it.

The tangle of feelings in my chest was nothing but chemical aftershocks, my body's way of making sense of pleasure that intense. I'd felt it before. I'd forget it again.

The shower squeaked off.

I tensed, listening to water droplets hitting tile, wishing I could fast-forward through whatever came next, the inevitable crash after the high.

Aidon stepped out from behind the shower door, steam curling around him. Water traced down his body, following every line, every dip, like it knew where it wanted to go.

His dark hair hung in thick, wet strands over his neck and shoulders. My mouth went dry. I couldn't help but imagine my tongue replacing the water, following the same route, inch by inch.

"Shouldn't you be in bed?" he asked, one dark brow arching as our gazes locked in the mirror's steamy reflection.

"I could say the same to you," I murmured, unable to tear my eyes away from the water droplets racing down his skin.

My throat tightened as he snatched a towel from the rack and dried himself with military efficiency, each movement deliberate and unhurried.

The air between us thickened, making it impossible to draw a full breath.

I ran my tongue over my bottom lip, making no attempt to disguise my hunger. His eyes locked with mine in the mirror, dark and unblinking, holding me captive as he closed the distance between us.

A droplet escaped from his wet hair, landing on my bare shoulder with the lingering warmth of his shower. His thumb brushed it away, the corner of his mouth lifting in that knowing way that made my pulse quicken.

His heat radiated against my back, too near, overwhelming. His nakedness crowded the space between us.

The way he just stood there, bold as hell, left me shaking.

He was naked, his cock hard and bobbing between us, a fraction from my ass.

All I could think about was turning around, dropping to my knees, and taking him in my mouth. The urge was immediate, impossible to ignore.

And he knew it. God, he knew it.

He crowded me against the sink, caging me between his arms, his naked skin radiating heat like desert asphalt at midnight. That knowing smirk played across his lips as his exhale brushed my cheek like a whisper of flame, igniting something primal that raced down my spine and pooled between my thighs. My body had already surrendered before my mind caught up.

Game over.

The man was a human inferno. Standing this close felt like dancing too near a bonfire.

I tried creating distance, but the air itself seemed to scorch my lungs. And still, I found myself leaning back into his space anyway, surrendering to that dangerous warmth, addicted to the exquisite burn of him against me.

I craved it.

The white-hot pleasure this man unleashed in me, stoking a fire that roared through my veins, threatening to burn me alive.

I edged closer. More. More. I wanted everything.

The blissful heat. The pleasure he delivered was tangled up with the sharp pain of surrendering to him.

It was addictive, like watching a disaster unfold and being powerless to look away.

My thighs quivered as his mouth grazed my shoulder, just that, nothing more.

My breath caught in my throat like I'd been running.

Heat lightning flashed beneath my skin, crackling down my spine. I let out a breath that sounded more like surrender than I wanted to admit.

His cock pressed against me, a reminder of what was coming, what always came. I leaned back into him, my body betraying every resolution I'd made in daylight.

The air between us still crackled with all our unspoken battles. The constant struggle for control, the games we played, the wall of distrust I'd built brick by brick, none of it had vanished.

But my treacherous body had its own agenda. But lust was winning, and with Aidon, it always had.

I trembled for him, craved him, needed the intoxication that only Aidon could deliver. And beneath that hunger lurked something far more dangerous, an emotion I refused to name, swelling like a high tide I couldn't outrun.

I despised its power over me.

But God help me, I couldn't get enough.

His eyes peered into mine, a spark of raw, naked emotion flashing in his dark, stormy gaze. He raised his hand to my cheek, caressing the ugly yellow bruise. My breath caught in my throat, my heart racing like it always did when Aidon touched me.

The sound of my swallow echoed in the steamy bathroom.

My fingers whitened against the marble edge, anchoring me to something solid while everything inside me threatened to dissolve. I wouldn't give him the satisfaction of seeing me unravel.

Not this easily. Not this soon.

I sealed my eyelids shut, building a flimsy barricade between us.

"Aidon," I breathed, his name evaporating into the mist between us.

Against the curve of my backside, I felt him harden, and despite myself, my lips curved into something dangerous and knowing.

The radiating warmth of his skin against mine dismantled my defenses one by one.

His palm traveled from my face down the column of my throat, each vertebra acknowledged by his fingertips with methodical precision.

A sound escaped me—half surrender, half defiance.

When his hand claimed the flesh of my ass, my eyes flew open. Our gazes collided in the fogged mirror.

His mouth, that cruel, beautiful mouth, tilted up at the

corner—a look that made it obvious he knew exactly how much my body wanted him. And there was nothing I could do about it.

His fingers slid between my cheeks, moving down to my pussy.

With his other hand, he nudged me forward until I was bent all the way over the bathroom counter, my ass right there in the open for him to see.

He dropped to his knees, pressing those same feathery kisses that had been on my shoulder just seconds ago onto my ass. His fingers slipped underneath, found my pussy, and slid inside.

I gasped, startled, the sensation of him behind me so illicit it made my knees weak.

His fingers plunged deep, the slickness between my legs making it effortless, like my body just knew what he wanted.

One hand working inside me, he used the other to pull my ass cheeks apart, exposing me even more.

I felt so bare, so fucking vulnerable, and it made my heart race.

His breath ghosted over my skin.

"Spread your legs, Esme," he said.

It was pointless to argue or to pretend I didn't want this.

"Wider," he commanded, his voice a dark rumble against my skin.

And then his hair brushed against my ass, and he flicked his tongue at the entrance of my pussy. I gasped, way too loud, legs shaking, thighs trembling, and I opened them wider, shameless.

The way he was behind me, his mouth on me, was new. Naughty. Wildly exciting. It was nothing like the other times he'd gone down on me.

I couldn't think; I just wanted more. I'd never wanted anything more, ever.

"Fuck, Aidon, that's...amazing," I managed, breathless.

He slid his fingers inside me again, his tongue working long, lazy strokes up and down my folds, taking his time.

The way he fucked me with his hand, his mouth following, was slow and deliberate, each movement dialing up the heat.

My hips rolled without thinking, desperate, my eyes rolling back as I gave up any pretense of control and let myself go, lost in it.

It felt wrong in all the right ways, wicked and off-limits.

The heavy pulse of his breath on my ass and the way his tongue and fingers played with me had me completely undone, like I was drunk on him.

"Aidon, Aidon!" I yelled, wanton, shoving my ass higher so he could get at me. He slammed into me, harder now, his fingers digging deep inside. Then he curled them, scraping over my G-spot while sucking my clit from behind.

My brain just went off like a firework, pressure building deep in my core, higher and higher until it exploded.

My body twisted, my ass started wiggling and grinding, my release hitting so fast and hard I couldn't even breathe.

My arousal gushed down his hand, and he kept going, not hesitating, licking and feasting. He continued his delicious torment until he sent me over again, my pussy clenching and spasming, pushing me to the point I thought I might pass out.

Aidon growled against my quivering pussy, determined, relentless, as if he wouldn't stop until I was beyond undone.

And even then, he would expect more. Another shudder vibrated through me, his hands all of a sudden rough on my hips, shifting me around to face him.

My eyelids fluttered open, only to lock with his.

The lust and starvation in his eyes had my heart skipping a beat. His need was undisguised, Dark and concentrated, all focused on me.

He dipped his head again, mouth catching my clit in a hard, punishing suck, then flicking, sucking, flicking, while his fingers dug into my hips, holding me where he wanted me.

"Aidon, fuck! I'm coming again!" I cried out, the words tore from my throat as I clutched his hair, pressing him closer to my pussy harder.

My vision blurred at the edges as another climax ripped through me, each pulse stronger than the last until I couldn't tell where one ended and another began.

My legs trembled uncontrollably, my body no longer my own.

When he released my hips and rose to his feet, his lips glistened in the bathroom light. The look in his eyes wasn't just satisfaction. It was a triumph.

And we both knew he was just getting started.

His mouth crashed down on mine, his kiss hard, insistent, desperate, as if he needed to swallow my breath to survive.

I shivered at the way his lips moved against mine, the heat of his hunger only fueling the fire twisting inside me. His fingers caught in my hair, tugging at the roots, tilting my head back so he could kiss me deeper, his tongue tangling with mine and setting off sparks.

I tasted myself on his lips, sweet and wild and dizzying.

I locked my arms around him, dragging him closer, matching his urgency with my own.

His thigh wedged between mine, nudging them open, and he stepped in, closing the space between us so that his cock, hard and pulsing, pressed right up against my pussy.

I gasped into his mouth, and the raw, frantic need between us surged, a torrent I couldn't hope to contain.

He let go of my hair, hands drifting down, catching me beneath the thighs.

In one rough pull, he hoisted me up and set me down on the bathroom counter.

It was freezing, marble biting through my skin. His fingers dug into my hips, not soft, not gentle at all, holding me tight, like he owned the place.

He broke the kiss, breathing hard, his eyes even darker than before. Hungry. Always hungry.

"You're mine, Esme," he growled, and then his mouth crashed against mine, hard and hungry.

I twisted away, just a little, shaking my head, grinning up at him.

"You always say that," I whispered.

I drank in the spark in his eyes, the heat of his hands clutching my hips, his cock nudging at my pussy, the delicious haze of everything he'd done to me already.

That did it. I saw the fuse catch.

"Is that a dare?" he shot back.

Then he shifted, just enough.

The head of his cock at my entrance. One smooth thrust, and he was inside.

A guttural cry tore from my lips, the feel of him inside me sending sparks racing through every nerve ending.

He was hard, thick, unyielding, and I spread my thighs, bracing myself against the counter, letting him in as deep as he could go.

I caught the smug pride flickering in his eyes.

Let him have it. Let him believe he fucking owned me. Let him think whatever he wanted, just so long as he kept driving into me like this, shattering every thought until there was nothing left but raw, desperate pleasure.

His strokes were long and relentless, each thrust purposeful and raw.

He dragged his hips back, slow and deep, only to slam forward again, sending bright sparks of pleasure through my every nerve.

His hands tightened around my hips, holding me in place as he fucked me, hard and unyielding, his cock sliding hot and smooth inside me, stroking every sensitive inch.

"Yes, god, Aidon!" My head tipped back as he drove deeper, harder, taking what he wanted.

The sight of him above me burned into my mind: naked,

muscles flexing, his shaft buried deep, wet hair plastered to his temple, eyes wild and hungry.

He looked like a god, feral and unrestrained, fucking me with a savage, desperate need.

I never wanted him to stop.

"Fuck, Esme, your pussy feels like heaven." His eyes found mine, dark and wild and so fucking desperate.

The words slammed into me and sent jolts everywhere.

His cock was buried deep, impossibly deep, and he held me there, fingers biting into my hips as he ground in slow, punishing circles.

My lips parted. My thighs shook.

"I can't get enough of you," he bit out, shaking his head like he couldn't believe this, couldn't believe me.

"Then don't." I forced my chin up and met his gaze, refusing to look away.

"Goddammit, woman," he growled, pulling out only long enough to slam into me again, hard and fast, each thrust a demand and a promise wrapped together.

His grip tightened around my hips as if he needed to ground himself. In one swift motion, he lifted me, carried me to his bedroom, and dropped me onto the bed.

He was on me in an instant, covering me completely, his cock plunging into my soaked pussy all over again.

He fucked me with a ferocity that bordered on savage, every movement designed to make a point I already understood.

Aidon needed me to know who I belonged to.

That my body, my pussy, even my thoughts, were his to

claim. That letting him between my thighs was more than surrender—it was ownership.

He was relentless, taking everything and leaving no doubt.

Me. My body. My pussy.

And with the way he filled me, stretching and owning every inch, I was more than willing to let him believe it.

"Harder, Aidon, please," I begged, spreading my thighs, arching my hips up to meet him.

He responded instantly, hips thrusting in a wild, reckless rhythm, driving into me with a force that bordered on madness.

Each motion sent pleasure shuddering through me, deep and overwhelming.

He bent his head, mouth closing over my nipple, teeth catching the tender flesh with a gentle bite.

I jerked, pleasure spiking so sharply it was almost pain.

"Yes, god, yes; just like that," I gasped, raw and desperate. "I'm going to come, Aidon! Don't stop fucking me, please, please don't stop."

"Never!" He moved faster, harder, wringing every ounce of sensation from my body with his thick, relentless cock.

I stared up at him, drinking in the sight of his face twisted in fierce concentration, brow drawn, eyes wild and hungry and full of need.

The realization that what he craved was me, that the aching, desperate need in his eyes was for my body, my pussy, above all else.

It rattled something loose inside me. I wanted to give him

everything, every last ounce of myself, until nothing remained but the way he filled me and the way I belonged to him in that moment.

I would have said anything, promised anything, to keep him moving inside me with those relentless, perfectly controlled thrusts.

Each time he drove deeper, precise and unyielding, I felt myself unravel further, clutching at him in a futile attempt to anchor myself.

"Yes," I gasped, barely coherent, my pussy clamping down around his cock, rippling with spasms as I shattered apart in his arms.

He powered through my release without pause, like my body's grip around him was fuel rather than friction. Wave after wave crashed over me as he maintained his relentless rhythm, dissolving the boundaries of where I ended and he began.

Time stretched and compressed until my universe contracted to a single point, the place where our bodies joined, where Aidon took everything I offered and still demanded more.

The world dissolved around us.

He took me with savage intensity, his primal sounds vibrating against my skin.

His cock jerked and swelled inside me, each thrust harder, deeper, sending shockwaves through my entire body.

The relentless rhythm of his hips stole the breath from my lungs, forcing raw, helpless sounds from me as he claimed me again and again. Perspiration glistened across his forehead.

His flushed face, those wild eyes burning with untamed hunger, the merciless intensity of his movements—all of it held me captive. This possession was unlike anything I'd ever experienced, a claiming so absolute it bordered on transformation.

"Esme, I'm going to explode inside you!" he choked out, his beautiful face twisting, eyes gone dark with longing and something feral and secret.

"Yes, baby, yes," I gasped. "Give it to me, Aidon. I want every drop you have, deep inside me. Come in my pussy, baby, please," I begged, so close to the edge.

He shouted again, this time so loud it seemed to shake the room, his hips slamming against me with a final punishing thrust. The pleasure was white-hot, searing through me as he spilled inside, his heat flooding my aching, desperate pussy and making me shudder all over again. The sensation of him filling me, the wetness and the rush and the sheer need sent me spiraling, raw and wild and undone by it all.

His arms stayed locked around me, possessive and desperate, as if letting go would mean losing me forever.

We remained tangled, sweat cooling, clinging to every inch of contact. His grip was bruising, fingers dug deep, like he needed the ache to remind him this was real. Between us, the silence buzzed, heavy with everything we couldn't or wouldn't say.

I traced his spine, slow and deliberate, feeling the shiver

ripple through him at every touch. He trembled, a live wire, all that raw energy still crackling just beneath the surface.

When he lifted his head, his mouth found mine again, slow this time, reverent.

His kiss lingered, full of a tenderness that threatened to undo me even more than his hunger. The need between us was still alive, insistent, coiling tighter with every heartbeat, even as exhaustion threatened to drag us under.

It wasn't enough. We hadn't sated anything, only stoked the fire.

I said nothing.

I didn't trust myself, not with the way my chest ached, or how every breath seemed to risk shattering whatever fragile thing we'd just made.

Instead, I just held him closer, refusing to let go, desperate to keep this moment whole for as long as I dared.

But I taught them. Those thoughts and emotions twisted in my skull, making me dizzy with confusion, need, and the kind of deep, aching satisfaction that lingered like a bruise.

Hours later, we crashed together in sleep, tangled up in the sheets and each other.

My pussy was still warm and full of him, his cock slick with the echo of my pleasure.

Outside, the lights of the Vegas Strip flickered through the windows, painting the dark with neon.

When morning came, the first thin slash of sunlight broke through the glass, turning everything gold.

I rolled over. Aidon was there, still sleeping, his face soft and unguarded.

His eyes were closed, his mouth slack, no hint of the ruthless, ferocious man I knew him to be. Just a man, vulnerable and beautiful in the dawn.

I rolled onto my side, letting my gaze linger on him, the slow, steady rise and fall of his chest hypnotic in the dawn's hush.

My fingers traced the lines of his torso, featherlight, savoring the quiet solace that settled between us.

Here, in this hush, there was no struggle for dominance, no silent war simmering beneath our skin. Not yet.

The day hadn't truly begun.

Instead, we floated in that fragile space between the heat of last night's hunger and the inevitable cold distance daylight brought. Our bodies still belonged to each other, tangled in sheets and memory.

He was still mine. I was still his.

There was nothing left between us but skin, bone, and the thunder of two hearts beating, unguarded. The usual tension, the power, the push, and pull. All of it faded away, leaving only stillness. Only an aching sweetness.

For once, my mind was quiet. All the noise, all the chaos fell silent, replaced by the simple intimacy of his warmth, his scent, his nearness.

I wanted to stay like this forever: watching him, touching him, worshipping him with my hands in the gentle morning light.

Of course, I knew it was doomed from the start. That didn't mean I could stop myself from wanting it to last, from wanting him.

Sunlight crawled in greedy streaks over his naked body, and I let a ragged smile split across my lips.

My gaze devoured him, drinking him in inch by glorious inch. The sight of his cock shooting raw, desperate shivers through me, down to the bone.

His voice was a low, rough whisper. "Hey."

It punched through the haze of morning and snapped my gaze up to his face, sharp and electric.

"Good morning, sleepyhead," I whispered back, words trembling between us, both of us holding onto the quiet like it might shatter if we moved.

His eyes flicked down, catching the way my fingertips traced over his chest, lingering on the hard lines of muscle.

He smirked, "This is new."

My lips curled into a smile, slow and defiant, and I shook my head.

"Don't ruin it," I breathed, the warning raw in my throat.

He laughed, a deep, hungry sound, and caught my hand, dragging my fingers to his mouth.

His lips were hot on my skin, burning a trail into my bones.

My head dropped to his chest, heart pounding so hard it felt like a challenge, and his arms caged me in, pressing every inch of me into his bare heat.

He tangled a hand in my hair, his breath ghosting over my scalp. "Good morning, beauty."

We stayed there, suspended, each breath synchronizing until it was impossible to tell where I ended and he began.

But the questions wouldn't stop clawing at me, demanding answers. I couldn't hold them back anymore.

I broke the silence. "What happens now, Aidon?"

He exhaled, the sound ragged and final. I looked up, finding him staring at the ceiling, jaw clenched, eyes dark with something I couldn't name.

"Now, we end it."

His words were immovable, a final verdict, and the echoes of yesterday's arguments still tangled in my mind.

He'd said 'we,' and I clung to the hope that meant he wouldn't fight me anymore, that I was truly going with him to face Rhea.

"Together?" I breathed, needing to be certain, holding his gaze and searching for any flicker of doubt.

He pulled me into him, gentle but sure, guiding my head back to rest against his chest. I could hear the steady beat of his heart when he finally spoke.

"Always, Esme. Always."

His promise lingered between us, light and soft, curling around me and making me feel weightless, a kind of happiness swirling in my chest because I knew the fight was over. I didn't have to argue with him again.

Not about this.

I melted into the safety of his arms. For the first time in longer than I could remember, I felt like I belonged somewhere. Like I was home.

I could get used to this, I realized.

If only it wasn't so dangerous.

TWENTY

Aidon

The overhead lights caught only half their faces, leaving the rest to darkness. The air felt dense enough to choke on. These men, rivals, not friends, sat too close in my private room, the same room where I'd made men beg, where the carpet still held secrets no cleaner could remove.

Rhea's downfall required this unholy alliance, this fragile scaffold of mutual need.

My eyes never stopped moving.

I cataloged every micro-expression, every shift in posture, waiting for the mask to slip. We shared a common enemy in Rhea, each nursing wounds too personal to name aloud, but that didn't make us brothers.

It made us wolves circling the same carcass.

Thalassios Adrias claimed the seat nearest to mine, his gaze slicing through the shadows between us.

The Atlantis Casino stood as his crowning achievement, a temple where the elite came to worship at the altar of chance.

Within those walls of his creation, velvet drapes absorbed whispered confessions while gold fixtures reflected the hollow eyes of those who'd lost everything.

Through perpetual clouds of cigar smoke, the wealthy, the famous, and those with blue blood in their veins all bent to the same primal urges.

Thal hadn't just gambled, he breathed it, inherited it, craved it like a man possessed.

When his father built that first casino in Atlantic City, little Thal had stumbled his first steps across that floor, chips clicking and cards whispering all around him.

His father's approving nod that day might as well have been a blood oath. The man raised him on hushed lessons between hands, molding him into something with edges that could cut, a mind that calculated odds before most kids learned multiplication, a face no one could read even when he was bleeding inside.

Thal cut through the casino world like a shark through still waters—deliberate, patient, lethal.

His mind calculated odds faster than dealers could shuffle, his face betrayed nothing while others sweated their tells. In penthouses where champagne flowed and million-dollar bets were placed with casual nods, he moved with the easy confidence of someone born to the rhythm of chips clicking against felt. The air of belonging clung to him like expensive cologne.

Once he'd conquered dealing, he flipped the script.

He was the one raking in chips while others watched their stacks dwindle. Night after night, he'd rise from tables surrounded by hollow-eyed men who couldn't figure out how he'd gutted them.

The whispers started before he could legally drink, wonder boy, card savant, as he dismantled veterans who'd been playing since before his birth.

By twenty-five, his name alone made players fold. He'd shattered his father's achievements, turned legends into footnotes, and collected fortunes with casual indifference.

Then came his father's slow-motion collapse, bad debts, desperate deals, and dangerous associations. The day they found the old man in the trunk of a car with broken fingers and a bullet hole, Thal built walls around himself that no one would ever scale again.

He'd already pocketed a small fortune when he bolted from the East Coast, drawn west by the promise of neon on the Las Vegas strip.

Vegas swallowed him whole. Here, at last, he could shake off the heavy weight of his father's broken legacy, carve out something of his own.

He slipped right in among those who mattered, the men and women who truly ran the city, and he did it with the same sharp instincts and fast-talking charm his father had drilled into him, only now he was the one holding the cards.

It didn't take long. He hustled, he gambled, he won.

Soon enough, he had the capital he needed, and with it, his first casino: The Atlantis.

The whiskey bottle emptied between us that night, glass by glass, as Thal unraveled his past like a deck of cards while we sketched plans to dismantle the new real estate hotshot.

Three years back now. Some New York developer who'd strutted down the Strip signing checks with a flourish, thinking Las Vegas would spread her legs for anyone with deep enough pockets.

In Vegas, a fat wallet isn't a skeleton key. I've watched men worth millions stand outside velvet ropes, desperate eyes darting for someone, anyone, who might recognize them.

Meanwhile, guys with empty pockets but the right handshake glide past security without breaking stride.

Cash was vapor here.

It materializes in stacks on felt tables, disappears into cocktail waitress tips, and reappears in jackpot sirens. We all participated in the charade, pretending those green rectangles mattered, when they were just paper totems in our collective hallucination. The developer never understood this particular mirage.

Trust was our currency, more valuable than the chips that changed hands across felt tables.

When I called Thal at three in the morning, he answered. When Zeno needed someone silenced, I made it happen without question. We traded favors like breaths, held each other's darkest moments in closed fists. Vegas ran on this invisible ledger of who owed what to whom.

The tourists never understood this.

They flooded our casinos in their polyester shirts and flip-flops, wallets fat with cash they thought mattered.

We let them believe their money bought them status.

They remained outsiders, temporary amusements who'd be gone by Monday.

Our inner circle had no vacancy sign. No application process.

Over decades, we'd drawn the lines tighter around ourselves until power concentrated in just a few hands.

And tonight, those hands were all clasped around whiskey glasses in my private room.

Thal occupied the leather armchair to my left, while Zeno claimed the one beside him, bringing a thundercloud into my office with every breath.

For twenty minutes, he'd hammered me with questions about his half-sister.

"Where's Esme hiding?" and "What the fuck did you do to her?"

Each one deflected with practiced indifference.

I'd sooner walk barefoot through hellfire than position myself between blood relatives with unfinished business.

Zeno's reflection glared back from the polished tabletop.

Shoulders bunched beneath his tailored jacket, jaw muscles working like he was grinding glass between his teeth.

His fingers curled into bloodless fists against the armrests, trembling with barely contained violence.

Ares maintained his post at my right flank, eyes constantly scanning, cataloging, assessing, my human security system with a trigger finger.

Four crystal snifters sat untouched between us, amber

liquid catching the low light, condensation sliding down expensive glass like nervous sweat.

Thal's fingers drummed a silent rhythm on the armrest. Zeno's jaw twitched. I caught myself holding my breath.

The air between us felt charged, like the moment before lightning strikes. We watched each other's hands, tracked each subtle shift in posture, listened for the slightest change in breathing. Three predators sharing the same cage.

We carried matching bullet scars, different locations, same caliber.

Had pulled each other from burning buildings and wiped blood off marble floors together. Our truce was written in scar tissue, not paper.

Zeno still wouldn't drink anything I poured him. Thal kept his back to the wall whenever we met.

I never sat without a clear path to the door. And here we were, because our empires had grown so entangled that cutting one free would collapse them all.

Vegas had forced our hands together, fingers interlaced but palms never quite touching. This meeting wasn't about friendship. It was survival, ugly, necessary, and inevitable.

The blueprints of Rhea's compound lay spread across the table between us, each hallway and exit point marked in red.

Three kings of Las Vegas, leaning over the same map like generals plotting an invasion. I held nothing back, every detail, every weakness I'd discovered.

Not out of loyalty. Not out of friendship. In our world, information was currency, and I was investing. They'd do the same if Rhea had targeted me first.

I jabbed at the blueprint, my fingertip leaving a sweaty print on Rhea's compound perimeter.

"Divided, we're dead men. Simple math." The whiskey burned in my throat as I swallowed. "She's holed up near Blue Diamond for now, but Rhea never stays put. Always three steps ahead, always watching us scramble." I dragged my finger across each entry point marked with crimson X's. "Guards at every door, every window, every goddamn air duct. You try going in alone?" I locked eyes with each man around the table. "They'll mail pieces of you back to Vegas for weeks."

Thal sank deeper into his leather chair, face carved from stone. "We approach this strategically."

I nearly laughed. Fucking obvious. I bit my tongue, but Zeno had no such restraint.

"Strategy?" Zeno's fist crashed onto the table, rattling the whiskey glasses. "I want her bleeding out at my feet."

Each word escaped through clenched teeth, something feral lurking behind his eyes, something that had tasted blood before and wanted more.

My molars ground together as heat crawled up my neck. These peacocking bastards would get us all killed with their dick-measuring.

"Both," I sliced through their bullshit. "We move smart, we move lethal. One shot, clean execution. Rhea disappears, and everything she built?" I spread my hands. "Becomes ours for the taking."

Zeno's shoulder rolled in a dismissive shrug while Thal

lifted his whiskey to his lips, sipping with calculated slowness, eyes narrowed to slits.

The silence stretched taut between us. When I caught Ares's gaze, I recognized the readiness in his posture, the slight forward lean, the hand positioned inches from his holster.

His eyes flicked between the other two men, assessing threats, but I felt no concern. These men might fantasize about putting bullets in me, but they wouldn't.

Our empires were too intertwined, our secrets too deeply buried together. They'd sooner cut off their own hands than destroy the man who kept their worlds intact.

I leaned forward, my fingertips hovering over the blueprint.

"Here's our approach."

The door crashed against the wall before I could continue.

Esme appeared in the doorway, silhouetted against the hallway light.

Four hands moved to four weapons in perfect synchronicity, then stopped mid-motion.

The room went still. Esme. Here.

Zeno was the first to snap, "You shouldn't be here!"

Without flinching, she closed the distance in three sure steps, dropped a folder onto the table with a dull slap, and leveled us with a gaze that dared us to move. Unbothered, she glanced at Zeno's pointed finger, a slow, wicked brow arching.

"Try to stop me, dear brother," she murmured, mouth

curling into a smirk. The challenge hovered, thick and electric, between us.

My eyes locked on her before I could stop myself. The black satin of her blouse caught the light as she moved, the fabric shifting against her body with each breath.

Her hair was pinned up, but rebellious strands had worked themselves free to frame her face, drawing attention to the yellowing bruises beneath.

Those marks were healing day by day, though the memory of her injuries still cut through me like a blade.

She was a force of nature standing there. But what held me captive was the steel in her gaze, that unflinching challenge that dared anyone to question her presence.

I adjusted my position, fighting for composure as I watched her square off against the others.

Her chin tilted upward, eyes narrowing as if silently daring them to try removing her from the room.

The already dense atmosphere in my office transformed instantly, charged particles seeming to dance in the space between us, her arrival turning our careful détente into something far more combustible.

"Esme. Sit," I said, nodding at the empty chair beside Ares. "Tell us what's in the folder."

She inhaled, deep, steadying, then let it out. "It's my contribution."

"Nobody asked you to get involved," Zeno snarled.

She shot him a look, cool and edged. "Didn't realize I needed an invitation, Zeno. Did you get yours delivered by pigeon, or...?"

The sarcasm dripped off every syllable, baiting him, and she didn't even bother to hide it. Their battles were old, ugly, bruised from years inside the ring. I knew better than to step in.

"We're all here for a reason," I said. "That includes Esme."

"Thank you, Aidon," she murmured.

Her smile cut through the professional facade I'd constructed for this meeting like a stiletto through silk.

"I've gathered intel on Rhea, everything from guard rotations to property holdings. But the real prize?" She tapped a manicured nail against the folder. "Access codes. Not just her digital systems, but banking credentials. Those offshore accounts funding her operation? We could freeze them with a keystroke."

Thal leaned forward, elbows on the table. His gaze traveled from the folder up to Esme's face, then dropped to where her blouse gaped open at the collar. My fingers tightened around my glass until I feared it might shatter.

"What's your angle here?" he asked, while his eyes remained predatory.

"To help," Esme said, brittle and blasé. "I want to see her destroyed just as much as the rest of you."

Thal's gaze lingered, his nod slow, deliberate. "Is that so? Why?"

She shrugged, evasive. "I have my reasons."

Zeno's eyes roved over her face, lingering on the mottled bruises. "Would those bruises be part of your motivation?"

A ghost of a smile flickered at the corner of Esme's

mouth. "Is that a hint of concern I hear, dear brother?" She was provoking him, toying with matches in a room drenched in gasoline. Maybe she wanted to watch it all go up in flames.

He only grunted, jaw clenched so tight it might shatter.

Zeno vibrated with contained violence—a grenade with its pin half-pulled. His reputation for unpredictable brutality preceded him like a shadow.

Esme wasn't alone in that.

"I like her," Thal murmured, sidelong glance at me, lips curling into a smirk.

Zeno bristled, rage radiating from him in waves. At any moment, I expected him to snap, shatter the tension with an outburst. "This isn't a fucking game."

"It never was."

Esme's accusation lingered in the air like gunpowder after a shot. Zeno's silence was admission enough. Four pairs of eyes locked in a Mexican standoff, muscles tensed, jaws clenched, waiting for someone to crack first.

"Enough," I growled, my palm slapping the table. "This isn't helping." The temperature in the room dropped ten degrees, but nobody moved.

"If I may," Ares leaned forward. "Our intelligence suggests a three-point strike would cripple Rhea's entire network."

My eyes met his. A nod passed between us, an unspoken understanding that the real enemy wasn't sitting at this table.

"Yeah, Ares is right," I said. "We hit her all at once. First, the power grid. We tear it down, take the lights, kill Rhea's eyes and ears. Then we go in, every team, everybody we've got, right through the perimeter. Flash bombs next. It'll blind them, confuse the hell out of them, and we move while they're staggering, attacking from every side all at once. Our people, her people, it's chaos, and we want it that way. And while everything's burning, we lay into them online. We hit the banking system, the comms, everything she needs to crawl out of there alive. Rhea's not getting away this time."

"Just for good measure," Esme said. "I had her put on the no-fly terrorist watch list. She's not going anywhere. Not by plane."

That got my attention.

I stared at her, thrown off-balance. She hadn't told me that part. I wasn't sure I liked it.

I respected her for being ruthless, but did that mean she thought we'd lose?

Was she hedging her bets?

The doubt nagged at me, but I forced myself to nod, to keep moving forward. Zeno shot us a look, all suspicion and heat, but I ignored it and kept going.

"Can I say something else?" Esme asked. "It's obvious. Rhea wants Aidon. She used me, dangled me in front of him like bait, to lure him out. She said so herself. So we need to remember that. She'll use me however she can to get at him." Esme's eyes flashed, her breath catching. "I don't know what you did to her, Aidon, but she wants you ruined. She'll stop at nothing."

"She can try," I muttered.

"She's not getting anywhere near you," Ares cut in, his gaze flicking to Esme, all steel and resolve. He'd heard her.

Esme nodded, slow and deliberate, a shiver running through her. "Thank you. Rhea won't hesitate to twist whatever is unresolved between us. She'll use every crack. We can't forget who the real enemy is."

"Esme's right," I said, rising to my feet, the words slicing through the thick tension in the room. "Are we all on board here?"

Thal nodded, mouth set, eyes hooded. "I'm down."

The finality of it was a heavy weight between us.

"Yeah, me too, I guess," Zeno muttered, reluctance clinging to every syllable.

Ares was already pushing to his feet, energy crackling from him, turning toward me with a sly tilt of his head.

"I'll send you all the detailed plans on an encrypted chat tonight." There was something hungry in the way he watched me, waiting for my command. "Anything else for now, boss?"

"No, thank you, Ares."

He left, boots echoing in the hallway, and then it was the four of us and the air bristling with old grudges, exhaustion grinding down whatever patience I had left.

"Okay, we'll be in touch. Thank you for coming." I moved toward the door, needing space, needing distance, but Zeno spoke, cutting through the haze.

"Aidon. A word?"

I stopped, turning to face him.

However, my gaze flicked to Thal and Esme, dismissing them.

They slipped out the door, closing it behind them.

"What can I do for you?"

He studied me, his focus intense. "Listen. Esme can be a problem, Aidon. She's unpredictable and fucking wild half the time. The rest, she's plain stupid."

"She's your sister," I shot back.

He smirked, not the least bit offended. "Yeah, and I know her a hell of a lot better than you do. I'm just saying: call it however you want, let her come or not. But if she gets in the way, you'd better know what needs to be done."

His gaze cut straight through me, cold, expecting.

Rage tore up my spine, hot and sudden. My hands balled into fists at my sides. I stepped in, close enough to smell the smoke of his threat, my eyes locked on his, daring him to look away, daring him to test me.

"Zeno," I bit out. "I don't give a fuck who you think you are. If you touch even one hair on Esme's head, you won't live long enough to regret it."

His eyes darkened, pupils blown wide with fury.

Every word I said, I meant, loud and raw and right between us. The tension was electric, a current snapping in the air as Zeno stared me down, chest rising and falling, lips pressed thin. This dance between us was old, practically ritual by now, and neither of us ever knew how to let it go.

"We can end this now, if that's what you want, brother."

The words came out sharp, biting, almost a dare. I wanted him to take the bait. Needed it, truth be told. After everything with Esme, my nerves were shot to hell, and the anger roiling inside me was a live wire, sparking and begging to be unleashed.

I raised my chin, meeting his gaze, refusing to blink first.

For a second, he looked like he might lunge.

Instead, Zeno pivoted, boots heavy over the floor as he stalked out, leaving me alone with the fire raging in my blood. I huffed out a breath, a jagged smirk twisting my lips. The fury had nowhere to go, not yet.

But it was still there, burning.

I stalked to the balcony, staring down at the club.

It was a riot tonight, the crowd wild and oblivious, drunk on music and booze and the illusion of safety. No one below had a clue what was being plotted above their heads.

If we pulled this off, everything would change. There'd be no going back. Vegas would bear new scars, and half these people would find their lives turned upside down by morning.

The risk loomed large. I clenched my jaw, my eyes fixed on the target. Rhea had to go. There was no other option. I would see her destroyed or die trying.

Esme came up without warning. One moment I was alone, the next her arms closed tight around my waist, a blindside, a comfort, and a demand all at once. I closed my hands over hers, our fingers locking together.

I drew in a breath, and the world steadied. Christ, the things she did to me. How the hell could she light me up like an inferno and, in the same breath, soothe me to the bone? I'd never get used to it. I didn't want to.

She slipped past me, forcing me to look at her. That face: gorgeous, battered, defiant.

Her eyes locked on mine, electric, and for a second, I couldn't breathe.

She'd been through hell, and she was still here, shining up at me. The storm inside me stilled, went calm, and I knew what I had to do.

"Ready for war?" I asked, cupping her cheek like I needed her to know I was right there, that I wasn't going anywhere.

"With you? Always," she answered, not even blinking, just leaning into my touch and letting me in.

I yanked her closer, arms circling, desperate and all-consuming.

For the first time, it hit me, raw and real, just how much I needed her, how I couldn't stand the thought of letting this woman go—not now, not ever.

TWENTY-ONE

ESME

From Aidon's penthouse, the view stretched down the entire Strip, glittering and endless. If I narrowed my eyes and leaned just right, I caught the garish, leering faces of the clowns on the Circus Circus sign, all the way at the far end. But the Strip at night was something else.

Gone were the tourists darting for shade, desperate to escape the sun's relentless glare. Now they spilled in waves onto the neon-soaked street, stumbling and shouting, high on too much alcohol and the thrill of being somewhere they'd seen in movies.

The women wore sequined dresses so tight they shimmered like scales, clinging to every curve. The men strutted in shirts loud enough to stop traffic, their arms draped around each other, sloshing oversized drinks.

Under the pulsing lights, the scene was electric, feverish, almost hypnotic. I wondered what it felt like to experience

Vegas as a visitor. To not know what lurked behind the glitz, or the power games that kept the city alive.

They were clueless. They had no idea that everything was about to change.

I hugged myself, drawing in a shaky breath as the tension coiled deeper in my gut. Aidon hadn't tried to talk me out of it again, but I knew better than to trust the calm.

The closer we got to go-time, the more my anxiety twisted and sharpened. I wouldn't put it past him to try to stop me at the last possible second.

But my determination burned hotter than his stubbornness, hotter than anything he could throw at me. No way was I going to let him stand in my way.

My muscles still ached from our last fight, and the memories kept looping in my mind like some broken record.

Rhea's army was no joke. They'd put everything on the line to stop us from getting to her. One wrong move, and any of us could end up seriously hurt or worse.

The thought of Aidon getting hurt made my skin crawl.

I hated it. We were getting closer, whether we liked it or not, even if both of us seemed hellbent on pretending otherwise.

The push and pull, the constant friction, it was driving me insane. I couldn't settle, couldn't breathe right.

Yes, I knew I was part of the problem. Maybe the biggest part. It was like self-inflicted torture, and I just kept coming back for more.

If I wanted it to end, I could walk away. Nothing was stopping me. No one was holding me hostage. I'd had more than enough chances to pack up and disappear for good.

"You're not going to disappear on me again."

I hadn't heard Aidon approach, but his words sliced through my thoughts like he'd been eavesdropping inside my skull. My spine stiffened. The space between us felt too small, too charged.

I turned to face him, stalling with a deliberate exhale.

"Every instinct I have is screaming at me to run," I said, the confession tasting strange on my tongue.

His lips curved upward, predatory and pleased. He crossed the distance between us with measured steps, his fingers finding my jaw and tilting my face until I had nowhere to look but into those eyes that saw too much.

"So, stop thinking," I felt his words, soft and low, settle over me.

Simple enough, but it landed like a gentle touch, smoothing out the roughness in my head.

Then his mouth found mine.

Slow, sure, a little desperate. Not like before. Nothing rushed.

He kissed me with a kind of longing that curled through me, warm and steady. I pressed closer, every inch of me greedy for it, for the feeling of being held tight in his arms and pulled right up against him.

His tongue teased at my lips, careful, testing.

I let him in, easy, no resistance. My mouth opened, and the kiss deepened, heat and comfort tangled together.

Oh, fuck.

I moaned before I could stop myself, and then Aidon kissed me harder, like he was trying to drown out my thoughts and feelings with his mouth.

And honestly? It worked. We were just there, all lips and tongues and raw hunger, until it was impossible to ignore the way my whole body wanted him.

It was real. Straight up honest, no bullshit. Intimate in a way I didn't even know I needed, but damn if I wanted to let go.

This wasn't about winning.

It wasn't about keeping score.

Not about power, or playing games, or who could resist the longest.

None of that crap.

It was just...a kiss. For pleasure. For comfort. For the hell of it.

And holy shit, it was good.

With all the other stuff stripped away, it was just pure, stupid bliss. The second Aidon's shoulders relaxed, and he held me against him, soft and careful, I freaking knew he felt it too.

Not that either of us would ever say that aloud.

Feelings? For each other? Yeah, right. Let's not get carried away. Neither of us were anywhere close to that mess.

But in that weird, quiet moment, with no drama, no tension, just us and the way being together felt...it was deep. Uncomplicated. Unflinching.

And I wanted more.

So much more.

Before I could overthink it, I wrapped my arms around his neck, and he lifted me like I weighed nothing and carried me to the bed.

He set me down, but the second he looked at me again, any hint of tenderness vanished.

His eyes were wild, greedy, like he was going to devour me.

I could see it all over his face: he thought I was his. Which was cute because there was no way in hell I'd ever belong to anyone.

Not even someone like Aidon, who was the definition of sexy, successful, and impossible to resist.

Nice try, though.

"You don't own me, Aidon," I said, forcing the words out.

Even as I tried to talk tough, my body wasn't getting the message.

That look he gave me. It should have pissed me off.

Instead, it sent a shiver all the way down, making my whole brain short-circuit with lust.

The war in my head? Alive and well, and there was no sign of a truce.

And I was soaked between my thighs. Every nerve was on fire.

I told myself to get a grip, but my libido just laughed in my face.

Brain versus body? Ha. Not even a contest.

Aidon nudged my thighs apart, slow and deliberate, and leaned in over me on the bed.

His face hovered just above mine, close enough that I could feel his breath.

Then he grinned that way he does, a crooked, cocky smile that made me want to smack him and kiss him, all at once.

Infuriating. And irresistible.

"If you're not mine, then why do you keep coming back to me, Esme?" He caught my lower lip with his teeth and bit down, just enough to make me shiver.

I moaned. It slipped out, and I pulled back, trying to think, to weigh my options.

I could push him away.

That would be the smart, sane thing to do.

It would also be the easiest, or so it was supposed to be.

In reality, it felt goddamn impossible.

So, the other option. The reckless, delicious one. I didn't even debate it. I spread my thighs, wrapped my legs tight around his waist, and tugged him closer.

His cock pressed against my pussy, and the sensation made me gasp, my head spinning.

His pupils went dark, all storm and sex, and it sent a jolt straight through me.

He cupped my cheek again, fingers firm and gentle, and shook his head.

"Esme, you're fucking killing me; you know that?" His voice was rough, jagged. "Can you see it? I need this. I need you, Esme. Not anyone else, not ever. I don't even know why. I don't know what happens after tonight. Maybe I'll never see you again, maybe this is it. But right now, we're here. Right now, I don't want to waste another second not touching you. I want to forget all of it, just for tonight. I want to lose myself in you and pretend nothing else matters. Shut everything out. " He dragged a hand through his hair, eyes wild. "Don't you want that, too? Tell me you do, Esme. Please."

Hearing him talk like this, the vulnerable, it was a risk. He knew it. He knew I could laugh at him, push him away, slam the door in his face. He knew how high my walls were, how far I'd go to keep him out if I wanted to.

And still, he said it.

And yet, he still went for it and opened up.

Like, against all odds, he put his messy, stormy feelings right on the table for me to see. Same kind of chaos I was dealing with.

Without thinking twice, I grabbed him and kissed him, hard. His mouth was hot, hungry. The passion of it hit me right in the soul.

Smashed through all the walls and all the "no, don't go there" and every little bit of caution I'd ever built up.

Hit me straight in the center, no mercy.

We must have been making out for what felt like hours. City noise drifted in through the window, while our bodies were so intertwined that nothing else seemed to matter. All other thoughts vanished.

Alone, in the darkness of his bedroom, we dropped every worry and inhibition. There was nothing left between us but raw nerves and skin, stripped bare.

His hands, rough and sure, slid over my skin, tugging at my clothes until they fell away. I fumbled at the buttons of his shirt, peeling it off his broad shoulders as soon as I managed.

Then the jeans; I popped the button, shoved them down his hips, and onto the floor.

I needed him. I needed the heat of his body pressed against mine, the way he burned from the inside out, the way his essence seemed to blanket me.

It felt like I might die if I didn't get it.

Once his shirt hit the floor, my hands were all over him. Hard shoulders. Biceps that probably bench-pressed small cars. Forearms, taut and corded, my fingers lacing with his as he kissed me like he hadn't eaten in days.

I felt the same. Starving for him. Ridiculous, because we'd just had sex a few hours ago.

And his little speech? About how I should go with it for tonight, just for now?

My brain decided to buy that. Like he'd slipped me a hall pass to drop all my usual hangups, at least for tonight.

Surrender, he'd said. And then, if I wanted, I could bolt those walls back up tomorrow, no harm, no foul.

But right now?

I was doing what he wanted.

I found myself just giving in to him, letting my body go, allowing every part of me to react to every kiss, every touch, every single thing he pulled out of me, even the stuff buried way down deep where I didn't like to look.

But submit? Hell no. Not even close.

There was a difference, and it mattered. Aidon wasn't trying to boss me around. He wasn't looking to make me heel. He wasn't trying to win or prove anything; he just took what I wanted to give.

And the truth was, I wanted him to have everything. All of it. In that wild, rough, no-holding-back kind of way.

The kind that burned.

Bodies tangled together. Wanting to get hotter and louder, until it felt like too much.

Skin against skin.

Mouths meeting, hungry.

Hearts beating, hard...

Yeah. That.

He broke away from my mouth, lips drifting to my neck and pressing kisses along the side, soft and slow. I let my head tip back, a shudder running through me as his mouth worked over that sensitive skin.

A low sound slipped from me, something between a moan and a gasp, my back arching so my breasts could press harder against his chest.

He trailed tiny kisses down my neck, stopping at my collarbone. His tongue flicked out, a quick dart that made me shiver. He didn't stop there.

He kept going, lips slipping down the top of my breasts until he was at my nipple, his mouth closing around it.

A cry tumbled out of me, sharp and needy, as my nipple hardened under his touch. He bit down, just enough for a jolt of pleasure, his teeth grazing, teasing, until I was gasping again.

"Harder!" I demanded, arching my back like I was offering him everything.

He made a sound, a low, rough growl, and his teeth sank harder into my nipple, making me cry out, not in pain, but something filthy and bright.

He let go, leaving my nipple wet and throbbing from the attention, then dragged kisses across my chest, stopping only when he bit down on my other nipple.

"God, Aidon," I groaned, fingers tangled in his hair, yanking his head closer, as if I could pull him through me.

He bit again, sharper this time, and the sensation ripped the breath from my lungs. Every bite sent shocks straight to my clit, which was now throbbing and desperate for more.

He moved further down, licking and nibbling at my belly, before pausing at the top of my pelvis. His tongue darted out to lick that sensitive spot just above my pussy.

My thighs twitched in response, and my entire body felt like it was strung tight and blazing with need.

I almost gave in to the urge to grab him by the hair and beg him to finish me off, but I knew we were both trying to drag this out. I wanted slow, yes, but the slow I had in mind and the almost torturous pace he was going for were two very different things.

And he knew it.

If I had to guess, I'd say he was taking a little too much enjoyment in how much he was driving me up the wall.

His tongue skimmed along the edge of my pubic hair, slow and deliberate. I couldn't help but lift my hips, a silent plea that he chose to ignore. As always, he liked having his way too much and drawing out his fun.

His tongue slid along the side of my pussy, right at the

top of my thighs, maddeningly close to where I wanted him. But still not quite there. I let out a shaky breath. He let out a couple of sharp, almost taunting breaths, the heat of them hitting my clit and pulling another gasp from me.

"Aidon! Please!"

He lifted his head. His eyes were full of mischief. "Please what, Esme?"

"God!" I couldn't help the sound of frustration that came out. "Just…"

"Just what?"

He was impossible. I glared at him, lifting my head, trying to look furious. It lasted not even two seconds. The sight of him there, between my thighs, looking up at me, just made me want him more.

He looked so damned good. Sexy as hell. Rugged, but refined, sophisticated, everything at once.

I couldn't get enough.

I looked at his mouth. "You know what I want," I said, trying to sound firm.

He just smiled. "And you know what I want, too, don't you?"

"Aidon, please…"

"That's a start," he said. "Keep going."

I couldn't do anything but shake my head and laugh at the mess I was in. Why was it so hard to say what he wanted to hear? It would be easy. All I'd have to do was give him what he wanted, and then I could have what I wanted, too. But nope.

This thing between us, the stubborn resistance, the weird

game we played, it was like it had gotten so tangled up in who we were that I wasn't sure we'd ever be able to quit.

Maybe this was how we started.

"Aidon, I'm dying with desire for you," I managed, the words feeling stiff and awkward in my mouth. "Please, will you give me your mouth? Will you eat my pussy and make my thighs shake, make my entire soul tremble with pleasure the way I know you can?"

He raised an eyebrow, looking too smug. Then he nodded, the smirk on his face back in full force.

"I thought you'd never ask."

His cocky grin stretched wide, eyes twinkling with confidence. If someone else had stood there, I might have pushed him aside, refusing to tolerate his arrogance. But now, I kept my distance, feeling Aidon's gaze on me, knowing he understood everything I needed to say without a word. Thankful he didn't force me into begging again.

He ducked his head and got to work, his tongue moving in and out of my pussy like it belonged there, like it didn't know how to stop. He fucked me with it for a few seconds, unyieldingly, before shifting to my clit, sucking and nibbling. Hard. It made me squirm, legs shaking, hair a mess, everything gone except the feeling.

"Yes, that's it; please don't stop," I said, not caring how desperate I sounded.

He sucked my clit even harder, tongue flicking at it, fast and slick, and the orgasm hit me, rolling over me before I could brace for it.

"Yes, god yes; I'm coming," I groaned, hips pushing up,

chasing his mouth, the pleasure sharp and sweet and so much I went limp, panting.

He pulled away, slow and gentle, and moved up to kiss me, deep and hungry. His hands were everywhere, sliding up and down my body, finding my breasts, cupping them, squeezing, his mouth never leaving mine.

Once I'd gotten my breathing under control and my brain started working again, I realized I was desperate to return the favor.

I wanted it so badly, the hot, heavy slide of his cock in my mouth, the weight of it on my tongue, pushing between my lips, all of it.

So I nudged his shoulders, and he let me, rolling onto his back and watching me with a curious look. I couldn't help grinning at the expression. I raised a brow at him, all mock-seductive.

"Your turn, handsome," I said, climbing over him and straddling his hips.

His cock was already hard as hell, pressed against my dripping pussy, like he wanted in. Not yet, though. That wasn't what I wanted, not for the moment.

Instead, I leaned down, my hair falling around our faces, shutting out the rest of the world. I looked straight at him. And for once, his face was soft, not just full of hunger, but something else, too.

He smiled at me, not cocky or teasing, just honest. For a second, I wondered if Aidon liked me.

Maybe this wasn't just about sex after all.

And maybe he saw me, too, with the same look.

My gaze flickered away, my pulse ticking with the uneasy truth: safety here was an illusion, at best. I didn't trust him. He didn't trust me, either.

Still, there we were, stripped bare, bodies and secrets and all. Letting each other in, inch by careful inch, even if it made zero sense. But I wasn't about to waste time or brain cells on the why. Untangling all that could wait. I had one thing on my mind.

His cock. Sweet, thick, begging for attention.

So I let him set the pace, following his lead. I trailed kisses along his neck, down to his chest, and clamped my teeth around his nipple to see him flinch.

He gasped, and I couldn't help grinning as I kissed my way lower, tongue skating down each line of his six-pack. My lips brushed his treasure trail, soft dark hairs rasping against my tongue, making my clit jolt and ache.

I didn't try to make sense of it. I just wanted more.

"Esme, fuck, woman!" I couldn't help but grin. I loved that I could do this to him.

I loved knowing I could make him lose control, make his toes curl, make him shudder from something only I could give.

There was a power in it, not the usual kind we fought over, but something different, something heady and addictive.

Knowing I could make him come, make his cock hard and flushed and aching for me? It was intoxicating. The best kind of rush. The kind I'd never give up without a fight.

I moved down, lips trailing toward his cock, but I didn't

touch it. Not yet. Instead, I kissed around it, careful to avoid any contact with my mouth. If he wanted to tease, I could tease right back. Fair is fair.

"You teasing little vixen," he growled, catching on.

That made me smile wider. I dragged my lips along the top of his thigh, slow and lazy, then dipped down between his legs, licking the skin right beside his balls, ignoring the way his cock strained for attention.

Taking a page out of his playbook, I exhaled, slow and steady, letting the warm rush of air drift over the bared skin of his upper thighs. He groaned, louder this time, and I couldn't help but notice how his cock twitched, straining up into the air like a plant starving for sunlight.

I dragged my tongue down his thigh, then back up again, this time grazing his balls. He moaned and lifted his hips, eager, but I shifted my mouth away.

"Dammit, Esme!" he grumbled, all protest and frustration.

I almost burst out laughing.

I was in control here, not him.

And I knew it drove him nuts, which just made me want to keep going.

I reached out and curled my fingers around his shaft, hot and velvety in my hand.

"Yes, fuck!" he gasped, keeping his eyes glued to me.

A teasing grin tugged at my lips as I drew the head of his cock close, letting it brush my bottom lip before moving away again.

"My god, woman, you're pure evil," he groaned.

I gave a little shrug and laughed. Then I stuck out my tongue, slow as molasses, letting it slide right over the tip. I knew he was dying for me to go for it, to get rough, fast. He had to fight like hell, not just to grab me and shove every inch straight down my throat.

But yeah, no, that wasn't happening.

I bent my head and focused on the underside of his cock, my tongue as smooth as silk, making the slowest trip possible up along the whole shaft. And then the same thing, but in reverse: dragging my tongue back down, flat and hot against him.

Up, down, again and again, I just kept licking, never hurrying, tasting every inch, loving every second of it.

My fingers joined in, wrapping around him and moving in sync with my mouth, squeezing as I licked up and down, up and down, setting the rhythm and not letting up for a second.

"Oh, baby," he breathed, his head tilting back, eyes squeezing shut, just lost in it.

I loved the way his cock slid through my fingers, how his skin yielded and flexed beneath my grip, the steady pulse beating against my lips.

But it wasn't enough. I wanted more. I wanted to give more.

I pulled back for a second, slipped my fingers into my mouth, then reached beneath him.

My lips found his cock again, letting it slide in and out while I pressed my fingertip against his ass.

He groaned, surprised, but didn't stop me. When I was

sure he was ready, I eased my finger inside, pausing, waiting to see what he'd do.

My tongue kept working, circling the head of his cock, and my finger slid in deeper. He was hot, tight. I moved further, searching until I found that spongy, throbbing spot.

I pressed into it and sucked him, hard, and he let out a cry, louder than I'd ever heard. That was all the encouragement I needed.

I kept going, sucking him harder and harder, my finger rubbing his prostate, working him until he was shaking.

"Esme, fuck! Esme!" he shouted, as his cock thickened in my mouth.

I could tell he was about to lose it, so I sped up, wrapping my other hand around him and squeezing while I sucked, my tongue flicking over the tip at the same time.

"ESME! Fuck yes!"

He was thrashing now, hips jerking up and down, and then everything just stopped. His whole body locked up, and he came hard, cock pulsing against my tongue, filling my mouth with that hot, tangy taste.

I slowed down, swallowing every last drop, my movements softening as I milked him until he had nothing left.

Then I let him go, grinning, and crawled back up to him. I watched as his eyes opened, all dazed and happy, pure satisfaction written all over his face.

"Did you like that?" I murmured, a little breathless.

He laughed, short and deep, and caught my cheeks in his palms, kissing me hard. His tongue curled against mine, hot and hungry, and for a second, I forgot everything but the taste of him.

When I pulled back, I found myself grinning down at him. "That's a yes, then?"

He groaned, dramatic, a hands-over-face mock agony.

"That's a very enthusiastic fuck yes, darling." He snatched my hand, pressed it between his thighs, and my eyes went wide at how hard he still was, the pulse of him unmistakable. "Can you blame me? Look at what you do to me, Esme."

"Good," I shot back, mouth already open to meet his lips again.

He rolled me under him, that body of his all warmth and weight, sliding against me until I shivered.

He nudged against my center, finding me soaked, ready and wanting.

His lips didn't leave mine, not once, as his cock, thick and pulsing, slid into me.

Our hips met somewhere in that impossible space between his body and mine, colliding and rolling together in perfect, mindless rhythm.

It was like we were made for this: to move as one, to lose ourselves in the same desperate need, to find relief tangled up in each other.

Aidon's cock was huge. There was no other way to put it. Every inch of him stretched me so wide I thought I might break, and the harder he fucked me, the wetter I got.

It was filthy, the way I drenched his length, but I didn't care. I wanted more of it. I needed more.

A moan escaped me, raw and loud, but he swallowed the sound with his mouth, kissing me. His tongue pushed deep, searching for mine, tangling and tasting while his cock drove in even farther, almost too much, but I craved every second.

He held me so tight I couldn't tell where my body ended and his began. His hands were everywhere, claiming, greedy. I let go, letting the pleasure take over as he fucked me slow and deep, again and again, each thrust winding me tighter until I thought I'd come apart.

My hands dropped to his ass as he fucked me, and I couldn't get enough of the way his muscles flexed beneath my palms, dragging him in even deeper.

He groaned, and the sound was almost a growl, sending a shiver through me. His cock thickened as he slowed down. He pulled away from my mouth and, when I opened my eyes, he was staring down at me.

With the lights from the Strip flickering across his face, he almost looked unreal.

I grinned up at him, and he shifted his hips, the head of his cock hitting my G-spot so perfectly I lost my breath for a second.

My eyes shot open at that, and a slow, smug smile spread across his face. He did it again, and I gasped, spreading my thighs wider, giving him all the access he wanted.

"I love to see you feel good, Esme," his eyes flashed.

"You make me feel amazing, Aidon. Please don't stop," I whispered.

"Never," He groaned. His cock slid out of me, slow and

deliberate. I watched him, watched the way his gaze never left my face.

Then he pressed his cock against my ass, waiting.

"Aidon," I hissed, every muscle tight.

He leaned in. "Let me give you the same pleasure you gave me." His eyes searched mine, questioning. My mouth fell open. A shock of raw, greedy want burned through my body.

I nodded, bracing myself for the pain and the pleasure.

It always went together. He caught my reaction, and his eyes lit up, like he was beyond thrilled to see me ready.

Then he pushed forward, just a little, and the tip of his cock slipped past that tight ring. I sucked in a breath, and he stopped, waiting for my signal, like he was determined to prove he could be patient.

The sting hurt, but then it faded, and I nodded again, opening my thighs wider. I even lifted my hips, wanting him inside me with such desperation.

He moved like he was afraid he'd break something.

Inch by inch, he kept going until I was squirming under him, filled up by his cock, all of me stretched around him.

It was intense. The way he filled me was almost too much, but not enough to make me want him to stop. If anything, the pressure made everything feel better, especially the pulsing in my clit.

I reached down and circled it with my fingers, like that'd help me handle how big he was. It did. Not that he got any smaller.

I sucked in a breath, so damn relieved he was taking it slow.

The way he moved gave me time to adjust to his size, and I was grateful for that. His eyes were locked on me, flicking from my fingers working my clit up to my face, then back down again.

"You're the sexiest woman I've ever seen, Esme. Are you going to come on the end of my cock, baby? I love watching you work your clit like that. Fuck, keep going, baby. I love watching you come. You're going to make me explode inside you just from looking at you."

"Aidon, my god," I gasped, my eyes going wide as he thrust faster.

The sensations rolling through me were wild and filthy and wicked. I clenched around him, and he let out a low moan.

His eyes darkened, crackling with pure, unfiltered lust. He fucked me deep and slow, and it was perfect, every stroke hitting just right.

Deep, rolling waves of pleasure curled inside me, pressure building until I thought my nerves would snap. Every thrust of his cock lit up some wild new center in my brain I didn't even know existed. My fingers sped up, chasing the rush. I was right at the edge, his cock pulsing, driving into me, hard enough I felt the press of his hips against me.

"Fuck, Esme, I can't hold off much longer, baby." He buried his cock so deep inside that it was almost too much.

His words shattered me. My orgasm detonated, pussy clenching hard around his thick cock, my body shaking, hips jerking up into him. I moaned, aware of the noises I was making, writhing under him as wave after wave crashed through me, each one somehow better than the last.

He slammed into me, fucking me through my orgasm until my eyes rolled back in my head. When I went limp, I just let him hold my hips up, his hands tight, determined. He kept thrusting, sweat beading on his forehead and dripping onto my bare chest as he moved over me.

I stared up at him, searching his face, desperate for something. Everything inside me was a mess, a whirlwind, a tornado, impossible to untangle. But in his eyes? I found it.

All of it. The things he tried so hard to hide.

The uncertainty. The honest-to-god naked hunger.

All those feelings...

He didn't bother to cover them anymore. They were right there. Raw. Vulnerable. Almost sweet, in a weird, sincere way that hit me harder than anything else had all night.

I smiled at him, drowning in the same flood of feelings, hoping he could see it, too. That he knew I was right there with him.

Always had been.

I was just as scared. Maybe even more. Too fucking scared to ever say the words out loud, or even admit they were there at all.

He leaned down and kissed me again, softer this time, his cock still driving into me, and something in me just...broke.

Not in a bad way. More like all my walls just gave up and collapsed, and we were drowning in the mess we'd made together, our own little fucked-up orchestra playing somewhere deep in the back of my mind.

Our bodies?

They were singing, like a bunch of angels or gods or whatever, except the thing we worshipped was the feeling of it, the pleasure, and how it made everything else disappear.

Aidon's cock throbbed inside me, and he moved faster, chasing his release, and my nails left angry tracks down his back, not that he seemed to care. He dropped his head to my shoulder, hips moving like he couldn't even stop himself.

"Yeah, Aidon, fuck, yes," I said, rocking my hips up to meet his, and then another orgasm hit me so hard I thought I might pass out.

It rolled through me, wild and sweet, and I wanted to stay in that river of sensation forever.

And then, with every push, every desperate thrust, I felt him lose it, hot and messy inside my ass, and that was it.

I shattered, lost in it, not even sure where my body ended and his began.

"Yes. Yes."

The two of us clutched each other with a desperation I'd never known, our bodies jerking and shuddering as pleasure crashed over us, unfiltered and raw.

We were both left panting, chests heaving, our skin slick with sweat.

I melted into him, my head pillowed on his chest, just listening to the wild, uneven beat of his heart and letting his fingers drift through my hair.

There was a hush in the aftermath, the kind of quiet that wrapped around you and made you feel...safe. Warm.

Like the world outside couldn't touch us here. I let out a deep breath, my fingertip tracing random patterns through the fine hairs on his chest while he held me.

Peace. That's what it was.

Real honest-to-god peace, a kind of comfort that made everything else in my life feel like a distant second.

For once, we'd found a way to drown out all the noise and exist, the two of us, together. It was like we'd carved out this tiny, sacred space where we didn't have to fight or hide or prove ourselves to each other.

And after this?

After this, I didn't think we could ever go back to being adversaries, always pushing and pulling and trying to get the upper hand. Something fundamental had shifted between us.

Deep down. Past skin and bone and muscle. I welcomed it with every part of me. It was right. It was easy. It was...fuck, it was healing.

For the first time, it felt like we were on the same side.

Not just allies in some war against Rhea, either. Something more than that.

I stayed there, stretched out across his chest, rubbing gentle circles over his skin and wishing the night would never end. And for once, I wasn't scared. Not of Aidon. Not of how I felt.

Not admitting that, maybe I was human after all, and I had needs, and those needs included him and every wild, addictive thing he made me feel.

I wasn't naive. I knew it wouldn't be simple. We still had enemies. We still had danger waiting for us, lurking around the next corner. None of that had changed.

But now, for the first time, I could imagine a future that didn't terrify me.

But these feelings? These emotions zipping between us? No doubt about them. I'd never been more certain of anything in my life. And I had a pretty strong hunch Aidon felt the same way.

A dozen conversations were waiting for us. Maybe more. All those words we'd left hanging in the air, unsaid, would have to come out.

In the back of my mind, I knew I'd have to tell this beautiful man how much I loved him, how much I needed him with me, walking through this insane world. He needed to know what he meant to me. And, hell, I needed to hear it too.

Clarity was important. We couldn't keep going without saying it. The silent thing was fine until it wasn't. Left too much space for confusion. For hurt.

Soon, I told myself, but not right now. The time would come when we'd be ready to say it aloud, every single thing that needed to be said.

For now, I was fine just in his arms, floating in the quiet afterglow only our bodies could make together.

I listened to the slow, steady rhythm of his breathing, my cheek rising and falling against his chest. I wondered what he was thinking, but I wasn't about to ask.

I kept my thoughts locked down and just let the silence settle for a while.

He broke the silence. His voice was so low, it almost didn't register. I looked up, caught off guard by the emotion shining in his dark, beautiful eyes.

"Esme, this wasn't about Rhea, was it?" he asked, tone too casual to be casual.

"What do you mean?" I played dumb. It never worked on him. Not anymore.

"This is about us," he said, all certainty and no hesitation.

I swallowed. Hard.

The words hovered between us, awkward and heavy, and for a second, I almost panicked.

If I agreed with him, what was I copping to? The old Esme would've spiraled.

Run a mental lap around this for hours. But that wasn't me anymore. Not really.

Everything had changed. The space between us crackled with something new, something raw.

Aidon wasn't trying to win. He wasn't playing some game or trying to trap me, or prove a point, or rack up some ego points for himself. That part was over. Dead and buried.

We weren't doing that anymore.

He just wanted the truth. So did I. Funny how easy it was once I admitted it.

So I kissed him.

Slow and soft, right on the lips. Let it build. Let it settle.

And then I gave him the answer he'd been waiting for, the answer I'd been carrying around since the start.

The truth. The real, messy, beautiful truth.

"Hasn't it always been about us, Aidon?" I said.

I couldn't help smiling, even if it was a little wistful.

His eyes lit up every shadow and corner I'd tried to hide for so long.

"I don't see anyone else here," he said, grinning, like the cat who got the cream.

"Neither do I." I kissed him again, this time longer, slower. "Honestly? I hope it stays that way."

He smirked, kissed my forehead, and pulled me in like he was never letting go.

"Me, too, babe. Me too. I'm all yours."

And just like that, I drifted off in his arms.

Safe.

Secure.

Surrendered.

Twenty-Two

AIDON

Our caravan cut through the Nevada desert, kicking up clouds of crimson dust in our wake. Five black SUVs, headlights extinguished, snaked along the back roads of Red Rock Canyon.

Even in darkness, we cast an imposing silhouette against the dusty pink hills. The stars hung overhead by the millions. It was a stark contrast to the artificial glow of the Strip I'd left behind.

Blue Diamond might only be thirty minutes from Vegas, but hugging these rugged mountain foothills under a blanket of stars, we might as well have been on another planet. Every element of our approach had been planned.

Rhea wouldn't see us coming until it was too late.

Her compound was a fortress of technological might. Her security rivaled military installations with motion sensors embedded in the perimeter, thermal imaging that could detect a coyote at five hundred yards, and guards who moved with the precision of former special forces.

We'd decimated her ranks in our last encounter, but I had no illusions. By now, she'd have recruited twice as many men, each one deadlier than the previous. This was Rhea's talent: building impenetrable walls around herself, layer upon calculated layer.

Rhea's compound rose from the desert like a fortress, all steel, silicone, and security systems that would make the Pentagon jealous. She'd escaped us once. That wouldn't happen again.

As we approached, I pictured my hands around her throat, her pulse fluttering beneath my thumbs as realization dawned in her eyes. Her empire would fall tonight, payment for the bodies she'd left scattered behind her.

But I wasn't the only one with a score to settle. We were all sharks in these waters, circling for the kill.

Zeno was a powder keg ready to detonate. The man hadn't slept in days, his eyes bloodshot and wild. Rhea was just the target he needed.

Thal saw this as his chance for glory. Taking down Rhea would cement his reputation and feed that insatiable ego of his.

Then there was Esme. The bruises on her ribs had faded, but I'd caught her wincing when she thought no one was watching.

She'd spent hours in my penthouse gym, learning to throw punches that could break bones. This wasn't her usual game.

She was a chess player, not a boxer, someone who destroyed opponents without ever throwing a punch.

Yet there she'd been in my gym, hammering the heavy bag with such precision that Ares, a man who'd killed with his bare hands, had watched her with newfound respect. The woman who once wielded only words now moved with the lethal intent of someone who'd tasted their own blood.

Nothing was stopping her from disappearing. She had resources, connections, escape routes I'd never be able to trace.

Most people, after what Rhea put her through, would vanish into anonymity to heal. I would have understood that impulse.

Instead, she stayed. That's when I recognized our shared affliction: neither of us could stomach an unpaid debt. We both carried ledgers in our souls, and every entry demanded balance.

Now Esme's eyes held that dangerous gleam I knew too well, the look of someone who wouldn't rest until they'd carved their vengeance into flesh.

My allies were all racing toward Rhea, each for their own reasons.

But watching Esme's profile in the dim light, I wondered which of us would reach her first.

Thal and Zeno were with their men in the other cars, but I'd insisted Esme ride with me. She'd protested, of course, but not for too long or too hard. I was still plagued with the immense need to keep her close to my side.

Even though she'd been hurt, I'd managed to keep her alive last time, and I intended to do better tonight.

"You good?" I asked, reaching over and taking her gloved hand. She was dressed like a fucking Ninja, with fingerless Kevlar gloves and a bulletproof vest strapped to her chest. Her hair was wrapped up tight in a bun on the back of her head, and her face was void of makeup, her expression somber, focused, and determined.

She'd never looked hotter.

My cock twitched in my pants, and I felt a smirk play on my lips.

Of course, I'd want to fuck her right now. I had half a mind to do it anyway.

"Do you have any idea how fucking sexy you look right now?" I growled.

She smiled and shook her head. "Down, Boy! We have a job to do."

"We're still a few miles out," I protested.

"It would take that long to get me out of this outfit," she said, raising a brow at me. "And twice as long to get back into it."

"Fair enough." I shrugged. "But afterwards you're mine."

"You keep saying that." She winked.

"I mean it," I said, growing serious and giving her a pointed look. "Every time."

The future stretched before us like an uncharted desert. I stared at the road ahead, my mind racing past tonight's mission to whatever might come after.

Would there even be an "after" for us?

Some ridiculous part of me imagined driving away from Vegas with her beside me, leaving the blood and bodies behind.

Pathetic fantasy.

Her silence on the subject spoke volumes. A woman who moved like Esme, who calculated three steps ahead of everyone else, surely had plans that didn't include a man like me.

I'd watched her navigate my world with lethal precision, yet I realized I'd never once asked what she wanted beyond survival.

For months, she'd existed in my mind as categories: Zeno's troublesome half-sister, my obsession, my conquest, my weakness.

My throat tightened. I knew the exact pitch of her moans in the darkness.

The way her eyes fluttered closed at climax, but she couldn't name a single thing she treasured. With death potentially waiting at our destination, this felt unforgivable.

What if I never got the chance to know her beyond the battlefield of our bodies?

"Esme, what's something no one knows about you?"

Her head snapped toward me, surprise flashing across her face before dissolving into laughter that echoed against the tinted windows of the SUV.

"Now? With Rhea's compound less than a mile away?"

"Yes, now," I said. "Humor me."

She studied me for a moment, then sighed. "I love flowers. I used to steal flowers from the botanical gardens when I was broke in college."

"What kind?" I asked, watching her lips part.

"Magnolias," she said, glancing out at the desert darkness. "They reminded me of something unattainable."

I committed this to memory, like coordinates on a map. "I'll remember that."

"Gardenias were what I wanted," she added. "The scent stays with you for hours."

"Planning my next gift already," I said, the corner of my mouth lifting.

"Aidon the romantic," she teased. "Who would have thought?"

"I'm not," I admitted. "I just want to know what matters to you."

"I'm an open book." She shrugged.

I gave her a look.

"What?" Her eyes widened with false innocence.

"You're a locked vault with booby traps."

"Not last night," she whispered, dropping her eyes.

I leaned over, brushing a gentle kiss across her lips.

Even in the dark, I saw the blush bloom across her cheeks. I kissed her again. And again.

Desperate, greedy, drinking her in, her taste, her mouth, her gasps swallowed into mine. This Esme, the one who spread her thighs for me, the one who let me inside, the one who still wouldn't admit she was opening her heart even as she opened her body, I couldn't get enough of her. Not ever.

Sure, her fiery side made my cock harder than a rock, but her softer side was going to be my undoing.

She'd changed these last few days. The hard edges of rebellion had softened, her stubbornness melting into something that looked a hell of a lot like partnership. I'd watched her in those meetings with Zeno, Thal, even Ares, holding her ground with a tenacity that would have sent a lesser woman scrambling for the shadows. She never backed down. Not once.

I kissed her again. Couldn't help it. She'd gone from a dream in my head to something real, solid, breathing beneath my hands.

Then her palm found my chest, a slow, careful pressure. She pushed me back, not hard, but enough.

My eyes flicked open. She was staring at me, searching, like she wanted to see what was there.

"We need to get our game face on," she hissed, breathless. "I can't do that with your tongue down my throat, as much as I'm enjoying it."

"Fair enough," I muttered, dragging myself off her.

I tore my eyes away. It was slow, brutal, like peeling flesh from bone, each inch separating with a raw discomfort that felt wrong, unnatural, desperate for more.

Having Esme close had become a habit I couldn't shake, a need more than a preference. I wondered, not for the first time, what would happen to us when all this ended.

The thought gnawed at me. Not now. I had to stay focused. Anything less, and one of us would bleed for it. That was not fucking happening.

A sigh left me as my phone buzzed in my pocket. I dug it out, thumbed it to life, and Ares's name flashed on the screen.

He was tailing us, his car close enough I could feel his presence at my back. I answered, quick and sharp, put him on speaker. Esme's gaze flicked to me, both of us hanging on for every word.

"Boss, we're just a mile out. Are you suited up?"

"We're ready," I said. "Any changes to the plan?"

"None."

"Good." My pulse kicked up. "What about our inside source? Rhea still oblivious?"

"She doesn't have the faintest clue what's coming for her."

A low, satisfied hum escaped me. "Perfect. This should be interesting. Stay sharp."

"Always," Ares answered. He hesitated, just for a heartbeat, and in the silence I felt everything between us. All the years. All the blood and loyalty. We never said what we meant, not out loud, but it lived in every pause.

"Alright," I said. "We'll pull off at the spot and take the back way through the trees. Quiet."

"Affirmative."

Ares hung up. No goodbye. No hesitation.

The sense of danger that lingered in the car between me and Esme thickened instantly, rolling in like a storm.

It was suffocating. Heavy. A warning neither of us could ignore.

I wanted to make her stay behind, keep her safe, but the idea alone was a loaded gun.

One pull of the trigger and the soft, open Esme I'd finally gotten to see would vanish, maybe for good. She'd walk away and never look back.

I wasn't willing to take that risk—not with her.

So I kept quiet, letting the tension fester, letting her see how serious this was. We were about to cross a line, and there was no room for mistakes or second thoughts. Our lives were on the line, and that wasn't something either of us could pretend away.

This was the life I'd chosen. Getting my hands dirty wasn't an accident—it was survival. You learned fast, or you got buried.

Zeno knew it. Thal, too.

We all had something to gain from this scheme.

Our business would thrive off the bones of Rhea's empire, splitting her assets between us. But Esme?

All she had was vengeance, that cold, sharp promise lodged in her heart. Was that worth the risk, the danger that could easily swallow her whole?

I wanted to roar at her, grip her shoulders, and shake her until she saw sense, pin her to the bed and leave her there, seething, while I walked away to deal with it myself, only to come back, gather her in my arms, and fuck away all the bitterness until she forgave me.

But I knew none of that would work. No amount of shouting or rough hands could change Esme's mind. She wouldn't forgive, not for this.

This was a path she had to walk, pain and all, to reach that jagged place of satisfaction. If I tried to stop her, it would destroy us both.

So I kept it all locked up inside, the words burning my throat.

When the driver finally slowed and the tires crunched off the dirt road, dust swirling in the headlights, relief crashed through me. I wanted it done.

Over. For the first time, the future didn't look like a threat.

It looked like a fucking promise. I glanced at Esme, unable to offer her one last chance to escape. There was no turning back.

"Esme, you know you can change your mind. It's not too late."

Instead of anger flashing in her eyes, she just smiled, something almost gentle about it.

"I'll be okay, Aidon," she said. "I promise. You don't need to worry about me. But thank you for caring."

I nodded. "Alright then. Let's do this."

"Yes. Let's go. Together. Like we planned."

I leaned in, crushing my mouth to hers in a hard, hungry kiss before wrenching myself away and reaching for the door.

When all the cars had finally pulled over, we assembled in the shadow of the mountain, the air thick with anticipation. Every man in our group fell silent, waiting.

"We head north," Ares barked, cutting through the night.

He took command of all three groups, and it was a sight:

Thal's small coalition, dwarfed by Zeno's army, but together with my own security team. Every man was huge, intimidating, and armed to the teeth—the kind of force that left nothing to chance.

We moved in silence, every step toward Rhea's compound feeding something wild in my chest. Confidence burned through my veins, hotter than blood, a wildfire swelling as the moon carved silver into the darkness.

Esme kept pace beside me, head high, eyes flashing with a terrible, beautiful certainty. Her mouth was set, unyielding. The only light was the moon, and it made her fierce, almost untouchable.

I had to look away.

I couldn't let myself slip. Couldn't falter. Couldn't drown in the sight of her. Esme, the woman I would destroy worlds for, was caught in the moonlight, surrounded by the storm she embodied. I told myself my job was to protect her, even when she said she didn't need it.

Even when she looked so fucking gorgeous and unstoppable, striding into danger, all that raw resolve on her face.

And I couldn't focus on the fact that I'd just called it love. That word. That feeling. Thundering in my chest, a secret I could barely admit to myself.

I shoved it all down, knuckles white on the steering wheel, refusing to let myself glance at Esme and the way her beauty threatened to pull me apart from the inside out. Later, I promised myself.

Later, when the world wasn't hanging by a thread, I'd let myself drown in her. But right now?

Now I had to focus, keep my pulse steady, my hands sure. Except a vision of her cut through the darkness anyway: sprawled out on my bed, hair wild around her, thighs parted and slick as I drove my cock into her again and again, her moans echoing somewhere deep in my chest.

Fuck. What was she doing to me?

How had she burrowed so deep under my skin, turned my bones to fire and my thoughts to chaos?

I made a vow right then, teeth clenched and jaw aching: if we survived tonight, just barely scraped by, I'd take her out past the city lights tomorrow and fuck her under the moon until I forgot my own name.

But there was no room for that now. Not with so much riding on my back. I shoved the hunger down, locked it tight, and forced every cell in my body to remember what was at stake. I wouldn't let my weakness cost us everything.

Not Esme. Not any of us.

And she was my weakness. Everyone knew it by now.

Rhea had figured it out even before I'd admitted it to myself, and she'd twisted the knife without hesitation, the way only someone like her could.

She wouldn't hold back tonight, either. Not even for a second.

That was why I wouldn't let Esme leave my side. If she slipped too far, Rhea would snatch her up in a heartbeat, and this time, she wouldn't settle for a warning shot. She'd finish what she'd started. Maybe worse.

The thought made me flinch, muscles tightening. I forced it away, dragging in a breath, shaking my head as though I could rattle the anxiety loose. Couldn't afford that now. Couldn't risk it, not with everything on the line.

Not with her on the line.

Fuck. The only thing I loved.

Love. Love. Love.

The word pounded through me, an endless echo every time my boot hit the dirt. Step after step, the word drove itself deeper into my chest, into my bones, until I half-expected the others to hear it, especially Esme.

She glanced over, breath brushing my arm. "Are you okay?"

"Yeah." My answer was rough, unsteady. I tipped my head back, eyes fixed on the moon, letting its cold light flood over me and spill into the cracks.

If tonight were the night I died, this wouldn't be the worst way to go. My best men stood beside me. My pride remained intact. Hands steady, heart ready to spill whatever blood was necessary.

For her.

If I had to die tonight, it wouldn't be so bad with Esme beside me. It would be alright, whatever happened. In fact, I could almost believe it would be perfect. But I wasn't about to die, not tonight, not here, not like this.

That fate belonged to Rhea now. Poor Rhea. She'd sealed her fate ages ago, and there was no walking it back. No one fucked me over as hard as she had and lived to gloat about it.

Honestly, she had to know her time was almost up. She had to feel it every time she looked over her shoulder. It almost made me laugh, the thought of her believing she could be the first to take me down without paying the price.

No.

Tonight, Rhea was done for. And I couldn't lie, I was almost giddy at the thought of being the one to end it for her.

The compound slid into sight as we rounded the edge of the rocky bluff. It sprawled behind chain link fencing, barbed wire curling along the top, every inch washed in glaring white from the oversized floodlights that cut through the darkness and made the shadows scatter.

My pulse thrummed, half anticipation, half something sweeter, and I could almost taste the coming surrender on my tongue.

"Looks like a fucking prison," Zenos bit out.

"Looks like a fucking good place to destroy our enemy, if you ask me," I shot back.

The rage I'd been carrying for Rhea had been simmering just beneath my skin, threatening to crack me open. Now, knowing she was just beyond that wall, I let it flood through me, let it burn hot and wild and hungry.

"Everything looks peaceful," Ares observed, as if he didn't trust the calm.

"Calm before the fucking storm," I muttered.

My eyes swept the compound, memorizing every inch, every shadow, every threat.

Ares shifted, straightening his spine, his presence suddenly all leader. With two fingers, he pointed into the darkness ahead.

"North side. Compound's got a massive gate. Main entrance. Security booth with one guard. He's loaded for war, and the booth's got eyes all over it, straight from the security hub inside. One button, and he can call in a shitload of backup. If he spots us, we're fucked."

"So, we make sure that doesn't happen," Esme said.

Zenos shot her a glare, still pissed she was here at all, but I ignored it.

"Exactly," Ares replied, not missing a beat. "We do it by coming up behind him. I'll handle it alone. Less noise, less chance of tipping him off. Once he's down, we move in. Cameras will still see us, but my guy inside will keep security distracted. Timing is everything."

Ares checked his watch, every movement crisp, sure. Then he nodded once.

"We're right on time." He pulled out his phone, thumb moving with quick precision, and sent the alert to our man inside.

We'd finally managed to sneak someone into Rhea's operation, a spy who'd survived when so many before him had not.

He'd gone in undercover, smooth in his interview as a new guard, and she'd hired him without a second thought. His presence was everything; the mission hinged on him.

"You got this," I said to Ares, locking eyes with him and letting the silent message settle between us before he turned and sprinted off.

No goodbyes, no hesitation, just the pure, electric trust of brothers in arms.

In the darkness, we watched him move. He zigzagged through the shadows, limbs taut and low, silent as a predator closing in.

My heart hammered in my chest so loud it was all I could hear. I couldn't look away. Every muscle in my body was wired and waiting, my gaze flickering between Ares and the guard, my finger ready on the trigger if things went sideways.

A quick scan told me the others were just as tense, crouched in position, all of us coiled tight, ready to strike if it meant saving our brother.

The guard sat slouched in the dim, suffocating heat of the shack, screen glow painting his broad face a sickly, unnatural green. He was massive, dwarfing even Ares.

There would be no force against force here. The only option was surprise. I watched as Ares slipped into that familiar predatory quiet.

It was almost funny, the way he deployed the very skill I'd so often cursed him for. God, how many times had he startled me just for the hell of it?

Swore it was a habit from his military days, prowling through sleeping barracks like a shadow. I always found it unnerving. He found it hilarious.

Now, though, I watched him like an apprentice studying the master.

He moved with an almost unnatural patience, a slow, deliberate drift through darkness, every movement measured and spare. Not so much as a crunch in the red Nevada dirt. His gaze locked unblinking on the guard, the way a wolf might fixate on the softest part of its prey. The tension in our little group was electric, thick enough to choke on, humming through the hot night air.

The guard snorted at his phone, oblivious. Instantly, Ares paused, every muscle tensed mid-motion, a statue sculpted from midnight.

I barely breathed. The moment stretched and snapped, and then Ares was moving again, circling behind the shack, keeping low, slipping out of the cameras' sight lines as he closed in on the open entrance.

A handful of feet. That was all that separated them now.

Ares crossed the threshold, soundless, a ghost. The guard never stood a chance. One heartbeat, he was scrolling, chuckling under his breath, and the next, the cold mouth of a gun pressed into his temple, a bullet tearing through bone and brain before he could even scream.

He hit the floor with a wet, conclusive thud.

Ares didn't hesitate. He dropped low, listening, every sense straining for footsteps, alarms, any sign the kill had been noticed. I swept the property with my eyes, heart hammering, searching for movement.

Nothing. Not a whisper.

Whatever strings we'd pulled inside, they'd worked. The guard was dead, and nobody else was any wiser.

Perfect.

"Let's go," I hissed, the instant Ares raised his hand. Instinct took over.

We dropped low, melting into the shadows, every movement silent and calculated. Ahead, Ares reached for the button.

The gate responded with a tortured, bone-deep groan, metal scraping against metal, as it yawned open.

We slipped through the gap like smoke, leaving the dead guard sprawled behind us in his gory, makeshift coffin. The coppery stench of blood clung to my nostrils.

I kept one eye on Esme, the other on the door ahead, lungs tight with anticipation. A silent plea flickered across my mind: let us survive this.

Ares moved first, stalking ahead with predatory grace. He pressed his ear to the door, hand hovering over his weapon. Tension thrummed in the air.

He tested the knob, slow and cautious. "Locked," he murmured, voice barely audible.

He didn't waste time.

A single shot. The handle exploded in a violent spray of metal shards, echoing through the corridor like a war drum.

"Guess if they weren't awake before, they are now," I muttered, adrenaline sharpening my words.

"Damn straight," Ares shot back, a wicked grin flashing across his lips. "Brace yourselves, kids. Here we go."

We stormed through the door.

As expected, enemies surged down the corridor toward us, heavy boots pounding, weapons raised and lethal. The crack of gunfire shattered the air.

I shoved Esme behind me. Zeno, Thal, and Ares fanned out, unleashing a torrent of bullets. Bodies crumpled, momentum lost, blood painting the walls as they fell.

"One battle down," Ares growled, stepping over the fallen

with ruthless purpose. Thal grabbed their discarded guns, arming himself and the others. We pushed deeper, hearts thundering, into Rhea's stronghold, every sense straining for the next fight, the next threat, the next inevitable clash.

We didn't slow down. We couldn't—not now.

Esme tried to shove past me, but I blocked her path, stepping in front again. She let out an annoyed scoff, sharp, brittle, but I ignored her. I wasn't about to let a fight with her distract me—not now, not here.

Our leadership circle was small: Ares, Zeno, Thal, and me. But with our soldiers supporting us, we were like a small militia. If I failed, I knew the others would do whatever it took to keep Esme safe. But until that happened, she was mine to protect. My responsibility.

We marched down a dark corridor, boots echoing as we turned a corner. The hallway opened suddenly into a cavernous two-story warehouse, shadows stretching high overhead. Boxes lined the walls from floor to ceiling. A balcony ringed the upper level, doors spaced evenly along the edge, the whole place wrapped in silence. The kind of silence that prickled the skin. Too fucking quiet.

Ares strode over to the nearest box and cracked the lid. Inside: six assault rifles, stacked with precision, strapped down, and ready to ship.

"There must be hundreds of these," Ares muttered, sweeping his hand over the endless rows of identical boxes lined up along the warehouse floor.

"They're all boxed up to go," Zeno said, flipping open a

lid with an impatient flick of his fingers. His eyes scanned the label. "Colombia."

Thal drifted over. He didn't bother opening the box. He read the shipping label taped to the cardboard.

"Honduras," he said.

Esme tilted her head back, gaze skimming the web of thick steel beams overhead, the iron hooks, that ancient pulley system clinging to the ceiling like it was waiting for someone to give it purpose again.

"What did this place used to be?" Esme asked.

Ares answered without glancing her way, "Old lumber mill."

"That's what I'm smelling," she murmured.

"Sawdust," he told her.

In the farthest shadows, beyond the reach of the dirty light, I caught the shapes of rusted saws scattered across the cracked cement, half-buried in piles of wood shavings and splintered, rotting logs.

In the corner, lumber racks hunched beside a kiln so ancient it looked like it belonged in a museum, not a warehouse.

Ares's eyes went up, tracking the metal stairs to the balcony overhead.

He jerked his chin at it. "She's up there. Word is, she knocked down the old office walls to make herself a little suite."

"God forbid Rhea settle for anything less than a luxury hideout," Esme said.

Ares's jaw clenched. "Always wanted to be a fucking Mafia princess," he growled.

The smallest smile tugged at my mouth. I didn't take my eyes off the balcony, not even as I spoke. One door at the end glowed faintly, the glass catching a thread of light.

Every other room up there was dark, abandoned, empty as a tomb.

"Something's off," I said, the unease crawling down my spine.

"Yeah. Too quiet." Ares's tone was low, all tension. "Where are her men?"

"That's just what I was—"

My words died on my tongue as the overhead fluorescents blasted the warehouse in stark, blinding light. The metallic zing of bullets ricocheted everywhere, slicing the air with a barrage of violence.

Instinct took over, I grabbed Esme's arm and yanked her with me, pitching us both behind the closest stack of boxes as rounds tore through the shadows.

We hit the concrete hard, ducking low, my heart pounding so loud I could barely hear her furious whisper.

She shot me a glare, eyes burning like wildfire.

"What?" I snapped, adrenaline spiking.

"I can take care of myself!" she hissed, jaw clenched, fury nearly vibrating off her.

"I never said you couldn't!" I barked back, but before I could say more, a bullet punched through the box right beside her head.

She flinched, ducking even lower, arms coming up instinctively to shield herself.

"Fuck, Esme, stay down!" I choked out, and without thinking, I threw myself over her, shielding her with my body as the world erupted in gunfire.

She squirmed in my grasp, desperate for freedom, and managed to scoot away, dragging herself backward on her ass until the crates shielded her body.

I let her have the space. For now, we were both half-hidden, crouched low, as bullets tore through the warehouse, ricocheting in sharp, metallic shrieks.

Gunfire exploded all around us, ours and theirs, so loud it made my teeth ache.

I risked a glance around the corner, pulse thundering in my ears, searching for the source of Rhea's men and the direction their shots were coming from.

Up on the balcony, I caught a flash of movement.

Three men, guns drawn, hunched and firing. Behind them stood Rhea, untouched by the chaos, her silhouette striking in a gauzy, lemon-yellow dress that shimmered in the half-light.

Dark sunglasses perched, almost arrogantly, on her sleek hair. She looked every inch the socialite, more suited to a summer cocktail party than a midnight firefight on the edge of the desert.

But her expression...God, she was radiant.

A twisted sort of joy played across her lips, her mouth stretched in a wild, delighted smile as she watched the violence unfold.

A delicate flute of champagne dangled from her hand, red manicure immaculate even as bullets screamed through the air.

The surreal image burned into my brain, but I forced myself to focus. Where the fuck was Ares?

My eyes scanned the shadows until I spotted him, crouched low behind the kiln with Zeno and Thal, the three of them exchanging fire with Rhea's crew. Ares moved with lethal precision, lining up shot after shot, and I watched as he dropped one man, then the next. Rhea's smile faltered when only one remained; then she slipped into the office, her last guard scrambling behind her.

For a heartbeat, quiet reigned, a brief, tense pause as we all recalibrated. My chest heaved, lungs burning, but the silence didn't last.

Another door burst open at the far end of the warehouse, spilling out a fresh wave of Rhea's men. They moved as a pack, laser-focused on Ares and the others, unleashing an avalanche of bullets that chewed up concrete and metal alike.

"Fuck," I hissed under my breath, snapping off return fire.

My aim was steady, and I dropped three, watched them crumple, but five more kept coming, relentless. They were going to overrun Ares if I didn't do something fast.

Distraction.

I needed to draw their focus, buy Ares time. But a cold knot twisted in my gut at the thought of leaving Esme exposed, even for a second. Instinct made me turn, searching for her, and my heart stuttered, thudding painfully, when I realized she wasn't there.

The space behind me was empty. She was gone.

What the fuck.

I hissed under my breath, catching the flash of her darting away, a spectral blur melting into the shadows and toward the open door, the staircase gaping beyond.

"Esme!" I shouted, but she was already gone, her feet hitting the steps before I could even push myself upright.

I glanced back at Ares, Zeno, and Thal, a split-second calculation, primal and electric.

Three of them. Only one Esme.

They'd be fine.

I lunged forward, adrenaline hot and reckless, chasing her into the dark, following every wild step as bullets tore through the air around me.

One clipped my arm, pain exploding, sharp and immediate, but I shoved it aside, teeth bared, rage at Esme burning brighter with every stride.

I wouldn't stop. Not for anything.

Twenty-Three

ESME

The scent of sawdust and gunpowder clung to my skin, a rough, gritty haze burning in my lungs as I sprinted up the stairs.

I'd caught sight of Rhea on the balcony, laughing, drinking, like she was a queen presiding over carnage, and the fury that slammed into me was primal and hot, obliterating all reason.

My grip tightened around my weapon as I took the steps two at a time.

The world narrowed to the cold metal door ahead, the threshold I knew would unleash chaos the second I breached it. Rhea had ducked behind her guard, but I could feel the others lurking, their presence thick and unspoken.

Somewhere behind me, Aidon's voice crashed through the haze, shouting my name. I ignored him. I'd deal with that later.

My hand closed around the door handle, ready to rip it open, when the pounding of footsteps sounded behind me. I spun, pulse stuttering, only to find Aidon storming up the stairs, his face twisted in fury. Dark, dangerous, and commanding.

God, it was fucking hot.

For a split second, I wanted to shove him against the wall, sink to my knees, and swallow him whole, tasting that wild, forbidden heat as the world burned around us. The image flashed through me, sharp and electric.

But Aidon? He'd never let me. Not when he was this angry.

Especially not now, with blood and adrenaline singing through both our veins.

"I told you to stay close to me!" Aidon's eyes were blazing, nearly unhinged.

"Did you?" I tilted my head, feigning curiosity, though I could feel the sharp heat of rebellion sparking in my chest. Maybe I was baiting him, but I didn't give a single fuck.

"Look," I said, "we came here to destroy Rhea. That's the mission. I'm not the one off task."

"Off task? Off task, Esme?" he shouted, face twisted in disbelief. "This is a goddamn war zone! We're fighting for our lives, not punching a clock at some shitty mall!"

"Don't you think I fucking know that?" I shot back. "I'm the one who took the beating, Aidon. Or did you forget already?"

His jaw flexed, muscles working as he glared at me. "You aren't doing this alone."

"That was never my plan," I hissed, every syllable laced with venom. "We're supposed to do this together. That's what you said."

For a heartbeat, the fury in his eyes flickered then softened. "Fine. Together. But don't you dare run off like that again."

I arched a brow, refusing to break his gaze.

Ignoring the warning, I asked, "Ready?"

He still thought he could cage me, order me around, but I'd never let him win that easily. If I needed to run, I would. And nothing, not even he, would stop me.

"Stay behind me," he growled, stepping forward to shield me, as if I was something fragile, breakable.

"No," I snapped, matching his intensity. "We fight together, side by side. That's what you promised me, Aidon. Don't you dare forget it."

I met his gaze head-on, holding it, daring him to push back. The echo of gunfire in the warehouse fractured the silence, then stopped, so abruptly it left us both frozen, breath caught.

For a split second, all I could hear was the pounding of my heart, then a thunder of heavy footsteps filled the stairwell, vibrating through the floor.

We looked down, and there they were: Zeno, Thal, and Ares at the front, bloodied but unbowed, their men close behind, every single one of them still on their feet.

"Fuck yeah," Aidon muttered, low and savage, and something hot twisted in my chest.

We waited, tense, until the whole crew was packed in

behind us, a wall of bodies and guns and grim determination. I wrenched the door open.

Together, we moved down the hallway, shoulder to shoulder, a bulletproof phalanx blazing toward the door where Rhea had vanished.

We were ten feet away when it exploded open, and a dozen guards poured out, weapons drawn. The air came alive with bullets, a crackling storm of death. Instinct took over: move, shoot, survive.

One guy charged straight at Aidon, firing wild and missing every shot. Aidon let him come, then slammed the butt of his gun into the man's chin with brutal efficiency. The guard crumpled at our feet, red leaking from his mouth, groaning. I kicked his gun away and watched as Aidon, without a flicker of hesitation, put a bullet through his skull.

"Jesus," I muttered, but there was no time to dwell.

Another man barreled toward me, rage twisting his face. I steadied my hand, aimed for his forehead, and squeezed the trigger.

The gun kicked, and so did fear, electric and sharp. My shot punched through bone and flesh, and the man dropped, limp and sudden, a sack of dead weight.

All that mattered was getting past these bastards, breaking through, closing the gap between me and the only thing that mattered.

"Good shot," Aidon muttered, flashing me a quick smile of approval before turning away to help Zeno, who had been disarmed and was tangled up and wrestling with one of Rhea's men on the ground.

All around us, the battle raged, our own little army fighting valiantly against Rhea's men.

Aidon was there in a heartbeat, his gun drawn, and he didn't hesitate. He shoved the barrel against the back of the man's skull, the one tangled with Zeno, and pulled the trigger.

The body went slack, crumpling in a dead weight over Zeno, pinning him beneath. For a moment, Zeno was lost in the mess of limbs and blood, but then he shoved the corpse off, breathless, grabbing both the dead man's gun and his own as he scrambled upright.

The room spun with chaos. Thal and Ares were locked in combat near the balcony, three men pressing in on them, fists and elbows flying.

The fight was merciless, bone on bone, and though Thal and Ares were holding their ground, it was clear they were getting pushed to the edge.

Aidon charged forward, Zeno at his side, and I followed, heart pounding, the metallic taste of fear on my tongue.

Before I could even raise my gun, Zeno and Aidon crashed into the fray, drawing two of the men away from Thal and Ares, giving them just enough space to gasp for breath and regroup.

One of the men landed a savage punch to Aidon's jaw, knocking him flat. It was brutal, and for a second, I lost sight of him in the violence, but then I saw Aidon pinned, the man straddling him, driving fist after fist into his face. I moved, instincts taking over, gun raised, hands shaking as the fight writhed across the floor.

Aidon twisted, bucking hard, and suddenly he was on top, then back underneath, both men rolling and thrashing, bodies slick and desperate.

I tried to draw a bead, tried to steady my trembling hands, but every wild movement forced me to readjust my aim. I couldn't risk hitting Aidon, not even by accident.

My heart slammed against my ribs, the noise and bodies and panic threatening to drown me.

But then I saw Aidon, blood streaked down his cheek, teeth bared, eyes wild. It was like something inside me snapped into place.

Calm, cold, certain. I closed the distance, blocking out everything but the target on the floor.

I pressed the barrel against the back of the man's head, inhaled, then squeezed the trigger. The retort shattered the air, the heat of the recoil biting into my palm, and the acrid tang of gunpowder curled around us as the man's body went limp beneath Aidon, dead weight and blood pooling fast.

I jerked the gun up and squeezed off two more shots, dropping the last of Rhea's men who stood between Thal, Zeno, and Ares. Then it was just us on the balcony again, the floor a graveyard of Rhea's loyal dead.

All four of them stared at me, open-mouthed. I lifted my chin, pride humming through my blood.

"Onward, gentlemen," I said, stepping over a corpse and dodging the red, glossy pool bleeding from the hole in his head.

"Fuck, Esme," Zeno muttered, a crooked smile splitting

his face. "You're making me goddamn proud to be your brother right now."

"Half-brother," I shot back, arching a brow. "Don't get cocky."

He grinned. "I like to think we got the bad-ass half of the DNA."

I let him have that one. There were bigger things at stake. Like the door Rhea was hiding behind. I could feel Aidon's stare burning holes through me, the taut line of his jaw. I knew every muscle in his body was straining not to shove me behind him. But I was leading now.

I'd saved these bastards. I wasn't going to fade into the background. Not when I could practically taste Rhea's blood.

Anticipation shimmered through every nerve ending. I saw Rhea's face, clear as day. Revenge was so close, I could almost reach out and crush it in my fist.

I was at the door when it swung open.

Rhea stepped out, flanked by two more men. Her gaze swept over the carnage, lingering on Aidon, and then she laughed. Threw her head back, hair gleaming, sipping champagne like she was holding court at a palace and not surrounded by corpses.

It was an act, a perfect, icy illusion.

But underneath? She was a monster, a polished, beautiful nightmare with a heart made of razors.

"Oh, Aidon, you are so predictable."

Her voice dripped with arrogance, every syllable heavy

with mockery. She stood there, cool and composed, as if she were untouchable.

As if the world bent to her will and we were nothing, a laughable threat at best. Her confidence was almost impressive, except for the fact that she was so very fucking wrong.

She prowled toward us, her gaze locking onto mine with a predator's delight.

"Esme, Esme, Esme," she purred, each repetition a taunt, tongue clicking in feigned disappointment. "You've stuck around, I see."

I said nothing. Let her fill the silence with her poison.

She kept going, relentless, her smile razor-sharp and cruel.

God, I wanted to wipe it off her face with a single bullet. But she just kept circling, trying to get under my skin, even now, moments from destruction. It was almost impressive, the audacity she wore like a crown.

"Did Aidon tell you about the first time he doubted you, Esme?" she murmured, as if she was holding the winning card. As if that might split us apart. Pathetic.

She had no idea with whom she was dealing.

I stepped forward, pulse pounding in my ears, and felt Aidon tense at my side. But for once, he didn't hold me back. Neither did the others. For a split second, I almost smiled. Maybe I'd finally proven myself.

I squared my shoulders and looked Rhea dead in the eyes. No fear. No hesitation. Just cold resolve.

I lifted my gun and aimed it right at her face.

Her guards reacted, weapons swinging toward me,

fingers tightening on their triggers. Behind me, the sound of my own people raising their guns rang out, a chorus of threats in perfect harmony: my army, my family, my choice.

I held her gaze and shook my head.

Unmoved. Undaunted. Ready for whatever came next.

"Rhea, you're pathetic; you know that, right?" The words dripped from my mouth, cold and sharp, as I stared her down. Disgust curled through me, so hot it almost burned, but the only thing I felt for this woman was contempt. "It might almost be sad, if you weren't such a complete fucking cunt. But you can't change what's already been done. You're not in control anymore. Can't you feel it slipping away?"

The way her twisted smile faded.

It was almost satisfying. She tried to meet my glare, tried to match my ice with hers, but now she was the one faltering.

"You're wrong, Esme," she spat.

Her words came out brittle, desperate, even if she tried to cover it.

"No, you're wrong, Rhea," Zeno cut in, a dangerous rumble.

He stepped forward. Aidon fell in beside him, Thal on the other side, all of them closing in. "Your little act, your bullshit grip on this town and on us. It's done. When we end you, we're taking every last scrap you've got, torching this place for good measure. But first, we're stealing your weapons and getting paid. You're finished. Canceled. Without our empires backing you, you're nothing but a shadow."

She tilted her head, arching a brow, still clinging to her goddamn pride.

"And still, here I am, standing alone," she shot back.

"We let you get away with it for way too long," Aidon said, edged with years of repressed fury.

"The power's shifted," Thal added, his gaze all lethal intent. "We're the ones in charge now."

But listening to them bicker about who ran what was pointless. I didn't come here to argue.

"Enough," I snarled. "Let's finish her."

She laughed, a low, mocking sound that rippled through the air.

"Gentlemen," she started, a smirk curling on her lips, "I'm afraid you've got it all wr—"

I launched myself at her, the urge to get my hands on her too much to resist. She was so close I could touch her. Sure, guards surrounded her, but so was I.

She cried out in surprise as I made contact, my fingers snaking around her throat as I threw her to the ground. The sounds of chaos and fighting ensued around me, but I didn't look over my shoulder. I was confident the men I'd surrounded myself with could take care of themselves just fine.

We'd come this far, hadn't we? The moment stretched, a taut wire between us, thrumming with something wild and electric.

The sheer thrill of it, the pleasure that ripped through me at the sight of Rhea's fear, so fresh, so real, painted her blue eyes wide as the sky, raw and desperate.

Her fingers scrabbled at mine, her mouth open in a silent gasp, lungs greedy for air. I smiled down at her, letting the dark satisfaction roll over me.

Delicious. Twisted. Mine.

I squeezed, knuckles whitening, but released her. No. Suffocation would be too easy, too merciful. I wanted more. Needed more.

She thrashed beneath me, hips bucking, but my thighs pinned her tight, a low, throaty noise caught in her chest. I made a fist, raising my arm high, heart hammering, before I brought it down.

The sick crack of flesh-on-bone echoed. Rhea's nose split open, blood blooming beneath my knuckles. She howled, shock and anguish mixing in the air, and I hit her again, the crimson rush spilling hot and fast.

Yes. That was better. So much better.

I struck her again and again, losing myself in the rhythm.

The jolt of muscle and bone, the rawness of power that pulsed through me. I cared about nothing else in the room, not the world. Only Rhea. Only the way she broke.

My fist rose once more, and then someone seized my arm, yanking me back.

I crashed to the floor, breath knocked from my chest.

Before I could lift my head, a boot connected with my ribs, brutal and unyielding, stealing the air from my lungs and leaving me gasping.

I fought to suck in air, the sting of desperation burning in my lungs. Rhea scrambled upright beside me, but all around us the fight raged on, a storm of gunshots echoing, the guttural sounds of violence swirling through the space.

A flash of metal caught my eye. There was a gun just feet away. I clawed toward it, gravel biting into my palms, my fingers curling around the grip as I looked up and saw Aidon.

His face was a bloodied ruin, streaked with crimson and swelling.

One of Rhea's guards had him by the shirt, pounding him with savage satisfaction. Rage ignited inside me. I lifted the gun, aimed, and squeezed the trigger.

The shot cracked through the air, striking the man in the back of the head. He went down instantly, a puppet with cut strings.

I crawled to Aidon, struggling to breathe, my chest raw and burning.

He lay limp, blood soaking his shirt, and the sight of him like that gutted me. I pulled him onto my lap, cradling his broken body, my hands shaking.

"Aidon!" I sobbed, slapping his cheek, desperate to keep him tethered to me. "Stay with me, Aidon!"

His eyelids fluttered, his lips parting as he struggled for consciousness, for breath.

Panic clawed at my insides. I whipped my head around, searching for help, but the world had narrowed to this: Zeno, Rhea, and one last guard, the barrel of a gun leveled at Zeno's chest as he lunged for her.

Rhea's face was unrecognizable, battered and swelling fast. I wanted to put an end to her, to finish what I'd started.

But I couldn't leave Aidon, not for anything in this world.

She looked past Zeno, her eyes landing on us in the wreckage, and she laughed, a low mocking sound punctuated by a shake of her head.

"What a sight you two lovebirds are," she taunted, before locking eyes with Zeno. The tension between them was electric, crackling in the battered silence. "It's time for me to leave now."

"This isn't over, Rhea," I spat. "Not even close."

She laughed again, ignoring every word I said, her eyes locked on Zeno like I wasn't even in the room.

His shoulders stayed rigid, unflinching, but something flickered in his gaze, a glimmer of something raw and sharp that made me wonder just what the fuck had gone down between them. Later, I told myself. That was a question for later.

"Zeno, tell me something, old friend. Do you still think you're different from me? That you have more power than I do, that you deserve more?" Rhea's words dripped with a lazy, dangerous kind of amusement as she clicked her tongue. "Zeno, Zeno, Zeno. We both know power is just another kind of cage."

He sucked in a breath, jaw clenched so tight it looked like it might break. Rage rolled off him in waves.

Aidon wheezed in my arms, fighting for air, and I held him closer, bracing myself for the possibility that I'd have to drag him out of here myself.

Rhea leaned in, her lips curved in a smile meant just for Zeno. "The throne is never secure, my friend."

And just like that, Rhea and her guard slipped away, vanishing into her office. The only sign they'd ever been here was the echo of their footsteps thundering down the staircase.

Zeno turned to me, eyes blazing with fury, a storm barely held in check.

"You alright?" he asked, raising a brow.

"Yeah. You?"

"If you can call being so fucking angry I could tear someone's head off 'okay,' then sure."

A ragged laugh slipped out of me. Relief, exhaustion, the adrenaline dump of having survived the whole thing. I shook my head, so fucking glad it was finally over.

It was just a battle. The war still gnawed at our heels, jaws snapping, always hungry.

Maybe it would never be over. Perhaps another would rise, someone to take Rhea's place, someone just as ruthless, just as hell-bent on ruin.

She'd run.

It mattered not. She was gone, whether by death or disgrace.

We'd won.

I stared down at Aidon, hands shaking as I brushed the blood slick from his brow then traced the line of his jaw. My fingers trembled, raw and aching. I fought to catch my breath.

"We did it," I said.

He bared his teeth in a broken smile, pain twisting his words.

"Together." The word shuddered out of him, ragged, desperate, and real.

My head dipped, lips catching his, the taste of iron between us.

"Yes," I breathed. "Together, Aidon."

TWENTY-FOUR

ESME

A WEEK LATER

Everything looked different.

Everything felt different.

I was different.

From the window in Aidon's office in The Underworld, I stared out at the city pulsing beneath us, my thoughts spinning.

It had only been a week since the confrontation with Rhea, the violence, the blood, but I was still here. I hadn't disappeared into the night. I hadn't shed my identity like a snake and slithered away to some new land, hungry for power.

Instead, I'd spent every day tending Aidon's wounds.

Every night, I ended up in his bed, curled around him.

And fuck, I was happy about it.

I caught sight of my reflection in the glass and for a moment, I didn't recognize the woman looking back at me. There was no urge to argue, no compulsion to fight Aidon for control every second. I'd already proven myself, and the confidence that came with that victory let me breathe. Let me be.

For the first time, I didn't feel like I was barely holding on to my power. I owned it. It was mine. No one could take it from me, not even Rhea and her men, even if they burst through the door with guns drawn and murder in their eyes. I would fight, and I would survive.

I could go to war and walk away with my head high. That knowledge changed everything.

I believed in myself now, truly believed, and the need to prove myself—to anyone, ever again, was just gone. Obliterated.

And it felt fucking incredible.

I knew Rhea would return. Eventually.

But I also knew we wouldn't see her for a long while, not after the hit we'd just delivered.

We'd crippled her. First, by taking her warehouse, then by crushing her security team, not once, but twice.

Every asset she'd built up, every weapon, every crate, every ledger.

It was all ours now, locked down and out of her reach. And when we finally had time to dig through the warehouse, we found more than guns.

So much more. Heroin. Cocaine. Enough to flood the

city and line our pockets tenfold. That was, if we moved it all.

That part? I left it to Aidon and Zeno. The two of them and Thal, too.

They had more skin in the game, more to lose and gain here, than I did. But that didn't mean I was stepping aside. Not a chance. I wanted my cut, my say, my power.

Vegas had shifted overnight. The balance of control, the money, the muscle, the kind of power only the city's elite ever tasted, all of it upended and redistributed.

We'd already sent the evidence packet, including manifests, faces, and burns, to Olympus Legal. The receipt notification still lit up Aidon's monitor.

My phone vibrated across Aidon's desk. It was an old Olympus number I hadn't seen in months. I almost let it go to voicemail, then hit the speaker.

"Esme," Zeno said, his voice sealed and sharp as steel. "One marker retired. Two remain."

"Lift the black book," I said.

"Limited privileges," he replied. "Medical reinstated. One monitored account. Full reinstatement requires the hardware and a verified copy, or another Konstantinou artery cut with proof. Don't mistake progress for forgiveness."

The line went dead.

Aidon's jaw clenched. "One down," he said. "We take the next."

I stared at my reflection in the dark glass and didn't look away. Progress, not absolution. Fine. I'd earn the rest.

Rhea was gone, and in that vacuum, something new had taken root.

Now, Aidon and I shared that power. Vegas was ours, and there was no going back.

He'd tossed the offer onto the table like it was nothing, a stake in his operation, my own piece of the action, and here I was, still pretending to consider.

Maybe I'd stay. Perhaps I'd walk. The truth?

I'd probably stick around to see what would happen next. But I wasn't about to let him see how much I wanted it. A girl's got to keep him guessing.

Funny, all that anxiety I'd had about running. The way I'd convinced myself I'd have to slip out in the night, before things got complicated or dangerous. But Aidon's urge to control me?

It had vanished, burned away by something new. Maybe it was always about protection; a twisted, overbearing kind, sure, but his own way of caring.

Now that he'd seen I could handle myself, seen me stand my ground, there was a shift between us.

I felt it every time he got close, a note of respect, sharp and electric, in the way he looked at me, in the way he touched me.

Not that he'd stopped being a man, with all the stubbornness and pride that implied.

I could sense how hard it was for him, the effort it took to loosen that grip, to accept that he couldn't shield me from everything, not after what happened last time. But these days, he seemed to have different priorities.

Mostly? Fucking me until I couldn't think, until my limbs went weak and my thoughts shattered into sparks.

We spent hours tangled in his sheets, mapping each other's bodies, learning every inch with hands and mouths and teeth, making up for lost time and then some.

Between bouts of desperate, frenzied sex, we traded stories and secrets, filling the silences with laughter and memories and half-formed plans for a future that might never come.

And in those moments, the urge to run didn't even cross my mind.

Maybe tomorrow everything would be different. Perhaps I'd wake up and want out. But for now?

I was right where I wanted to be.

Outside this club, nothing had changed. The river of tourists below was just as oblivious as the locals. None of them had a clue that power had shifted, that the criminal masterminds running this city were suddenly different faces behind the curtain.

But here, in the smoky shadows of Aidon's club, the difference was unmistakable.

The air crackled with energy, as members swapped stories about Rhea's downfall. Some were already scheming, eager to slide into the vacancies left behind now that new blood held the reins.

Most of them had feared Rhea. She'd run guns and drugs through this city with ruthless precision, destroying anyone who dared to oppose her.

Now, rumor had it she'd resurfaced in New Jersey, which was hilarious.

Anyone who understood this world knew the Jersey syndicates were even more misogynistic than Vegas ever was.

Rhea wouldn't stand a chance at rebuilding there. The family heads would mock her, maybe even strip her of whatever scraps she had left, before laughing her out of town.

She was about to learn a brutal lesson, and I couldn't wait to watch it unfold.

I found myself smirking, satisfied with the way things had unraveled, even if I hadn't gotten to see the light fade from Rhea's eyes. Knowing we'd toppled her entire operation was enough for now.

The promise of sharing the profits with my colleagues was a bonus. I could only imagine how it burned Rhea to walk away from the empire she'd built.

Footsteps drew my attention, and I turned to find Aidon approaching, a snifter of whiskey in each hand. He offered one to me.

Our fingers brushed, the touch sending a shiver up my arm. I took a sip, my eyes lingering on him, measuring and waiting.

"It's over," I murmured, letting the whiskey burn its way down my throat, the fire spreading low and deep inside me.

Aidon nodded, slow and unhurried, his bruised, handsome face still marked but healing.

The evidence of what he'd been through was written across his skin, but if it bothered him, he didn't show it. I reached up, fingertips brushing gently along the battered line of his jaw.

He caught my hand in his, brought my palm to his lips, and kissed it. His gaze locked on mine, a slow, dangerous smile curving his mouth.

"Don't get too comfortable, Esme. I'm not trying to kill the mood, but you know as well as I do: our enemies are never gone for good. Rhea's out of the way, for now, but this war isn't done. Not really." He shrugged. "But I'll give you this; it's over tonight."

I exhaled, letting the tension bleed from my shoulders.

"I know. I remember. But it wouldn't kill us to relax for a little while."

"No, it wouldn't." His laugh was more a rumble than a sound, and when he bent to kiss me, it was so casual, so familiar, it almost startled me; as if we'd always done this, as if we'd always belonged to each other.

We hadn't talked about where we stood, or what we meant to each other, but maybe that was for the best. I wasn't sure I wanted to define it, not when just being with him felt like this.

"To a brief respite," he said, lifting his glass and clinking it against mine.

"To rest," I echoed, grinning at him before drinking again.

I turned toward the window, letting my gaze drift out over the city as the sunset bled fiery pinks and oranges across the horizon.

He moved behind me, sliding his arms around my waist,

and held me tight as he rested his chin on my shoulder. I felt the strength in his hold, the warmth, the safety.

"Beautiful," he rasped.

"The sunset?" I asked, watching the colors stain the wild city below.

Aidon shook his head, a long, shuddering sigh escaping him. "Not the sunset, beauty. You."

I shivered at the sincerity, the rough affection I heard. He kissed the side of my neck, making me tremble with a need that felt dangerous. I leaned back into him, savoring the iron-clad way he held me, the way we were stronger together than we'd ever been alone.

We'd learned that the hard way.

"Aidon," I breathed, turning in his arms to face him. I kissed him, soft at first, then deeper, letting him know what I couldn't say. "Thank you."

He cocked a brow, smirking. "For what?"

"For believing in me. For not getting in my way."

He laughed. "Oh, I tried, babe. But you're stubborn as hell."

I rolled my eyes. "That's one way to put it. So, did you learn your lesson?"

His grin was pure challenge, eyes dancing with heat. "Not a chance."

"Aidon!"

"I'm joking, sweetheart," he replied, that sexy rumble sending a jolt straight between my legs. "You proved you know how to kick ass when necessary. I believe that now. I'm a little scared of you, if I'm being honest."

"Oh?" I shot back.

"Please don't tell anyone else I said that," he murmured, almost pleading.

"Your secret's safe with me."

"That's ominous." He arched one eyebrow. "You know I deal in secrets for a living."

"Guess the tables are turned now, aren't they?" I threw back at him, feeling the thrill of the game all over again.

"Fuck, I'm in trouble, aren't I?" He shook his head, eyes narrowing as if he was concerned.

"Only if you try to double-cross me," I warned.

"How about we just work as a team and not threaten to betray each other?"

There was a smile on his lips, but underneath, I heard the seriousness threading every syllable.

Was that a real question? Was he asking for more, something deeper? The unspoken hovered, thick and heavy.

I could have kept it going. Played coy, teased him, fired back another clever line. That was what we always did, the back and forth, the chase and retreat. But suddenly, it felt empty. I was tired of the games.

I wanted what came next, the part where you could finally let someone in, let yourself trust, let yourself hope.

So I kissed him again, this time pouring everything into it.

The hunger, the relief, the silent promise. Words could simmer. We had time to say all the things that mattered.

Right now, all we needed to know was that whatever came next, we'd face it together.

He pulled away just enough to look down at me, his warm lips barely parted, eyes soft and full of something close to devotion.

"Aren't you going to say it?" he asked.

"Say what?"

"That you're never going to betray me again?"

"Oh, that?" I shrugged, giving a wicked little grin. "I mean, never say never, right?"

"Esme!" He feigned outrage before he scooped me up in his arms, carrying me over to the battered brown leather sofa in the corner of his office. He lay me down, looming over me, his body pressing between my thighs, his face just inches from mine.

He kissed me, hard and fast.

"You think you're funny," he rasped, the sound vibrating against my mouth. "But it matters to me. I need you to know that."

"I'm pretty sure your head's pressing against my—"

"Can't you be serious for one fucking moment, Esme?"

"I'm listening. Sorry."

He shook his head, and the frustration in his eyes was almost affectionate. No one else got under his skin like I did, and we both knew it.

He cupped my cheek, fingers gentle, gaze searching mine, like he could anchor himself in me.

"We built this together," he said. "You and me."

"Yes," I whispered, the word turning soft on my tongue.

"And together, we'll keep it."

He kissed me again, slower this time, luxuriating in it,

drowning us in the heat and certainty of what we could be. The promise was clear: whatever storm was waiting outside, we'd weather it side by side.

Ready for the next installment in the series?

She thought their island affair was buried in the past.
He thought he'd never touch her again.

In Vegas, forbidden love is about to ignite a war... Preorder *Dark Alliance.*

Their empire was only the beginning...
Las Vegas is still burning with secrets.
Zeno may think he controls the city.
But Daphne knows better—because her heart belongs to the one man she should never touch again.

Thalassios Adrias is power, danger, and temptation rolled into one. And when old rivalries ignite a war, every kiss becomes betrayal, every alliance a risk, and every choice could destroy them all.
The next chapter of the *Sinful Gods* series begins.
Are you ready for the alliance that could bring them all down?
Preorder *Dark Alliance.*

Dark Alliance

Preorder: https://geni.us/DarkAlliance

In Las Vegas, power is the ultimate gamble.

Daphne has always belonged to Zeno—at least in the eyes of the empire he built. But one forbidden glance across the poker table shatters her carefully controlled loyalties.

Thalassios Adrias isn't just a rival.

He's the man she should never want again...and the one temptation she can't escape.

As old enemies rise from the shadows, alliances blur, and every secret threatens to ignite a war. Desire becomes betrayal. Loyalty becomes a weapon. And when the city's most dangerous syndicate strikes back, Daphne must choose: the man who saved her life,

or the man who could set her free.

Dark Alliance is a dark mafia romance of forbidden love, dangerous games, and high-stakes passion. Perfect for fans of ruthless antiheroes, powerful heroines, and the intoxicating pull of love that should never have been.

Books by Sienna

Rules of Engagement

Rule Breaker

Rule Master

Rule Changer

Politics of Love

Celebrity

Senator

Commander

Gods of Vegas

Master of Sin

Master of Games

Master of Revenge

Master of Secrets

Master of Control

Master of Fortune

Sweetest Sin

Intrigued By Love

Street Kings

Dangerous King

Vicious Prince

Deceptive Knight

Ruthless Heir

<u>Violent Delights</u>

Claim

Defy

Own

<u>Sin and Lies</u>

Sin and Betrayal

Sin and Deception

<u>Sister of Wrath</u>

Legacy

Influence

Power

<u>Sinful Gods</u>

Forbidden Empire

Dark Alliance (May 2026)

Broken Crown (2026)

<u>Collections</u>

Reckless Romeo

Take Me To Bed (2019)

Meet Me Under The Mistletoe (2021)

Nightingale (A charity anthology in support of Ukraine) - (2022)

Darkly Ever After (An Organized Crime Anthology) (2022)

RARE Melbourne Anthology (2023)

About the Author

USA Today bestselling author Sienna Snow loves to craft dark and extremely sexy stories centered on anti-heroes and the strong, unapologetic women who bring them to their knees. Her books immerse you in a world of indulgence, suspense, and undeniable steam.

Her heroines are vibrant and self-assured, often discovering love and romance under unconventional circumstances. Sienna offers her readers enticing glimpses of steamy romance filled with empowerment and indulgent satisfaction.

Sienna loves a life filled with travel and adventure. She plans to explore even the farthest corners of the world and revel in experiencing the diverse cultures along the way. When she isn't writing or traveling, Sienna is focused on her "happily ever after" with her husband and children.

Sign up for her newsletter for notifications of releases, book sales, events, and so much more.
http://www.siennasnow.com/newsletter
contact@siennasnow.com